P9-DWH-186

NOW THAT I'VE FOUND YOU

Also by Kristina Forest

I Wanna Be Where You Are

NOW THAT I'VE FOUND YOU

KRISTINA FOREST

ROARING BROOK PRESS • NEW YORK

Published by Roaring Brook Press
Roaring Brook Press is a division of Holtzbrinck Publishing Holdings
Limited Partnership
120 Broadway, New York, NY 10271
fiercereads.com

Library of Congress Control Number: 2019948762

ISBN: 978-1-250-29502-6

Our books may be purchased in bulk for promotional, educational, or business use. Please contact your local bookseller or the Macmillan Corporate and Premium Sales Department at (800) 221-7945 ext. 5442 or by email at MacmillanSpecialMarkets@macmillan.com.

First edition, 2020
Book design by Cassie Gonzales
Printed in the United States of America

3 5 7 9 10 8 6 4

For my grandmothers, Peggy and Naomi

MAY

Article from FilmBuzz.com—May 2, 2020

ACADEMY AWARD–NOMINATED EVELYN CONAWAY TO RECEIVE FILM CRITICS CIRCLE LIFETIME ACHIEVEMENT AWARD

The Film Critics Circle just announced this year's nominations, and while some actors and films were snubbed, and others were nominated as suspected, the biggest surprise is that Evelyn Conaway will be honored with the esteemed lifetime achievement award. Conaway's career skyrocketed in 1970, when she starred in *Every Time We Meet* as the wealthy and doe-eyed Diane Tyler opposite leading man James Jenkins, who played Henry, a boy from the wrong side of the tracks. The film won an Academy Award for Best Picture and scored Conaway a nomination for Best Actress. It is arguably the greatest romantic film of the twentieth century.

Conaway quickly became a household name. For years, you couldn't go anywhere without seeing her face on a billboard or magazine cover. She and Jenkins would go on to star in five films together and were known for their dynamic chemistry on- *and* off-screen. They were married in 1970 and divorced after only two years before marrying again in 1974. After their second divorce in 1979, Conaway married movie producer Freddy Stevens, who died of lung cancer in 1988. In 1990, Conaway and Jenkins rekindled their romance and married a third time, only to divorce once again in 2012.

Many believe the incident at the 2012 FCCs was to blame for their last divorce. That year, Jenkins was set to receive the very same lifetime achievement award, and by then, he'd had a number of tumultuous years behind him. In the late '80s and early '90s, he struggled with drug addiction and had multiple stints in rehab, but by 2012, he was slowly putting his career back together.

The night of the ceremony, Conaway, who was still his wife at the time, made one of the most memorable speeches in Film Critics Circle history. Instead of praising Jenkins for his career accomplishments, she called him a liar and said he didn't deserve the award. And then, to everyone's astonishment, she walked offstage with his award in hand. She agreed to return it only after security chased her down. Jenkins's stunned face splashed across the theater's screens.

To this day, we don't know why Conaway reacted so strongly. She refused to give any interviews, remaining tight-lipped. She moved out of her Beverly Hills home and, essentially, dropped off the face of the earth. This year's FCCs will be the first time she's made a public appearance since that night. Meanwhile, Jenkins did, in fact, manage to turn his career around. He's now known to the younger generation as the beloved grandfather in the Aliens Attack Earth movie franchise.

In related news, this August also marks the fiftieth anniversary of *Every Time We Meet*, the film that shot both Conaway and Jenkins to stardom. There has been talk of a remake, and lately many have petitioned for Conaway's granddaughter, Evie Jones, to star as this generation's Diane.

Jones has been in the spotlight recently, as she was just cast as the lead in legendary director Paul Christopher's newest psychological thriller, *Deep Within*. She was only a week shy of graduating from Los Angeles's prestigious Mildred McKibben Performing Arts Academy when the casting announcement was made, and this will be her second feature film. Last fall, she had a minor role in Paul Christopher's *Mind Games*, playing Alanna Thomas, who was killed off early on but quickly became a fan favorite.

If we want Jones to play Diane in an *Every Time We Meet* remake, then who should play Henry? He'd have to be just as charismatic as Jenkins. Can we all agree that there is nothing more swoon-worthy than the final scene, when Henry says to Diane, "Well, darling, I'm sure glad you showed up"?

We here at Film Buzz are waiting in eager anticipation for Conaway to receive her award at the FCCs and for Jones's star to rise.

When asked about the recent developments in her burgeoning career, Jones stated, "I'm incredibly lucky to be in this position, and I'm grateful for all the support I've received."

Conaway could not be reached for comment.

Chapter One

FRIDAY, MAY 15

"Ms. Jones, how does it feel to have such a breakout role so early on in your career?"

This is asked by a press reporter who stands in a sea of other reporters, photographers, and fans. They stare at us eagerly, stare at *me*. I'm sitting onstage at the Los Angeles Palooza Film Festival on a panel with the legendary Paul Christopher to talk about his new movie, *Deep Within*. We start filming in a few weeks.

"It's *surreal*," I say with a small laugh. I swallow and remind myself to smile brighter. I cross my legs and will my heartbeat to slow down. I just want everyone to like me.

"I can't believe this is my life right now," I say. "When I got the call that Paul wanted me to audition for this movie, I almost fell out."

Everyone laughs at this, and I unclench a little. *Be cool*, I think to myself. *Be charming. Be the best that you can be!* God, I sound like an after-school special.

"Evie is one of the most talented students I've witnessed come out of Mildred McKibben," Paul Christopher says in his elegant British accent. He turns to me and smiles, adjusting the brim of his gray newsboy cap. His white hair is pulled back in a ponytail at the nape of his neck. "She really understands character in a way I haven't seen from someone so young. We've already done great work together on *Mind Games*, and I'm looking forward to working with her on *Deep Within.*"

I smile and try my best to pretend that I'm not completely freaking out at his praise. Paul Christopher is in his midsixties, not that much younger than my grandmother, and he's been making twisty, critically acclaimed thrillers for decades. I've sat at home on my living room floor, watching his movies on a loop, my bowl of popcorn sitting untouched because I was so engrossed in the story.

Now maybe someone will stop eating popcorn in order to watch me.

People in the room are recording us on their phones, and I'm once again thankful to my agent, Kerri, who hooked me up with a stylist last week. In my opinion, I've always had good fashion sense. I mean, that's what happens when your grandmother is Evelyn Conaway. (Yeah, *that* Evelyn Conaway. Basically the biggest movie star ever.) But the bright-orange

Carolina Herrera minidress and white Christian Louboutin pumps I have on today is maybe the best outfit I've ever worn.

I imagine the number of times I'll be tagged in videos and posts on Instagram and sit up a little straighter. I'll have a lot of DMs to respond to tonight.

I turn to Kerri now, who is standing off to the side. She gives me a subtle thumbs-up, and I nod. As thrilling as this is, having her here makes me feel less alone, less like I'm in a fishbowl.

"Ms. Jones, you have quite the family legacy," another reporter says. "Do you feel any pressure now that you are following in the footsteps of your grandmother, specifically?"

"Of course," I say, answering honestly. "But I've wanted this my whole life, so I feel ready. I've been waiting for a really long time."

A really long time meaning basically since birth. I grew up watching my grandmother's movies. My parents wanted me to have a "normal" childhood, so the plan was that I couldn't go on auditions until after I graduated high school. But then Paul Christopher came to our spring showcase last year and was so impressed with my performance, he offered me a role in *Mind Games* on the spot. Technically I didn't break Mom and Dad's rule because I didn't have to audition. And then they couldn't really say no when I was invited to audition for *Deep Within* after the senior showcase a few months ago.

"It was just announced that Evelyn Conaway will receive

the lifetime achievement award at the FCCs this year," a third reporter says. "Do you have any thoughts about the stir she caused at the FCCs eight years ago, when James Jenkins received the same honor?"

I blink and glance at Kerri, who glares at the reporter. She looks at me and tightly shakes her head. That's our sign for *no comment*. But I do have a comment about this.

"My grandmother is one of the most talented actresses of all time," I say. "She couldn't be more deserving of this award. If it were up to me, she'd have received it in 2012, every year before that, and every year after."

There's a collective "aww" from the crowd. I'm glad they find my honesty so endearing. I shoot another glance at Kerri. She gives another thumbs-up, and I relax again.

Thankfully, the rest of the questions are directed at Paul Christopher. Then the panel ends, and I'm ushered offstage toward Kerri.

"You are a rock star," she says, grinning at me like she might burst from excitement. Kerri looks more like a fashion model than an agent, tall and slim with flawless dark-brown skin and long, sleek extensions in her hair. She's only twenty-two and fresh out of college. Paul Christopher cast me in his movie before I had an agent, so I had to act fast. Kerri was referred to me by my school advisor. And I'm glad I went with her, because she's a shark. In one month alone, she's secured a stylist, hairstylist, makeup artist, and two endorsement deals.

She talks a mile a minute as we walk, her heels clicking with each step. "I would have never believed that was your first panel. You were so well spoken, and you didn't get off topic. And you—"

I turn to her when she abruptly stops, and that's when I realize Paul Christopher has appeared on my other side.

"I'll see you in a few weeks, Evie," he says. "Take care." He tips his cap in goodbye and walks away, surrounded by his team.

Paul Christopher just tipped his hat to me. He told me to *take care*. What is life, even?

Said life gets even more exciting as we make our way outside and are hit with a wall of sound.

"Evie! Evie! Evie!"

Fans and paparazzi always wait outside the festival to see their favorite stars, and I can't believe that some of them are waiting out here for *me.* Mostly it's because Paul Christopher has a cult following. Ever since my role in *Mind Games* last year, I've gained hundreds of thousands of followers on social media and people recognize me at the most basic places, like Target and McDonald's. Two girls even recognized me once while I was waiting in line at the DMV.

"Hi, everyone!" I wave enthusiastically, and a security guard appears to escort Kerri and me, whisking us away into a black Expedition. My best friend, Simone, is waiting inside.

She was in the audience at the panel, and now she stares at the crowd with wide eyes as we drive off.

"That was nuts!" she shouts, grabbing my hands. Her thick box braids are pulled back and wrapped in a tight bun at the top of her head, and her bun wobbles as she scoots toward me. "Oh my God, Evie."

"I *know*." I give her hands a squeeze and match her wide grin.

She continues to stare at the crowd in wonder until we can't see it anymore. We've been best friends since our freshman year at McKibben, and we used to sit at lunch, dreaming about the day we'd experience what's happening right now. I'm so glad she's here to witness all of this with me.

Our hands are still clutched together when Kerri, who has been busy clicking away on her phone answering emails, suddenly shouts, "YES!"

"What?" I say, spinning to face her.

She turns her phone so that I can see the email she just received. "Guess who has just been asked to be the face of Beautiful You's newest campaign?"

Beautiful You is the number one Black hair-care company in the country. I've only been using their products for, I don't know, my whole life?

I blink at Kerri. "*Me?*"

"Yes, you!"

The three of us squeal so loudly the driver swerves in shock.

"But, I mean, of course they want you," Kerri says. "Your hair is already amazing." She nods at my curly hair, which frames my face and head like a cloud, then adds, "Oh, and someone from James Jenkins's team reached out again for another meeting. I said you weren't available."

"Good." I frown. "I don't know why they're trying to get in contact, but he is persona non grata in the Jones/Conaway household."

Kerri nods. "I know. I basically told them as much."

"Thanks, Kerri. For everything." I hug her, and she stiffens for a second because she thinks physical contact is unprofessional. But she eventually relaxes; I'm starting to wear her down.

I lean back in my seat, grinning. I can't believe this is all happening. I know it sounds cheesy, but dreams really do come true.

After Kerri and I go over plans for the next few weeks, I'm finally off the hook. Simone and I are dropped off at my house in Malibu, where I live with my parents.

It's empty once we walk inside, of course. My parents, Andrew and Marie Jones, indie darlings of the documentary genre, are hardly ever here. Right now they're working on a new doc about the horrors of elephant poaching in Botswana. They'll be back in August for Gigi's FCC ceremony. Their long absence is nothing new, really. And they trust that I won't do anything out of control while they're gone.

"I'm heading out to the deck," Simone says, grabbing a can of soda from the fridge and opening the patio door.

Simone basically lives here. The guest bedroom is filled with all of her things. She has free rein of the house, just like me.

I nod and say, "I'm gonna call Gigi. I'll be out in a few minutes."

"Okay," she says over her shoulder.

I take off my heels as I walk upstairs to my room and close the door behind me. I sit on my bed and dial Gigi's number, glancing at the framed photograph of the two of us on my nightstand. It was taken the day I was born. Gigi is holding me, and I'm wearing one of those little pink hospital hats, and she's dressed glamorously in a white wrap dress. Her hair wasn't so gray then, but it was still curled the same way she wears it now.

Gigi lives in New York City. I used to see her every day when I was younger, back before she divorced James Jenkins and moved out of Beverly Hills. Now she never comes out to LA. She never leaves New York, actually. For almost a decade,

I've had to settle for phone calls to keep in touch, only seeing her in person when I visit. Most recently, that was last Christmas.

The phone rings one more time before someone finally picks up.

"Hello?" A boy's voice.

I frown and pull my phone away from my ear. Did I call the wrong number? No . . . this is Gigi's number. The same number I dialed just two days ago.

"Um, who is this?" I say slowly.

"Milo . . .," he answers. His voice is deep and melodic. "Who is this?"

"*Milo?*" I repeat, bewildered. "This is Evie. I'm calling for Evelyn Conaway? I'm her granddaughter."

"Oh, Evie! What's up?" His voice immediately brightens. "How's it going?"

How's it going? Who is this guy? Has some mad fan broken into Gigi's house and taken her hostage?

"Um . . . where is my grandmother?" I ask, growing frantic.

"She's in the sitting room," he says calmly. It sounds like he's moving pots and pans around in the background. "I'm answering phones for her. She said you might call."

"Oh, you're her new assistant," I say, relieved. This all makes sense now, and I stop thinking about calling the cops. "Wait, what happened to Esther?" Esther has been Gigi's personal assistant for as long as I can remember, since the '70s or something.

"She retired." He laughs a little and adds, "And I'm not your grandma's assistant, just a friend."

"A friend?" Now I'm wondering if Gigi has turned into some kind of Manhattan sugar mama. Or worse, is this guy trying to take advantage of her somehow? Horror stories of old ladies giving strangers their Social Security numbers flash through my mind.

But no, Gigi is smart. She wouldn't let something like that happen . . . would she?

Before I can really start to freak out again, Milo says, "And I deliver her groceries. That's why I'm here right now. Just dropping some stuff off."

"Oh." But I'm still feeling a little suspicious. "Can you put her on, please?"

"Of course. And hey, congrats on the Paul Christopher movie. Great stuff."

"Thanks so much," I say. *Odd, so odd.* I can hear the sound of him walking through the house and carrying the phone to Gigi.

"Hello, Evie Marie, my love," she says, her voice husky and velvety. Gigi and my parents are the only ones who call me Evie Marie, my first and middle names. Evie is for Evelyn. Marie is for my mom. "How was the film festival?"

"Oh, it was amazing, Gigi," I say, flopping backward onto my bed.

"You deserve it, baby. You've worked really hard at that school. I'm proud of you."

Hearing those words means so much coming from her. Especially because Gigi never wanted me to get into acting. She thinks everyone in the film industry is untrustworthy and that my grandfather Freddy was the only person she could depend on.

"A reporter asked me about the FCCs, and I told them you should've received the award years ago," I say.

Gigi sucks her teeth. "I wish everyone would just be quiet about this ceremony. You should've told them to mind their business."

I laugh. "I'll make sure to say that next time."

I don't bother telling Gigi that James Jenkins has been trying to get in touch with me. It would only upset her. I'm not sure why she hates him so much or what he did to make her blow up at him on live television. I just know it's bad, so bad that she still refuses to talk about it eight years later. I don't even know what he wants, but I have no interest in finding out. My loyalty is to Gigi. James might have been like a grandfather to me the first few years of my life, but I haven't seen him since they divorced when I was ten. He's a stranger now.

In the background, I can hear Milo say something to Gigi.

She mumbles in response. Then, "Evie Marie, my love, I have to go. It's time to cook dinner."

"*Cook?* You?" I've never known Gigi to even boil ramen noodles.

"You can learn new things, even in old age!"

I laugh again. "Okay, Gigi. I'll talk to you soon. I love you."

"I love you too." She sounds distracted for a moment, the sound of Milo's voice getting louder. But then she's back. "I'm so proud of you, baby."

When the line goes dead, I remind myself to ask for more information about this Milo kid the next time I call her. Gigi is smart and a great judge of character, but we all have our lapses. I'd hate it if he were some gold-digging boy looking for a handout. But I'll think about that tomorrow. Today is meant for celebrating.

Simone is slouching in a deck chair when I finally make it outside. I've changed out of my dress and put on a T-shirt and cutoffs. LA is the best city in the world, especially during summer, and we have an awesome view of the ocean from the patio. The perks of living in Malibu. I take a deep whiff of the salty air and plop into the seat next to Simone.

I check my Instagram, and like I guessed, I have thousands of tags and DMs from today's panel. Everyone loved the outfit and my hair. Lots of people want to know when I'll be in their cities next or when I'll start filming *Deep Within*.

I post a selfie that I took with Paul Christopher right

before the panel started, and within five minutes I have over two thousand likes.

All the love is making my heart grow ten sizes. It's wonderfully overwhelming, like a rush. All these people—strangers—who are invested in me, people who take time out of their day to say the nicest things. Their support makes me feel so worthy of the roles that have come my way.

"I could get used to this," I say to Simone, showing her the post of Paul Christopher and me. The likes keep ticking up and up.

She smiles a little and looks down at her own phone.

I wait for her inevitable wisecrack about how I always hold the camera too close to my face when I take selfies, but she's staring off into space, unusually quiet.

"Hey," I say, waving to get her attention. "Everything okay?"

She pulls her legs up onto the chair and wraps her arms around her knees. "I'm just wondering when all of these great things are going to happen for me too."

I wince and look down at my toes. Simone and I were in the same play during the senior showcase. After watching in the audience, Paul Christopher asked a handful of us to audition for *Deep Within*. Simone and I both auditioned for the lead role of Shay, a girl who investigates a classmate's murder at her ritzy New England boarding school. But Paul Christopher chose me. It was a little weird between us at first, but that went away eventually. I didn't know she was still upset.

"Your big break is coming," I say. "I just know it. You're way too talented."

And I mean that wholeheartedly. Simone was one of the best actresses in our senior class. Hell, even at all of McKibben.

"Sometimes I just feel like you get everything so easily," she says, still not looking at me.

Her words are like a punch to the gut. That's what everyone at McKibben used to say, that every lead role I got came down to nepotism because of my parents and Gigi. No one thought about how I had to audition just like everybody else or how hard I worked to prove I wasn't some legacy with a name. It's why I don't have any friends, except for Simone. She never seemed to care about any of that.

Except maybe she did.

"You know that isn't true," I say quietly.

She glances at me and shakes her head. "Never mind, don't listen to me. I'm just being stupid." She jumps up out of her chair, a mischievous look on her face. "This is a cause for celebration! I'll be right back."

The tension in my stomach recedes as I watch her skip back inside.

I take a deep breath and wait for my heartbeat to slow down.

Gigi is all the way in New York, and my parents are never around. Simone has been my family since our freshman year.

Our white classmates at McKibben thought we actually were related, even though we look nothing alike and all we have in common is our light-brown complexions. After a while, we began tricking people into believing that we were sisters.

If I lost Simone, I don't know what I would do.

When she returns, she's carrying a bottle of champagne from my parents' bar, which is strictly *off-limits*. But they're never here, and Simone is grinning, so I reach for the champagne flute she hands me. With a flourish, she pulls the cork, and it shoots out with a loud *pop*. We both jump back in surprise and laugh.

Simone pours the bubbly champagne into both of our glasses. "To your much-deserved success," she says, holding up her flute in cheers.

I don't usually drink, because I hate the taste of alcohol. But I'm so happy, and I do deserve a little celebration.

"Cheers," I say, knocking my flute into hers.

We sit back down, and I pull up a playlist to match our good mood. Every time one of our glasses is close to empty, Simone quickly fills it to the top. The warm summer air feels amazing on my skin, and I take a deep breath every time a breeze blows. I feel myself swaying in time to the rhythm of the ocean waves, and that's when I realize I'm buzzed. I'm such a lightweight.

We're both humming along to Janelle Monáe when Simone

suddenly smiles and says, "Hey, do that Paul Christopher impression."

"No," I say, laughing. "It's *so* bad, and it does him no justice. I don't sound nearly as dignified."

"Oh, come on!" Now she's laughing too. "Your British accent is so good."

"*No.*" I shake my head, laughing even harder. "I did it that one time because I thought I could pull it off! I won't embarrass myself again."

"Do it, do it, do it," she chants.

I easily give in to the peer pressure. "Okay, okay." I stand up and push my thick curls away from my face, pulling them into a ponytail just like Paul Christopher's. In my best British accent, I say, "The psychological-thriller genre continues to grow more and more each year. You'd better bet your fannies that *Deep Within* will be my greatest work yet. Better than anything you've seen thus far, because I am better than every other director there is, and you'd be a fool to think otherwise."

Simone giggles, whispering "fannies" to herself. She pulls out her phone to record me. She hiccups and says, "Keep going."

I start laughing again but force myself to stop, schooling my face into seriousness. I sit up straight and look down my nose at Simone. "Everyone is always going on and on about the awards I've won, but is it real talent on my end? Or have I just hypnotized you all with my posh accent?" I say, giggling. "Oh, who am I kidding? Of course it's talent! Tarantino who? Christopher Nolan? Please. Scorsese? Not bloody likely. I'm leagues better than the rest of these sorry chaps. Cheeky bum, bloody numpty, knickers, knickers, loo."

As my performance devolves, we laugh so loudly I'm nervous the neighbors might hear us. All the tension and awkwardness from a few moments ago slide away, and what's left is a feeling of extreme contentment.

"Okay, that's enough," I say, flopping back down in my chair. "Paul Christopher is one of my heroes, and I hope he never hears my terrible impression."

Simone stops recording and puts her phone away. She wiggles her eyebrows at me. "I don't know, that accent is pretty great. Maybe he'll cast you in the next movie he films in the UK."

I snort. "Yeah, right."

I lean my head on Simone's shoulder. After a moment, I say, "Thanks for being here for me. I'll be right there with you when it's your turn."

She doesn't say anything in response, just wraps her arm around me and gives me a sideways hug.

As I watch the sunset in my backyard, I figure today has probably been the best day of my life.

Article from TMZ.com—May 16, 2020, 11:45 A.M. PST

EVIE JONES, WOULD-BE HOLLYWOOD STARLET, HIRED THEN FIRED!!!

Just a month ago, it was announced that **Evie Jones**, granddaughter of the great Evelyn Conaway, would star in the next **Paul Christopher** thriller, *Deep Within*, alongside a slew of other A-list actors. But that excitement was short-lived to say the least. This morning, footage leaked of Evie mocking Paul himself!

In the video, she's visibly drunk, swaying side to side as she makes fun of Paul's accent in a surprisingly good impression.

Apparently, Paul was so offended by the video, he fired her on the spot! He's already hired another newbie, **Simone Davis**, as Evie's replacement. And get this, Simone went to the same high school as Evie. Apparently they were best friends. Can you say *awkward*? We doubt that friendship is gonna last . . .

A petition (most likely created by Paul Christopher superfans) went around online, begging directors and producers not to work with Evie. Our sources tell us that some big-deal people in Hollywood are already way ahead of them and Evie's name has made it onto a blacklist.

Evie has yet to make a statement, and she hasn't been seen out in public. Sounds like a certain grandmother of hers . . .

AUGUST

Chapter Two

WEDNESDAY, AUGUST 12

This has been the worst summer of my life.

I think it's safe to say that this has been the worst summer of my parents' lives too. Because here they are back at home, nowhere near Botswana, their film nowhere near finished. And it's all my fault.

They sit across from me at the dining room table, silently watching as I push scrambled eggs around my plate. My mom went through the trouble of cooking breakfast this morning. She clears her throat, and I glance up, but she doesn't say anything. I look at my dad and wonder if I'm the reason he has new gray hairs sprouting in his low-cut afro. He takes a sip of his orange juice and steeples his fingers, like he's thinking hard about a way to start conversation. But he doesn't say anything either. Instead, they both look at me with matching frowns—a mixture of disappointment and confusion. This is how it's been between us all summer.

"Kerri will be here soon," I say, breaking the silence.

My mom nods, rubbing her eyes. Her usual light-brown skin is a few shades darker from all the time she's spent in Botswana. "Are you all packed?" she asks. I nod. "Well, you should finish your food before Kerri gets here."

I look down at my eggs, which have gone cold. It's weird to try to eat food with actual protein or vitamins. For weeks I've survived on nothing but Cheetos and Sour Patch Kids as I lay in bed, bingeing cartoon shows from my childhood. *Total Drama Island* was the only thing that could keep my mind off the disaster that is my life. "I'm not that hungry."

Dad gets up and starts stacking plates. "Do you need help bringing down your luggage?"

"No, I've got it." I take this as an out to excuse myself from the table. "I'll be back down in a few minutes."

My parents share a look and only nod in response.

They came back from Botswana the day after the video leaked. All it took was my life blowing up for them to finally come home. First, there was a lot of yelling. *What were you thinking, sneaking into our bar and* drinking*? Didn't we teach you better than that?*

After the anger, there was embarrassment. Not that they'd say so. But I could tell. Usually, when my parents get back from a documentary trip, our house is bustling with their friends who haven't seen them in so long. This summer, the house has been a dead zone. It's just been me wandering to the bathroom at 2:00 A.M. while my parents act like I killed their real daughter along with my career.

Now they're just coming to terms with the fact that I'm not as exemplary as they thought I was. My mom wanted to send me to rehab. She thought I'd been sneaking into their bar behind their backs for months. Gigi is the one who persuaded her not to go through with it.

Gigi, who I haven't spoken to since the night before the video leaked.

She's called, but I've been too ashamed to speak to her. I deleted all of her voice mails except for the last one from a few weeks ago. "I know what this is like, Evie Marie, I do," she says. "If there was anything I could do to help you through this, baby, you know I would. I *hope* you know I would." She heaves a sigh, and there's a long silence before she hangs up. I've listened to it so many times that I have it memorized.

We communicate through my mom, mostly. Meaning my mom tells Gigi that I'm still alive, and Gigi tells my mom that she loves me and hopes to see me soon.

Well, I'm going to see her now, and she won't like why I'm coming.

On my way to my room, I pass the guest room, where Simone used to sleep. It was once filled with her things, and now it's empty, save for the neatly made bed and unused dresser.

The morning after we recorded the video, I woke up with a killer headache. I shuffled down to Simone's room, and she was in the middle of packing her things.

"Just taking my winter and spring clothes home," she said when I asked what she was doing. She turned around and flashed a bright smile. "I'll come back with my summer things tomorrow."

I said okay and even helped her finish packing. I should have paid attention to how she barely spoke to me. How she couldn't get out of my house fast enough.

Later that morning, when the video leaked, my phone was buzzing like crazy with alerts. Texts from classmates (who never talked to me otherwise) and Instagram DMs and tags. I rewatched the video a dozen times in complete horror. I kept trying to get ahold of Simone, because I was convinced that there was some mistake. Did someone hack into her phone? Did she accidentally send it to someone else and then they leaked it? She couldn't have done this on purpose. But I couldn't get in touch with her. She'd blocked my number and blocked me on social media.

Paul Christopher's fans flocked to my comments and said I was ungrateful and spoiled. How could I make fun of him after what he'd done for my career? They called me names that I don't even want to repeat. All that love turned so easily to hate. It's a little baffling when I think about it now.

I grab my suitcases out of my room as the doorbell rings

downstairs. And then there's the sound of Kerri's bright and firm voice.

"Good morning, Mr. Jones," she says to my dad.

I hustle to carry my luggage down the steps, eager to see her.

She walks into the living room, dressed in an all-black suit and pointy black pumps. She gives me a reassuring smile. "There's our girl," she says, sitting down on the couch. I quickly plop right beside her. I just saw her last week, but I've also been alone with my distant parents for days on end. Kerri is like a breath of fresh air.

"How are you?" she asks, quiet enough that only I can hear, as my parents sit down on the love seat across from us.

I shrug. "The same." Meaning *terrible*.

Her smile is a mix of softness and sympathy. "Don't worry. It's going to change soon. That's why we're doing this. It's going to work out." She turns to face my parents. "Do either of you have questions before I take Evie to the airport?"

Mom's full lips are set in a thin line. "Are you sure you don't want us to come with you now?" she asks me.

"I'll be fine, Mom," I insist. "I want to spend some time with Gigi, just the two of us."

She doesn't look comfortable with this, but she doesn't push it either. She's never tried to put herself between Gigi and me.

I'm flying to New York tonight for two reasons. The first

is that the FCC committee has asked me to present Gigi with her lifetime achievement award during Sunday's ceremony. After everything that's happened, I have no idea why they want me to be there. Before, the thought of getting up in front of all those people would have thrilled me, but now I'm just terrified.

The second reason is because I have to tell Gigi about a deal I've made, one that I hope will save my career. One that I hope won't make her hate me. This is my second chance, and my stomach churns at the thought of everything slipping through my fingers again.

"I know it's been a hard couple of months, but things are looking up for us," Kerri says confidently. "What happened in May was unfortunate, but we have to keep going, full speed ahead." She turns to my parents. "We'll fly into New York on Sunday before the ceremony like we planned." She looks at me. "You just worry about talking to your grandmother."

My mom's pinched expression still hasn't eased. My dad glances at his watch. "Well, I guess you'd better get going."

I stand and cross the room to hug them. Stiffly, my mom wraps her arms around me. The hug lasts a millisecond. Dad follows up with a similar hug, but he includes a shoulder pat.

"Be careful," he says sternly.

"Call us as soon as you get to Gigi's," Mom says. "And we'll see you on Sunday."

"I will," I promise.

Kerri and I go outside, where a car is waiting to take us to the airport. Once we're in the back seat, she reaches into her huge purse and hands me a plain black baseball cap and black cat-eye sunglasses. Last, she hands me a wig cap and a black wig. It's a French bob with bangs.

"It's a lace front, like we talked about," she says. "Human hair, so it looks real."

"Thanks," I mumble.

Last month, between cartoon episodes, I cut off all my hair. I'm not even sure why. I just know that one day, I was staring at myself in the bathroom mirror, thinking that I didn't recognize the person staring back at me. The next thing I knew, I was holding scissors and the bathroom tiles were covered with curls. I had shorn my hair so close to my head it gave not recognizing myself a whole new meaning. Then, naturally, I screamed. When my mom ran into the bathroom, she screamed too.

My Beautiful You campaign was officially out the window, right along with my career.

I haven't really been out in public since the video leaked. I went to In-N-Out once, but the paparazzi chased me down and I almost crashed my car. We decided for this New York trip, it would be best if I go incognito. I don't want anyone to know where I am or what I'm doing until the FCCs. It's possible that people won't recognize me without the wig anyway, since my hair is so short, but it's better to be safe than sorry.

"It's cute," I say, examining the wig. I just wish I were wearing it for a different reason.

"Of course it's cute," Kerri says. "I wouldn't have you out here looking a mess. You know me better than that."

She winks and smiles. To be honest, I don't understand Kerri's unending optimism or why she hasn't just quit yet. She's anchored herself to a sinking ship, and for some reason, she's decided not to abandon me.

The morning that the video leaked, Kerri practically flew to my house to do damage control, but by that point it was already too late. Someone from Paul Christopher's team called and dropped the news that I was fired. Paul didn't want to work with someone who had so little respect for him. I tried to explain that it was just a joke. I respected Paul more than anyone. But it didn't matter. The video was already out, and the media was running with it.

Kerri camped out at my house and decided that the best thing would be to issue a statement with a public apology. She wanted to get the right terminology, to make sure that my words couldn't be misconstrued. She wanted to wait at least a day in case things blew over. But Kerri wasn't the one getting all of the hateful messages. *I* was. While she was busy thinking of the best way to release a statement, I locked myself in my room and recorded an apology video. Tearfully, I looked into the front-facing camera and told everyone how sorry I was.

"I have deep respect for Paul Christopher," I said. "It was just a joke. Please, you have to understand."

But the video just made things worse. The next thing I knew, people were re-creating it and mocking me. It was like revenge for mocking Paul Christopher. Someone even turned my apology video into a GIF, and it exploded all over Twitter. The jokes went on and on, and I read every single one.

I deleted all of my social media after that. We decided the best course of action would be no more public statements. I'd already apologized to Paul and his team, and I'd put out a video, even if it was a bad idea. I just needed to lie low for a few weeks until things died down. It soon became very clear that no one else in Hollywood would want to work with me. We couldn't get any meetings, and no one would send Kerri scripts for me to read. The endorsement deals I had fell through. It was a nightmare.

Now it seems like we might be coming out on the other side, but I won't know if that's true until I talk to Gigi.

Kerri helps me put on the wig cap and wig. I run my fingers through the wig until the hair falls smooth and straight, and I slide on the sunglasses and baseball cap. The cap does not go with the black-and-white Peter Pan–collar dress that I'm wearing, but I can't bring myself to care.

"Gigi used to do this," I suddenly say, looking at my reflection in my front-facing camera.

Kerri tilts her head. "Used to do what?"

"She would wear disguises when we went out together because she didn't want to be recognized. One time, when she was still living in LA, she took me to the drive-in movie theater, and she wore this long platinum wig and a huge beach hat. I mean, in all honesty, it made people look at her even more. But they never would have guessed that she was Evelyn Conaway behind the disguise."

I laugh a little to myself at the memory. It's ironic, really. I've always wanted to be more like Gigi, and this is the way in which I'm like her.

"She sounds wonderful." Kerri's smile is sad. "I can't wait to meet her."

The rest of the ride to LAX is quiet. When Kerri and I get out of the car, the paparazzi waiting outside glance at us but look away, uninterested.

"That's good," Kerri mumbles. "They have no idea who you are."

She walks with me to security and stops because she can't go any farther. I turn to her to say goodbye, and I'm surprised when she reaches out and hugs me. Kerri, who finds physical contact to be highly unprofessional. Her hug is so warm and tight, unlike the hugs I received from my parents.

"You've got this," she whispers fiercely. She pulls away and stares me dead in the eyes. "Look at me. You've got this."

I start sniffling and wipe my face as tears run down my cheeks.

"Thanks, Kerri." I take a deep breath and force myself to stop crying. She gives my shoulder a tight squeeze and waits to leave until I pass through security. I turn around and wave at her. She smiles and gives a thumbs-up.

I wish I could be as positive as her. But I *don't* have this. I have nothing. No fans. No career. No friends. My *best friend* was the one who did this to me. Looking back, maybe I should have seen it coming. The signs were all there. I was just willfully oblivious.

That might be the worst part about all of this. That, or the news I'm bringing to Gigi's doorstep. I just hope she understands. My entire career is on the line.

I've survived the world hating me, but I couldn't take it if Gigi hated me too.

Chapter Three

There's no one waiting to pick me up at JFK.

I step outside and search for Gigi's driver, Frank, who drives a black Mercedes. But he isn't here. New York in the middle of August is no joke. I haven't visited during the summer in years, and I'm clearly not used to it. It's so hot out that heat rises off the concrete in waves. My scalp is sweating, and I can't wait to take off this freaking hat and wig. After a few seconds in the heat, I quickly walk back inside through the revolving doors. I'd rather not melt before I even make it to Gigi's.

"Ma'am, do you need help?"

I blink and turn to see an airport employee staring at me. She's white and tall, with a wide and friendly smile. "Do you need to get a taxi?"

"No," I say, instinctively pulling my baseball cap lower, pushing my sunglasses farther up on my nose. "I'm okay. Thank you."

"All right, then." She nods and starts to back away.

I avert my gaze and brace myself for the inevitable moment when she realizes who I am and yells at me for mocking Paul Christopher. Or worse, when she snaps a picture of me and posts it on social media.

But surprisingly, the woman turns and walks in the opposite direction, intent on helping a family that looks lost. She doesn't even spare me a second glance.

Before I *do* end up being recognized, I walk back outside again, rolling my two huge suitcases behind me. I look to my left and right for Frank, but I still don't see him. There are tons of other cars here, though. Including a grocery store truck parked all the way at the end. A short Black man with a thick mustache and bald head talks loudly on his phone, leaning against the side of the truck.

I pull out my phone to call Gigi, and that's when I see that I've received two texts. One is from my mom.

Did you land? she asks.

I text back, **Yes. Going to Gigi's now.**

Her reply comes right away: **Good. Stay safe. And out of trouble.**

I've been in New York for barely twenty minutes. What trouble does she expect me to cause in that short of a window? Before I can even let her message get to me, I read the second text, from Kerri.

Hey, I tracked your flight and saw that you just landed. Was everything okay? I hope you got some sleep. Did you get picked up yet?

The flight was okay, I respond. **I'm waiting for my ride now.**

How long have you been waiting? Do you want me to call you a car? she asks.

I text back, **No, I'm okay. Gigi's driver is on his way. Thank you, though.**

Okay, let me know when you get there? 👍

Our exchange makes me feel a little better. **Yep, will do.**

I wipe sweat beads from my forehead and call Gigi again. She doesn't answer. I sigh and call once more. This time she picks up.

"Hello?" she says.

I don't know if it's the heat and exhaustion or the fact that I'm so happy to finally hear her voice, but I suddenly feel like crying again.

"Hi, Gigi." I hold back a sob. "I'm here at the airport."

"Oh, Evie Marie," she says, sounding relieved, "I thought it might be you calling. Is everything all right? Have you found Mr. Gabriel? He should be waiting there for you."

"Is that your new driver?" I ask, surprised that Frank must have retired too. "What kind of car does he drive?"

"Oh, no, Mr. Gabriel is a dear friend who was kind enough

to do me a favor," she says. "I haven't had a driver since Frank moved back to Florida. Are you waiting at arrivals? He's hard to miss." She pulls the phone away from her ear. "Milo, didn't you say he was at the American Airlines terminal?" I hear a boy's voice respond "Yeah!" in the background.

I blink, trying to process what's happening. Milo? The name sounds familiar, but I can't place it. "Gigi . . . who was that?"

"Oh, you remember Milo. He was here last Christmas. I'm going to call Mr. Gabriel right now and make sure he finds you. Hold tight."

"Gigi, wait—"

But she's already hung up.

He's hard to miss? What is that supposed to mean? I turn my head this way and that, looking for a bright-red Mercedes instead of a black one, but I don't see anything.

"Evie! Evie, is that you?"

I whip my head to the left and see the short, bald man who was leaning against the grocery truck walking toward me, waving his hands in my direction. Immediately, alarm bells sound in my head. I've been discovered, even in my carefully curated disguise. Is he paparazzi or something? He doesn't have a camera. Maybe he's a reporter? My eyes go to the cell phone in his right hand, and I take a step backward.

He smiles at me, relieved. "Evie! I'm your grandmother's

friend, Mr. Gabriel. I thought maybe you'd hopped into a cab. You look a lot different from the picture she showed me."

I squint at him. Now that he's closer, I see that his red T-shirt says GABRIEL'S GROCERIES in thick white letters.

Wait a minute. *This* guy is taking me to Gigi's?

"How was your flight?" he asks, and before I can answer, he's reaching past me for my suitcases. "Let me get those for you."

But I move to the side, blocking him. "I don't understand. How do you know my grandmother?"

"She buys her groceries from my store," he says, still smiling. "She's one of my most loyal customers."

Without asking, he takes both of my suitcases and begins rolling them toward his truck.

I know that I've been avoiding Gigi, but I still trust her with my life. She wouldn't send a serial killer to pick me up from the airport. Mr. Gabriel has to be legit.

And that's how I find myself climbing into a grocery store delivery truck and being driven to the Upper West Side of Manhattan. As if I needed a reminder that I've completely fallen from grace.

Marvin Gaye blares through the truck's speakers, and Mr. Gabriel shouts over the music so that I can hear him. I'm learning that he is a talkative man.

"Your grandmother said you went to a fancy school in Los

Angeles and that you were in some popular movie," he says. "What was it called?"

"*Mind Games*," I say quietly, looking out the window.

"What?" he shouts.

"*Mind Games*!" I roll up my window so that the wind isn't so loud.

"Ah, never seen it," he says. "I'll have to check it out. My niece, Janine, lives in Los Angeles too, you know. She writes plays. She's working on one right now . . . Um, I forget what it's called."

"Oh, cool." Whenever I meet people who aren't from LA, they just assume all the people who live in LA know one another. I was well connected before my life imploded, but there's not much I can do for his niece now, if that's what he's hoping for. I continue to look out the window as we drive through Times Square, hoping he stops the conversation there.

"I'll give you her number, and you can call her." He glances at me as he says, "You know, you really do look a lot different in person. Nothing like that picture I saw."

I cringe, finger-combing my wig self-consciously. "It's the hair."

And, irony of ironies, that's when I see it: Simone's face on a huge billboard for Beautiful You's newest hair-care line.

"YOU'VE GOT TO BE KIDDING ME!" I shriek.

Mr. Gabriel swerves, and the drivers around us lean on their horns.

"What? What is it?" he asks frantically.

Not only did she replace me in Paul Christopher's movie, she stole my beauty campaign! She knew how much I wanted to work with Beautiful You, what it meant to me. How can one person be so terrible?

"I hate her," I mumble, holding my face in my hands. I'm *seething*. I'm surprised steam isn't wafting off of me. "I hate her so freaking much!"

"*Who?*" Mr Gabriel asks. "What are you talking about?"

I sink lower into my seat and squeeze my eyes closed, reminding myself to breathe. In and out, in and out, again and again, until my pulse returns to normal.

Poor Mr. Gabriel is still confused and alarmed. I can't even bring myself to explain. I'll end up spiraling out again.

"Here we are," he eventually says, turning onto West Eighty-Seventh Street and heading toward Columbus Avenue.

He comes to a stop in front of Gigi's town house. I look out the window and stare at it. The last time I visited, I was happy, a different person. Everything was different.

"Thank you," I say to Mr. Gabriel, but my hand freezes on the door handle. "And, um, I'm really sorry for shouting out of nowhere and scaring you."

He smiles warmly and waves his hand. "Please, it's not a problem. I live in New York. I've seen worse."

He helps retrieve my suitcases from the back of his truck and rolls them onto the sidewalk. I stand beside them and thank him again.

"Don't worry about it. Anything to help your grandmother," he says. "You just take down my niece's number and promise to give her a call one of these days."

"I don't really know if that's a good idea . . ." Doesn't he know what I've done? I'm sure his niece does *not* want me calling her, especially if she's trying to break into the industry.

"Nonsense! You take her number down right now."

He actually stands there and waits as I enter his niece's number into my phone before quickly hopping into his truck and driving away.

And then I'm alone again.

Gigi's neighborhood is so quiet. Beautiful and affluent, but mostly quiet. I guess that's why she wanted to move here.

I always try to look my best, but as a rule, I want to look spotless when I see Gigi. I try to smooth out my wrinkled dress, but it's no use. I finger-comb my wig's bangs again and climb Gigi's front steps, dragging my suitcases behind me and hoping for the best.

I ring the buzzer, and there's the sound of feet shuffling down the hallway. After a moment, where I assume Gigi is peeking through her peephole, the door opens, and she appears.

She's dressed in a white linen suit, wearing a pearl necklace with pearl earrings to match. It looks like she's ready for a fancy evening out. But she's not. Gigi never leaves her house.

I take off my sunglasses, and I can barely finish saying, "Hi,

Gigi—" before she pulls me inside and wraps me in the tightest hug of my life. Suddenly, I'm a little kid again, coming to spend the day with her, and I feel a little less alone. I've *missed* her.

"I was so worried about you," she says when she pulls away. "When you said you couldn't find Mr. Gabriel, I was afraid that he accidentally went to LaGuardia."

Even when frantic, Gigi somehow manages to look composed and pristine. Her hair is gray now, but it's still thick and freshly curled. She smells like Chanel No. 5 and . . . fried chicken? Actually, it smells like fried chicken all over.

"Come, come," she says, motioning for me to leave my suitcases in the foyer. I slide off my platform sandals and leave them at the door before I follow her down the hall to the sitting room. I step gingerly onto her cream-colored carpet, and she sits down on her cream love seat, patting the empty space beside her. Everything in Gigi's house is cream, from the furniture to the walls. She says it makes her feel calm. Even her two Persian cats, Mark Antony and Cleo, are sort of cream-colored. They're glaring at me from across the room as we speak.

"I'm glad to know that your phone is working," Gigi says, eyeing me. "I haven't heard from you in quite some time."

"I know." I look down, a wave of shame rising up inside. "I'm sorry."

She leans closer and quietly says, "How have you been? How are you feeling?"

"Not great." I look back up at her calm face, and she looks so sad. Sad for me.

"I know you've had a rough time, baby. But it won't be like this forever. This too shall pass, as they say." She gently puts her hand on my cheek and reaches up to smooth my bangs aside. "So this is what you've gone and done to your hair? It's not as bad as your mother made it sound."

I take off my baseball cap. "That's because I'm wearing a wig."

"Oh?" She stares, waiting. It takes a minute for me to realize that she wants to see my real hair. I sit up straighter, fighting nerves as I remove my wig and wig cap.

Gigi sucks in a breath, and I wince. My hair is growing back slowly, but it's in that in-between phase where the growth is not cute. I'd die before I let anyone other than my family or Kerri see it.

"Why on earth did you do this, Evie Marie?" Gigi asks, running her hand tentatively over my head. "My goodness, girl."

"Well, I . . .," I start. But I don't know how to answer this question. "I guess I thought there was no point in having great hair if my life was so terrible."

She shakes her head, frowning. "You should have been proud of your thick curls. I have them too, you know."

"I know." People always tell me how much Gigi and I look alike. I've seen the side-by-side pictures, and I won't lie, the resemblance is a little freaky. We both have light-brown skin, round faces with high cheekbones, and almond-shaped eyes.

She continues to run her hand over my head, and I lean into her touch. My scalp welcomes her massage and the fresh air. It's just going to be Gigi and me here all week. I'll never have to put this silly wig back on again. I feel my anxiety melting away.

"I think it looks nice, actually."

I whip around at the sound of a deep, unfamiliar voice and quickly cover my head with my hands.

I find myself staring at a tall, thin boy with deep-brown skin. His hair is cut into a fade with short dreadlocks at the top. He's wearing ripped jeans and the same red GABRIEL'S GROCERIES T-shirt that Mr. Gabriel wore . . . along with one of Gigi's aprons.

He looks slightly familiar, but I can't place him. He's also seeing me without my wig and basically just heard me admit that I cut my hair because I hated my life! *That* is why I practically shout, "Who the hell are you?"

"*Language*, young lady," Gigi chides. Suddenly, it all clicks—his T-shirt, the voice I heard in the background when I called from the airport. This is the boy who answered Gigi's phone a few months ago.

"I'm Milo," he says easily. He walks closer and holds out his hand for a shake. That's when I notice his gold hoop nose ring. And the fact that he's cute. Really cute. Classically handsome, as Gigi likes to say, with a square jawline, thick eyebrows, and full lips.

I shove my baseball cap back onto my head.

A bright smile is plastered on his face. "Milo Williams," he continues. "We've met before and spoke on the phone once."

I stare at his shiny white teeth and shake my head. Pointedly, I say, "We've never met."

"You have," Gigi corrects, standing up and placing her hands on my shoulders, trying her best to soothe me. "Milo and his band sang carols for us last Christmas."

I blink at him, trying to think back. All I really remember from that night is Gigi "surprising" my parents and me with carolers. They were four boys around my age, and they wore ridiculously ugly Christmas sweaters. One boy had a guitar, and now that I think about it, that boy might have been Milo. Another boy had a saxophone, but that's as much as I can recall. I think they sounded okay. I don't remember them sounding *bad*. But I spent most of the time texting Simone, who was in Ibiza with her girlfriend's family for the holidays. I barely paid attention to the carolers.

I look him up and down, and my eyes freeze at the slippers on his feet. *Gigi's* slippers. I suck in a breath and point. "Where did you get those?"

"He got them from me," Gigi says. "He's my guest. Really, Evie Marie. What's gotten into you?"

I think the correct question is what's gotten into *her*? I look back at Milo, who is still sporting that easy smile. When he finally realizes I'm not going to shake his hand, he stuffs it into his back pocket and shrugs like it's no big deal that I'm being incredibly rude.

I'm remembering the phone conversation I had with him in May. He said that he delivered Gigi's groceries and that he was her friend. I figured maybe they chatted a little when he dropped off her food. I definitely didn't expect him to be walking around her house and wearing her apron and slippers!

"Milo helped me cook this wonderful dinner for you," Gigi says. "We've been in the kitchen since two o'clock."

Well, it's definitely time for him to go now. Gigi and I have important things to discuss, and we don't need an audience.

I stand up and force a smile. Curtly, I say, "Thank you so much for helping Gigi with dinner. I guess you'd better get going soon so that you can grab dinner for yourself."

Milo blinks. "Oh, um. Actually—"

"He's staying for dinner," Gigi finishes.

"I'm sorry, what?" I say, looking between the two of them. I have no idea what's going on here! Who *is* this guy?

Gigi shoots me an admonishing look. "He's staying for dinner," she repeats. "Now let's eat. I'm starving."

Milo and Gigi walk to the kitchen side by side. Her cats trail closely behind.

I stand there in confused silence. Gigi glances back and beckons for me to join them.

With heavy, reluctant steps, I walk toward the kitchen, feeling like I just stepped into an episode of *The Twilight Zone*.

Chapter Four

The three of us settle around Gigi's huge white dining table, she and Milo sitting side by side across from me. Otis Redding's "Try a Little Tenderness" is playing on her record player, and Milo is smiling as if this is all normal. Like *the* Evelyn Conaway offering you hospitality and claiming you as a friend is something that happens to people every day.

"Gigi, how long has he been delivering your groceries?" I ask.

"Since last summer," Milo answers, as if I directed the question to him. Gigi nods.

So it's been a year. Why didn't I know this?

Maybe you were so concerned with your own life you didn't think to ask.

I shake away that thought and look at the dinner in front of me. The table is covered with fried chicken (explains the smell), baked macaroni and cheese, collard greens, and corn pudding. It looks delicious, but this isn't the kind of food that Gigi usually eats. She's been a clean-eating vegan my whole life.

"I made everything except for the mac and cheese," she says proudly. "You can thank Milo for that."

"All I did was follow directions from your recipe," he says. "I really can't take credit."

Gigi frowns at him. "What have I told you about taking credit when it's due?"

He laughs and nods. "Okay, okay. You're right."

It sounds childish and unreasonable, but now that I know Milo made the mac and cheese, I don't want to eat it.

"I thought you didn't like this kind of stuff," I say to Gigi, while Milo rubs his hands together and licks his lips.

She shrugs, piling food onto her plate. "Life's too short, baby. We might as well eat whatever makes us happy." She pauses and then adds, "Within reason, of course."

Gigi says a prayer, and then she and Milo begin eating. He stuffs his face like a barbarian. Apparently, over the course of their friendship, Gigi's never made him sit through her infamous etiquette classes like I had to.

Gigi passes the salt to Milo, and he hands her the hot sauce. She compliments him on the mac and cheese. He tells her that her collard greens have just the right amount of kick. All the while, Otis Redding continues to croon softly in the background. It's clear that this is a routine for them. A regular dinner on a Wednesday night. Gigi is visibly more relaxed than I've seen in years, and I should feel more relaxed too, happy even. But I can't seem to pick up my fork and join in on this meal.

My confusion morphs into agitation. I came here to see Gigi and talk to her about the ceremony, to tell her about the decision I've made. It's too important not to discuss. I wish Milo would beat it.

Instinctively, I glance up at the clock above the stove to check the time. But this clock is new . . . and it's bright red.

"When did you buy that?" I ask, nodding at the clock.

Gigi stops chewing and uses a napkin to dab her mouth. "Oh, Milo bought it when my old one stopped working."

"But it's red," I state, almost accusingly. Gigi hasn't decorated her house with anything but shades of cream for as long as I've been alive.

"I know." She smiles. "It's so bright. I like it."

When I glance over at Milo, he's staring at me with a wary look on his face, a mouse waiting for the cat to pounce. Good. He should be wary.

"So you're in a band?" I ask him, raising an eyebrow. "What kind of band?"

"It's a funk and R&B mash-up," he says. "Like Bruno and his band, the Hooligans . . . just not as good."

"Oh, I think you could be better than that Bruno fellow,"

Gigi says. "Don't sell yourself short." To me, she adds, "They practice all the time. One of their videos even went virtual."

"You mean *viral*, Ms. C," he says, laughing.

Ms. C?

Gigi waves her hand and says, "Yes, yes, viral." Smiling, she turns back to me. "Milo is a very talented musician, Evie Marie."

This interaction is strangely similar to the way Gigi used to talk to her friends about *me*. I feel a tightening sensation deep in my gut. He has to want something from her. An industry connection? Money? Both?

But it's not just my skepticism that makes me feel this way. From the outside looking in, you'd think *he* was her grandchild and I was the guest.

"Your mother told me things were going well in Botswana," Gigi says. "I'm glad they decided to come home for a little while, though. I never liked the idea of you being there by yourself so much."

"I wasn't alone," I say, thinking of Simone. Which then makes me remember her huge Beautiful You ad in Times Square, which then makes me upset all over again.

"When I was in middle school, we watched your parents' documentary on global warming," Milo says. "It was really good, eye-opening. Do you know what they'll do after Botswana?"

"No." I try my best not to glare at him. Why won't he just go away?

Maybe the best tactic is to broach the subject little by little until he eventually leaves.

"Have you thought about what you're going to wear to the ceremony on Sunday?" I ask Gigi.

She looks at me and sighs. Before she can reply, the phone rings. Milo stands up to answer it, but Gigi stills him, placing a hand on his arm. "Let the answering machine pick it up," she says.

Milo sits back down, just as a woman's upbeat voice leaves a message.

"**Hi, Peg,**" she says. "**It's Candice calling. I was hoping you might have changed your mind about coming to the gala tomorrow night. Give me a call back. Love you.**"

Evelyn Conaway is just Gigi's stage name. Her real name is Peggy Connor. So this woman must be a close friend if she calls Gigi "Peg."

"Was that Candice, as in Candice Tevin?" I ask.

Candice Tevin is one of the most famous fashion photographers, like, ever. She and Gigi grew up together in Brooklyn, and she got her start in the '70s, when she took a bunch of pictures of Gigi for a *Vanity Fair* article. Since then, she's gone on to photograph anyone and everyone. She even took a few pictures of me once, when Gigi set up a photo shoot for my eleventh birthday. I've always wanted her to photograph me professionally, but who even knows if that will happen now.

"Yes," Gigi answers. She points at my plate. "You haven't eaten any of your food. Aren't you hungry?"

"Candice Tevin invited you to a gala?" I ask, ignoring Gigi's attempts to distract me. "What kind of gala?"

Gigi shrugs. "She thinks because I signed some photographs for her fundraiser tomorrow it means that I actually want to attend. That's what everyone has been doing for the past month, inviting me here and there. Calling, sending things in the mail. It's been ridiculous. I even think there was a paparazzi man outside of the house last week!" She turns to Milo. "I told you that, didn't I? He was sitting in a black car."

Milo nods, then glances at me. "I don't know if it was paparazzi, though. I don't think it's something either of you should worry about."

"Gigi, that's perfect!" I say, waving away her paranoia. "You haven't made a public appearance in so long. The gala can be like a warm-up for Sunday's ceremony. You have to call her back."

Suddenly, Gigi gets quiet, fidgeting with her pearl necklace. Then, "I'm not going to the ceremony. You'll accept the award on my behalf."

"What?" My empty stomach drops. "But, Gigi . . . you have to go. What are you talking about?"

"I don't have to do anything, actually," she says, finally putting her fork down. "And while I'm slightly flattered that they've chosen to honor me in this way, I'd rather not be bothered with any of it. You'll do as I say and accept the award on my behalf, Evie Marie."

No. No, no, no.

I stare at her with the sudden realization that my well-laid plans are unraveling in front of me. This is going to ruin everything.

"But you have to go to the ceremony," I repeat. "Gigi, everyone is expecting you to be there. Are you afraid because of what happened between you and James last time? It was so long ago, no one is thinking about that anymore."

She holds up her hand. "You know better than to mention that name in this house."

The room goes deadly quiet. Then Milo drops his fork on the floor and Gigi and I both jump.

"Why are you still here?" I snap.

Gigi looks as if she wants to jump across the table and shake me.

"I actually have a band meeting," Milo says carefully, sliding away from the table and excusing himself. "Thanks for dinner, Ms. C." He leans down to hug her and nods at me. "It was nice to meet you."

"Don't forget to put your hamper outside your room," she says to him. "I'm doing laundry tonight."

"*His room?*" My head is spinning. I feel like Gigi has been fully taken over by a pod person. "Wait a minute, he *lives* here?"

"Not exactly," Milo says. "You know, the grocery store is right around the corner, so—"

"I wasn't talking to you!" I snap again. I turn to Gigi. "You can't be serious! He's living with you?"

Distantly, I wonder if I'm overreacting, but I can't seem to calm myself down. After the worst summer of my life, I was looking forward to spending time alone with Gigi. By the end of my trip, she may very well hate me, and I can't help but feel like every second counts—like Milo's presence is ruining everything and pushing Gigi and me further apart.

"Evie Marie, where are your manners?" Gigi hisses, looking horrified. "And stop with all that yelling."

"Sorry," Milo says to me cautiously, and I realize that I've ruined *their* family dinner. Quietly, he says to Gigi, "I'll be back later."

He quickly exits the room and heads upstairs to what I assume must be his *bedroom* so that he can take off his *slippers*.

"Gigi, what is going on?" I ask. "Why are you letting this boy stay here?"

"He needed help, and I'm in a position to help him," she says.

Something about her sympathetic tone makes me even more upset, and I don't know why.

"You didn't think to tell me about this?"

"I tried telling you. I left you a voice mail last month. One of my many calls that you didn't answer." She pauses to level me with a look before continuing on. "As I've said, I am trying to help him."

"Okay," I say, feeling numb. It was the same way I felt for days after the video leaked. I had hoped coming to Gigi's house would be the end of that feeling. "But what about *me*, Gigi?"

She goes completely still.

"What about me?" I repeat. "On one of your voice mails, you said that you would do anything to help me through my situation. Why is it so easy for you to help him, but you won't help me, your actual granddaughter, by coming to the ceremony?"

"How would I be helping you by doing that?" she asks. I don't say anything for a moment. How do I tell her that my entire career is riding on this? "*Talk* to me, Evie Marie. You don't talk to me anymore."

This is the moment. Now is as good a time as any.

Quietly, I say, "Gigi, I have something to tell you."

"What is it?" she asks. Her expression grows increasingly worried. She reaches across the table and gently places her hands over mine. "You can tell me anything, baby."

I gulp. I guess I'm about to find out if that's true. I start with the first reason that I need her at the ceremony.

"Well, I think making an appearance together, no matter how brief, would really help. Just having *you* there with me. I think it would remind people that I'm not just some screwup. I'm Evelyn Conaway's granddaughter. I'm part of a legacy."

"What I don't understand is why you care so much about

what people think," she says, shaking her head. "Why are you letting that influence your decisions?"

I bite my tongue to stop myself from talking back. That's so easy for Gigi to say. She didn't grow up in today's world. It's so much easier to ignore what people say when you aren't bombarded with their opinions every time you open an app to check your mentions or casually go on the internet.

"This is a big opportunity for me, Gigi. I can still be a serious actress," I say. "I can still be great."

Just like you. Just like Mom and Dad.

She waves her hand dismissively. "You've had a little taste of how nasty people can be. I never wanted this life for you. You've lost sight of who you are, which is probably why that whole video business happened in the first place. You should be grateful that this has forced you to take a step back. You're saving yourself from a life of unhappiness."

You've lost sight of who you are. She sounds just like my parents.

I know exactly who I am and what I want. It's why I'm going through all this trouble. I thought that Gigi of all people would understand why I want to fix this situation, why I need her help. But she doesn't understand, and she's refusing to try.

"And you call yourself happy?" I ask, throwing my hands up. "How can you say that when you can't even bring yourself to leave this house? How can *you* judge me for my mistakes when you embarrassed yourself in front of the world and ended your career over a mean thing your husband did to you? What do you know about happiness, Gigi?"

My voice gets louder and louder until I'm practically shouting. But when I finally take a look at Gigi's face, all the fight in me dies.

"I'm sorry, Gigi," I quickly say. "I didn't mean that."

She turns away from me. Gigi doesn't yell. Her motto is that the quietest person in the room actually tends to be the loudest.

I try to apologize again, but she holds up her hand to stop me from talking just as Milo comes barreling down the steps. I forgot he was still in the house, and I suddenly feel even worse about shouting at Gigi.

"Milo," she calls, "take Evie out with you."

"*What?*" I say.

"*What?*" he says, pausing at the door.

"I need space." Her voice is quiet as she massages her temples. "I need to be alone. Completely." She means she needs space *from me*, and it's the worst feeling in the world.

"Gigi, I'm sorry," I say.

Ignoring me, she stands abruptly and walks out of the dining room.

I bite my lip, looking down at the spread of cold food

on the table. I don't want to leave, but maybe it's best that I give her space and try again tomorrow. I walk into the sitting room and put my wig back on, adding the baseball cap and sunglasses.

I watch Gigi as she climbs the staircase with Mark Antony and Cleo right at her heels. But she doesn't turn around to look at me.

Everything blew up in my face before I could tell her the most important reason I need her at the ceremony. As a last resort, Kerri and I finally took the call from James Jenkins's team. It turns out that he's producing a remake of *Every Time We Meet*, and he wants me to play the lead, Diane Tyler. Months ago, I would have laughed at this offer and said absolutely not. But now I am desperate and pretty sure my career might be over before it's even begun, so I said yes. There's only one catch, though. He wants Gigi's blessing and for her to meet with him after the FCC ceremony. If I can't get her blessing or convince her to take the meeting, I don't have the role.

This is what I've been so nervous to tell her. And now we can't even have a conversation about it because I ruined everything by yelling at her.

"It's nighttime," Milo says, pointing at my sunglasses as I meet him at the door. "You won't need those."

Does he actually think I plan on going wherever he's going? Yeah, right.

But then again, I could use this time to figure out his agenda. His days of Gigi-freeloading are over.

"I can see just fine," I say, sliding on my platform sandals.

Then I follow Milo outside into the summer night.

Chapter Five

"What do you want from my grandmother?" I ask Milo.

We've barely made it past Gigi's front stoop. The air is less muggy now that it's nighttime, but it's still pretty hot. The street is quiet, though. The only sound I hear is the clicking of my sandals and the lack of sound coming from Milo's mouth because he hasn't answered my question. His long legs quickly cover a lot of ground, and I have to walk twice as fast to keep up with him.

"Um, hello," I say. "Did you hear me?"

He stops abruptly and faces me, running a hand through his short dreads. He's traded in his slippers for scuffed white Vans, and he's wearing a plain navy-blue T-shirt.

"Look," he says, "I'm sure you think I'm some kind of gold digger or whatever, but I'm not. I told you, I'm your grandma's friend. There's not really much else to say."

"Somehow I don't believe that," I say, rolling my eyes.

He frowns. "I'm not a liar. That's something you should know about me now."

I'm so surprised by how serious he's become that it takes me a second to realize he's moving again. I hurry to catch up. Not a liar, my butt. "How old are you?"

"Nineteen." His easy smile is back. "And you're eighteen, right?"

"Yes," I answer automatically. Then, "Wait, we're not talking about me! What nineteen-year-old musician willingly spends time with a seventy-year-old woman, who just so happens to have been a *movie star*, if he isn't after her money or some kind of business hookup?"

"You wouldn't ask that question if you knew how lonely your grandmother is," he mutters, but I hear him perfectly fine and flinch.

"What is that supposed to mean?"

He doesn't answer and keeps walking. I still try my best to match his pace. Eventually, we turn onto Broadway, where the streets and sidewalks are more crowded. I stop and tense up. In my rush to interrogate Milo, I'd forgotten that following him outside meant I'd be surrounded by a bunch of other people on the busy New York City streets.

Milo turns around when he realizes I'm not walking beside him. "What are you doing?"

"Um." I clear my throat, tugging my baseball cap lower.

That's when I realize no one is paying me any attention. The disguise really is working.

"Evie?" Milo says.

"*Shh*," I hiss as I start walking again. "Someone might hear you."

His gaze trails from my head to my toes, and something clicks. "Are you in a disguise right now?"

"Yes. I'm not supposed to make any public appearances until Sunday's ceremony." I immediately regret saying so, because it's not any of his business.

He makes a face as if he's trying not to laugh, then gets serious again. "Even if you looked like yourself, people would still ignore you. You're in *New York City*. But regardless, don't you think you're being a little extra? I mean, you were only in that one movie, right? No offense, but it's not like you're Rihanna or something."

I do, in fact, catch myself taking offense! If Milo knew the nasty things people said about me online, he'd tell me to wear a hazmat suit. But then I remember that I don't *want* to be recognized. So if he thinks I'll go unnoticed, that's perfect. I'm still irritated at what he said, though. "You don't have to worry about why I'm dressed this way."

He shrugs. "Okay. Can you just try not to trip while wearing those sunglasses? Your grandma would be *really* pissed at me if you fell and wound up in the hospital while on my watch."

I glare at him, deciding I don't need to respond. I'm mostly annoyed because he's right. These glasses *are* pretty dark. When Milo isn't looking, I lower them a little so that I can see better.

When we reach the entrance to the 1 train, he turns to me and raises an eyebrow. "You're not actually coming with me to my band meeting, are you?"

Going to a "band meeting" sounds worse than being forced to do improv without notice. But he hasn't answered all of my questions, and I'm not ready to let go of what he said about Gigi being lonely.

"Yep," I say, walking down the steps, feeling blisters form on my pinkie toes. These are not the right shoes for walking across New York City, but I'd rather die than ask Milo to slow down. It's hotter down here, and it stinks. But one subway ride won't kill me. At least I don't think it will. "So, tell me, when did you transition from Gigi's friend to Gigi's roommate?"

"I don't live with her full-time," he says. At least he hasn't completely infiltrated Gigi's house, like how Simone did with mine. "I just stay there when I have to work late nights and early mornings back to back. I live in Crown Heights with my bandmates."

"Where's that?"

"Brooklyn." He pulls a yellow card out of his wallet. "You have a MetroCard?"

"A what?"

He waves his card in front of me. "You'll need one to get on the subway. How do you not know what a MetroCard is? How many times have you visited your grandmother?"

"She used to have a driver, remember? And if you know Gigi so well, you'd know that she barely leaves her house. Frank took me wherever I wanted to go." I fumble to open my clutch. "Can I buy one with my credit card?"

A voice comes over the loudspeaker, announcing that a train is coming in two minutes. I glance at the long line of people waiting to buy MetroCards and look back at Milo. He's watching me, slightly amused.

"Let's just get an Uber," I suggest.

His eyes widen. "We're going all the way to the West Village. You have that kind of money?" He pauses, then adds, "Never mind. I'm sure you do. I'll swipe you through with me. Just stick close."

We walk up to the turnstile, and I stand right behind him.

"Closer," he says, wrapping his hand around my arm, pulling me so that I'm right up on his back. He smells good, like cinnamon.

"Won't we get in trouble for this?" I whisper as he swipes his card and pulls me through the turnstile and onto the other side of the platform. I can already see the headline: EVIE JONES FINALLY REAPPEARS TO COMMIT ILLEGAL ACTS IN NYC. If Kerri knew what I was doing right now, she'd have a heart attack.

My heart thumps in my chest, and I'm not sure that it's purely from committing a crime.

Milo laughs. "They don't care." He nods at the MTA employee, who is sitting in the booth, busy texting with her head down.

The train pulls up to the platform, and Milo and I manage to get on just before the doors close. It's really crowded, so we don't get a seat. And that really sucks because my feet are killing me.

Milo leans against the door, and I stand in front of him, holding on to the pole. The train jerks when it takes off, and I stumble.

"Whoa, careful," he says, reaching out a hand to steady me.

Embarrassed, I mumble, "I've got it, thanks."

"You want to sit down?" he asks, eyeing my shoes. "We can switch train cars."

Ha, nice try, musician boy. You and your manners won't distract me from my mission.

"What I want is for you to admit what you want from my grandmother," I say, leaning closer. "Just tell me the truth."

"I already told you the truth," he says, frowning. "The better topic is, what do *you* want from her?"

"*Me?*" My hand flies to my chest like an offended woman in Victorian-era England. "What are you talking about?"

"Yeah, you," he says. "You're trying to force her to go to that ceremony when she clearly doesn't want to. That's pretty messed up."

I suck in a breath, literally speechless. Finally, I manage, "How dare you eavesdrop on our conversation!" People turn to look at us, and I lower my voice to a whisper. "That is *not* okay."

"I wasn't eavesdropping; you were shouting. I could hear you all the way upstairs."

"Gigi understands why I need her to be there," I say.

He raises an eyebrow. "Does she? Because it didn't sound like she did."

"You've got a lot of nerve," I say, narrowing my eyes.

He sighs and holds up his hands in surrender. "Okay, I think we've gotten off on the wrong foot. We should try to get along for your grandma's sake, so let's call a truce. Friends?"

He holds out his hand, and once again I just stare at it.

"No," I say.

"No?" he repeats. "Is the idea of being my friend that unappealing?"

I frown at him. "Yes."

"Let me guess," he says, smiling slowly, "you have something against musicians."

"Musicians are passionate people who are dedicated to their craft. As an actress, I can respect that. I'm not big on friends."

He looks at me like I just admitted that I hate babies or those YouTube videos where tiger cubs play with puppies.

"'Not big on friends'?" he repeats dubiously. "What does that even mean?"

I think of Simone and her bright smile. The way she laughed as we sat across from each other during lunch, or when we stayed up all night in my big, empty house. She was like my sister. Until she wasn't.

"Some people prefer solitude," I simply say.

"Hmm" is his only reply. He eyes me intently, and I don't like the way it seems as if he's trying to find some deeper meaning behind my words.

"What? Quit looking at me."

"Sorry." He turns away, not actually sounding sorry at all.

Behind me, two young boys walk through the subway car selling candy. Milo flags them down and offers a couple of dollars but refuses the candy. The boys smile, eagerly thanking him before moving on. Now it's my turn to eye Milo. Apparently, musician boy is generous. He glances down and catches me staring. I shove my sunglasses farther up my nose and look away.

"I really was sorry to hear about all that stuff with Paul Christopher," he suddenly says. "I've never liked any of his movies, to be honest. I think he's overrated."

I blink, taken aback at how straightforwardly he says this. Everyone else walks on eggshells around me when it comes to what happened with Paul Christopher.

"He's not overrated," I finally say, because it's true. Paul Christopher is brilliant. It's very rare for thrillers to win Best Picture at the Academy Awards, and he's done it twice. That role in *Deep Within* would have changed my life.

"If you say so." Milo shrugs and looks up to track our stop.

"What did you mean when you said that Gigi is lonely?" I ask.

He returns his attention to me and opens his mouth like he might explain. But instead he says, "That's something you should talk to her about. We're getting off next."

Obviously, I'm not going to get any real answers out of Milo. As far as I'm concerned, my job here is done. For now.

The train comes to a stop at Christopher Street, and I follow Milo out onto the platform and up the steps aboveground. He starts leading me in one direction, but I stop. "Yeah, I'm not actually going with you," I say.

He nods. "Right. You probably have a lot of friends—I mean, associates—in the city."

I know of a few classmates who are in New York for the summer, but it would be a stretch to reach out to them even if I weren't a pariah. I don't have anyone to see. Milo doesn't need to know that, though.

"I do," I lie.

He nods again, slower this time. "Well, if you want some good french fries, you're welcome to come with me. My bandmate works at Pommes Frites, but I get that you have better things to do."

French fries? My stomach grumbles at the thought. I barely ate anything at dinner. The last real meal I had was on the plane from LA hours ago, and even that was only crackers and a salad. But why would I settle for french fries with Milo and his bandmates when I'm in New York City and there are literally thousands of other places I could go?

"Um, no thanks," I say.

We stand on the corner and turn to look at each other. He's *tall.* And he really does have a handsome face.

Now would be a good time to stop staring at it.

"Okay, bye." I turn on my heel and hurry up the street.

"Bye!" he calls after me.

I walk faster and bump into a woman walking her dog. The dog snarls, and so does she. "Take off your damn sunglasses. It's nighttime!"

Jesus, okay. New Yorkers.

But she's right. I do need to ditch the sunglasses because it's way too dark now. I finger-comb my bangs over my eyes and pull my baseball cap down lower. I have no idea where I'm going. I pause in front of a Mediterranean restaurant. It's packed, so the food must be good. But before I open the door, I clam up. I've had luck so far without being recognized, but what if my luck runs out? Sitting alone at a restaurant feels like a bold move. I don't think I'm ready to be around all of those people yet. It's funny that I've spent all summer wishing I didn't have to be alone, but the thought of being in a room full of strangers makes my heart race.

I could catch a cab back to Gigi's, but she said she wanted space. I haven't been gone very long. If I want her to hear me out, I need to give her all the time she needs. But if I can't go back to Gigi's, and I can't bring myself to go into a restaurant, what am I supposed to do? I'm exhausted, and my feet hurt.

Before I can think better of it, I turn around and speed-walk back to the subway stop, looking for Milo's blue T-shirt.

And there he is, standing right where I left him, a full head taller than the New York City foot traffic swirling around him.

"I wanted to make sure you got where you were going safely," he says as I get closer, a tiny smile just short of smug on his face.

I clear my throat. "Um, those french fries . . . How good are they?"

The corner of his mouth twitches. "Best in the city."

He stands there, staring, that tiny smile still on his face. I wish he would stop looking at me so closely.

"Okay, well, are you going to take me there, or what?" I ask.

"Has anyone ever told you that you're kind of bossy?"

I cross my arms and frown. "No."

He laughs and steps aside, holding out his arms in a gesture for me to walk in front of him. "After you."

Pommes Frites is tiny and crowded, but it smells heavenly. Once we step inside, I put my sunglasses back on and stick close to Milo. There's a long line of people waiting to order, and a short boy with brown skin and a long ponytail stands at the register, looking annoyed and tired. His face lights up when he spots us.

"Milo!" he shouts, completely ignoring the customer in front of him. He waves Milo forward, and his grin widens when he glances at me. "You gonna introduce me to your friend?"

"Raf, this is Evie," Milo pauses, glancing at me and all the people in line. "Ms. C's granddaughter."

Raf's eyes bug out, and his mouth falls open a little. He reaches over the counter to grab my hand and brings it to his mouth for a kiss. This is *not* the reaction I was expecting. All I can do is stare at him for a surprised second before I pull my hand away.

"I'm Rafael Gonzales," he says smoothly. He runs a hand over his hair, flashes a smile, and winks. I can't tell if he knows how cheesy he looks or if he actually thinks he's charming. "It's a pleasure to make your acquaintance."

"It would be a *pleasure* if you took our order." A tall white woman stands behind us with her arms crossed, looking disgruntled. "Or should I ask to speak with your manager?"

Raf frowns and opens his mouth to respond, but Milo steps in. "We're about done here," he says to the woman. He turns to Raf. "Can you bring two large fries to the table? The usual sauces."

"Yeah, yeah, I know," Raf says, waving him away. "Ben and Vinny are already in the back."

Milo nods and steers me past the line, toward a table where two other boys are sitting. One is lanky, with medium-brown skin and curly hair. He's reading a thick paperback novel with a dragon on the cover. The boy beside him is Asian, and he's wearing gold circular, wire-rimmed glasses. He waves at Milo and shoots a quizzical look at me, elbowing the reading boy to get his attention. Now they're both watching us as we approach.

"Yo," Milo says, sitting down across from them. He motions for me to sit beside him, so I do. Quietly, he says, "This is Evie. You know, Ms. C's granddaughter."

I wait to see what their reaction will be. They don't need to kiss my hand like Raf. I just hope they aren't Paul Christopher fans who might hate me.

Slowly, the reading boy puts down his book. His friend beside him adjusts his glasses. And then . . . they stare at me.

"Hi," I finally say.

Milo clears his throat and gives them a look that says, *Stop being weird.*

"Sorry, they're awkward," Milo explains.

"I'm Vinny," the boy with the glasses quickly says, rolling his eyes at Milo. He leans forward and offers his hand for me to shake. "Vinny Oh. It's so nice to meet you. Well, technically we've met before, but super briefly. Last Christmas."

I cringe, hating that I barely remember anything from when they sang carols at Gigi's. Was I that checked out, so busy texting Simone?

"I'm Ben," the other boy says. His smile is wide and welcoming. He glances back and forth between Milo and me. "Um, are you here just visiting your grandma?"

"We have the FCCs on Sunday," I say, and Milo coughs. I glare at him, and he shrugs innocently.

"Alanna was my favorite character in *Mind Games*, even if she was only alive for, like, twenty minutes," Vinny says. "I always say she should have been in it longer, right, Ben?"

"Typical that the Black person got killed first," Ben says, nodding.

My character, Alanna, was a quirky girl who wore Crocs and braces, and she played the trombone in the school band. She's practicing alone on the football field when she gets murdered by the teens in a cult terrorizing her small town. I loved playing her because she was one hundred percent her own person. I guess that must have resonated with Paul's fans. Last year, Hot Topic's bestselling T-shirt had a picture of Alanna with RIP written underneath.

Ben leans forward. "Can you play the trombone in real life?"

"No," I say, smiling. "I can't play any instruments, actually."

"Oh, well, that's also cool," he says, smiling too.

Then that's it. No more questions. And best of all, they

don't bring up Paul Christopher firing me or the video. This is unexpected.

"Apparently, Raf has a surprise for us," Vinny says, frowning. "We probably won't like it."

Milo sighs. "Do we ever?"

"How much do you wanna bet that it's a new song idea?" Vinny says. "I'll bet five dollars. No, better yet, if I'm right, one of you has to do dishes every night this week."

Milo and Ben both balk. "Hell no, not worth betting on that," Milo says. "And you technically don't even live there, so it's not fair."

I relax a little, now that the conversation doesn't revolve around me. Just as I'm starting to remember how hungry I am, a large basket of fries appears before my eyes.

"For you, madam," Raf says, placing another basket in front of Ben and Vinny. He actually bows before he slides next to me on the bench. "I hope you like Thai chili ketchup and pomegranate teriyaki sauce. But if you don't, just say the word and I'll—"

"It's fine," I say quickly, placing my hand on his shoulder and keeping him in place. "It's totally fine. Thank you."

What I want to say is *Please just treat me normally*.

I hope that no one decides to sneak a picture of me and post it somewhere later on. I scan the table, but the boys have their phones put away. I sigh, relieved.

Milo reaches past me and grabs a handful of fries, shoving

them into his mouth. "The Thai chili ketchup is my favorite," he says to me, still chewing.

They all dig in, and I figure I better start eating before all the fries are gone. And Milo was right. The fries *are* good. I've had actual pommes frites in Belgium when I visited with my parents, and these are right up there. Even the Thai chili ketchup is pretty good after I get used to the tangy taste. I start taking big handfuls, just like Milo did. He smiles at me, once again with a tinge of smugness.

"Worth the trip?" he asks.

I nod but don't say anything else since he's gloating.

"So what's with this surprise?" he asks Raf.

Raf wipes his mouth with the back of his hand and excitedly rubs his palms together. "Okay, so boom. About a month ago I was scrolling through Instagram, looking for inspiration, you know, like usual." Milo, Vinny, and Ben all roll their eyes, but Raf continues. "And I came across this artist, some boy named Eli, and his illustrations were dope. So, being the genius that I am, I get the idea that he should design our band logo, since we've been talking about it for so long but haven't actually *done* anything about it. I messaged him, gave him some ideas, and he came up with this." Raf reaches down, unzips his backpack, and pulls out four black T-shirts, dropping them in the center of the table.

The other boys exchange a skeptical glance and sit motionless.

"Well, go ahead and look at them. Damn," Raf says.

Milo is the first to grab a T-shirt and hold it up. In the center, there's an illustration of four white birds flying in a circle. DOVES HAVE PRIDE is written underneath it in bright-purple letters.

"Doves Have Pride," I say, confused. "What's that mean?"

"You didn't tell her about the band, Milo?" Raf asks, incredulous.

"It's our band name," Milo explains, still staring at the T-shirt.

Frustrated, Raf takes it upon himself to elaborate. "We're like Bruno Mars and his band the Hooligans but better," he says. I hold in a snort. I bet he wouldn't be happy to know that Milo told me the complete opposite. "Or if you ask Milo's parents, they'd say we're making the devil's music."

Raf, Vinny, and Ben laugh. Milo smiles and shakes his head.

"Okay, and what does *that* mean?" I ask.

"Nothing," Milo says. "Just that my parents aren't happy I left the church choir to do secular music."

Raf adds, "And they gave him until the end of summer for something to finally happen with the band before they force him to start taking classes at CUNY."

"Can you please stop telling all my business? Damn," Milo says, reaching behind me to pluck Raf in the ear.

"What?" Raf swats him away. "I'm just saying, that gives

us even more reason to wear these shirts. We have to look our best to give ourselves the best chance, you feel me?" He pauses, suddenly focusing on me. "Can I ask a question? What's with the wig?"

Taken off guard, I say, "I'm trying something new."

"Oh." Raf nods. "I mean, I liked the curly hair, but I like this look too. I used to follow you on Instagram before you deleted your account. What was that about, anyway?"

I shake my head, unsure of how to answer. This is the last thing I want to talk about.

"*Raf.*" Milo's voice is sharp.

Raf looks at me sheepishly. "Sorry! I was just curious."

"It's fine," I say, wishing they'd go back to talking about their T-shirts. I contemplate leaving. Has enough time passed for Gigi to have a sufficient amount of space?

Of course, Milo is looking at me carefully when I glance at him. He pushes the basket of fries closer to me.

"Doves Have Pride is a line from 'When Doves Cry,' the song by Prince," he says. "You've heard it before?" I nod. "Prince inspires a lot of our music. So we chose that name, and it stuck. Or it was the only name we could all decide on, I guess."

"And because when I'm singing, my mic is *on*," Raf says.

"Oh, okay," I say. Then quietly, so that only Milo can hear, I add, "Thanks for explaining."

"Sorry to rush this, but can we focus on the shirts?" Ben

asks. "I'd like to be in bed before midnight after a band meeting for once."

"It's not our fault you have the bedtime of a senior citizen," Raf grumbles.

"I kind of like the logo," Milo says. "Ben, Vinny, what do you think?"

Vinny sighs. "I think that I'll add this to the list of Things I Shouldn't Show My Parents. They'll just say I need to quit the band and put all of my focus into music school. The logo is cool, though."

"Vinny is a music major at Brooklyn College," Milo whispers to me. "He's the only one of us who didn't take a year off after high school."

"I heard that," Vinny says. "I'm the only one who has a *backup plan*."

"Excuse me," Raf says. "Can we go back to how Vinny said the design was cool? That's it? Just *cool*?"

Vinny shakes his head, confused. "What's wrong with *cool*?"

"Nothing, just that *cool* means *mediocre*. The response I'm looking for is *Wow, Raf, this new logo is absolutely exceptional. Thanks for always being one step ahead of the game*."

Vinny snorts. "Do you want me to praise the logo or *you*?"

"It doesn't matter either way," Ben interjects. "No one pays attention to band logos anymore. It's not the 1970s."

"Ha! Okay, funny guy," Raf says. "They'll be paying attention to our logo tomorrow night, because this is what we're wearing to the gig."

"Now, wait a minute," Vinny says. "That's something we all have to agree on."

They start talking about their show and continue to go back and forth on the logo. Raf defends wearing the T-shirts like his life depends on it, and Ben and Vinny both oppose him. I get the feeling they're not doing so because they dislike the shirts as much as they enjoy poking fun at Raf. All this back-and-forth banter is fascinating to watch, like I'm getting an exclusive tutorial on the art of friend groups.

"I'm the lead singer!" Raf bursts out. "I should make all final decisions."

"Yeah, but Milo writes the songs," Ben counters.

Intrigued, I glance at Milo, who just shakes his head and sighs. "They're only T-shirts," he says. "It's not that big of a deal."

"It *is* a big deal," Raf says. "Everybody needs to love the shirts just like they loved the outfits I chose for our 'Leather Pants' video."

I guess that must have been the video Gigi mentioned earlier, because then Raf starts to argue that their outfits were one of the reasons their video went viral in the first place. I've never heard of their band or seen the video, obviously, so I have no idea what they're talking about. You fall completely out of the loop when you delete all of your social media.

Finally, when there are no more fries and the boys have more or less agreed to wear the T-shirts, one of Raf's coworkers appears at the table. She's short and curvy, with long Senegalese twists.

"If you're done eating, you need to go," she says to Raf. "You can't keep taking up the biggest table for your band meetings."

"Charisse, babe, there's no need to be rude," Raf says smoothly. "We're leaving now."

"We broke up three months ago," Charisse snaps. "Stop calling me *babe*."

"Okay, babe." Raf stands up and dodges out of the way just in time as Charisse swats at him. He laughs. "Okay, sorry! I was kidding!"

"Get out," she barks.

"We're leaving, I swear," Milo says, steering Raf toward the door. I follow behind Milo, and Ben and Vinny bring up the rear.

We cut through Washington Square Park to get back to the subway station. I lag behind the boys in my uncomfortable shoes as they continue to discuss their set list for tomorrow night. They keep mentioning their song "Leather Pants," and I can't even begin to guess how they came up with that song title.

We pass a row of nice town houses, not unlike Gigi's town

house on the Upper West Side, and it's funny that I've been to New York City so many times but never actually had the chance to walk around and explore the city on my own. These town houses are so different from the apartment where Gigi grew up in Brooklyn. Once, almost five years ago now, she asked Frank to drive us there so that she could show me what it looked like. She was dressed in one of her elaborate disguises, complete with a big, floppy hat and sunglasses. It was one of the rare times we left Manhattan or her house in general.

When we arrived, the old brownstone was abandoned and falling apart. She had lived on the top floor of a one-bedroom apartment with her parents and two brothers.

She looked so sad as she stood in front of her old home. "You are very blessed, Evie Marie," she said. "You've never had to struggle for anything. Be grateful for that."

At the time, that was true. I'd just found out that I'd been accepted at Mildred McKibben. My biggest struggle was dealing with the fact that Gigi lived across the country and that I had to get on a plane to see her.

Gigi was my age when she was discovered waitressing at a speakeasy on the Lower East Side. The owners let her sing every now and then, and my grandfather, who was an up-and-coming movie producer in LA, happened to be there on one of those nights. The way Gigi tells it, he approached her once she was done singing and told her that she was too talented to be singing in speakeasies on Saturday nights; she belonged in movies. He promised that if she came with him to Los Angeles, he'd turn her into a big star. For some reason, she believed him. Two years later, she filmed *Every Time We Meet*, and it changed her whole life.

I almost had a similar life-changing moment, and it blew up in my face. Starring in James Jenkins's remake of *Every Time We Meet* will turn things around for me, though. I just need to get Gigi on board, for her to realize how important this is. Once I explain everything to her, the deal with James Jenkins and why I made it, I'm sure she'll change her mind about going to the ceremony.

Ahead of me, Raf pops a squat on a bench and starts debating with Vinny on whether or not they should actually wear leather pants in honor of the song. Ben stuffs his hands into his pockets and yawns, sitting down on Vinny's other side. When he sees me watching them, he smiles and waves. This catches Milo's attention, and he glances back at me.

He walks over. "You okay?"

"I'm gonna head back." I step over to the sidewalk and put my arm up to hail a taxi. It's actually the first time I've ever done it myself, so I'm surprised when a yellow cab pulls over in front of me. It really does work, just like in movies.

I ask, "You want a ride back with me?"

Milo looks surprised that I offered. "Nah, I'm cool. I'm gonna stay here with them until we figure things out. Thank you, though."

I nod in reply, and as I get into the car, I hear Raf shout, "Damn, Evie, you just gonna dip and not say bye?"

I turn around, and he, Ben, and Vinny are all watching me. Raf is kind of a handful, but Ben and Vinny are okay.

"Bye," I call. "Good luck at your show tomorrow."

"Thanks!" they shout.

Milo leans against the open car door and looks at me for a moment. "Are you sure you don't want to stick around?"

Now it's my turn to be surprised. As suspicious as I've been of him all night, he actually wants me to stay? "No, I should get going. It's been a long day."

He nods. "Okay. I'll see you later." He shuts my door for me.

"Mm-hmm," I say, facing forward.

Milo seems okay . . . maybe. But Gigi didn't go through all her life struggles just to be taken advantage of now.

When I have the chance to talk to her, I'm going to try my best to convince her that this whole Milo situation needs to be nipped in the bud. He might not be that bad a person, but I still don't quite trust him.

By the time I get back to Gigi's, it's almost midnight. I assume that she's in bed, until I walk by her office and see that her light is still on. At first, I wonder if maybe she forgot to turn the light off before she went to sleep, but then I hear her chair scrape against the floor as she moves around.

Part of me wants to open the door and talk to her now. But I think it would probably be best to wait until tomorrow, when we can start fresh.

If I'm lucky, by tomorrow, everything will be different.

Chapter Six

THURSDAY, AUGUST 13

It's quiet when I wake up, almost too quiet. Gigi is an early riser. Well, at least she used to be. She's clearly made some changes since the last time I saw her, and sleeping late might be one of them. Or maybe she's still angry and staying in her room to avoid me.

I sit up and take in my surroundings. My bed at Gigi's is a huge canopy fit for a princess. I loved it as a little girl, and I still love it now, even if it does make me feel a little childish. The bedroom walls are pastel blue, the only room in the house where the walls aren't painted some shade of cream. Pastel blue used to be my favorite color, and when Gigi moved here eight years ago, we painted the walls together. It feels like a lifetime has passed since then.

My phone vibrates on the bedside table, and my stomach sinks as I glance at messages from Kerri and my mom.

Kerri: **Morning! Checking in to make sure everything is going smoothly. How are you? How did the conversation go with your grandmother?**

Groaning, I put my phone facedown on my lap and pick it up again. **I'm okay. Working on talking to Gigi**, I text back.

All right. Good luck! Let me know if you need anything. I hope you're getting some much needed rest. 👍

And there are two texts from my mom.

Mom: **Call us sometime today.**

Mom: **Better yet, FaceTime us. We want to see Gigi too.**

I text back, **Okay, will do.**

But that's going to have to wait until I get my chance to talk to Gigi.

I ease out of bed and retie my silk scarf around my head. I open my door and peek my head into the hallway. It's still eerily quiet, and Gigi's bedroom door is closed. Taking a deep breath, I walk down the hall and knock lightly on Gigi's door.

"Good morning, Gigi," I say. "Can I come in?"

There's no answer. Not even a shuffling sound on the other side of the door.

"Gigi?" I say, knocking a second time.

Again, not a peep.

She's still upset with me. Okay. I expected as much. Gigi is known for holding long grudges, but I'm not James

Jenkins. I'm her *granddaughter*. There has to be a way I can fix this.

I think about ways to lure her out. I could cook breakfast. The best way to say you love someone is to say it with food, right? The only issue is that I can't cook to save my life. But how hard is it to make eggs and bacon? I'm not saying that presenting her with breakfast will suddenly smooth things over between us, but at least it's a start.

I rush down to the kitchen and almost trip over her cats, Mark Antony and Cleo, who yelp and dash out of my way. God forbid I fall and break my neck three days before the FCCs because Gigi's cats were willing to kill me for food. They follow me into the kitchen and circle my feet as I open the cabinets.

"You don't even like me," I say to Cleo, glancing down as she rubs her whiskers against my shin. For years I've been trying to get on her and Mark Antony's good side. What's suddenly changed?

Wait . . . why are Mark Antony and Cleo even down here? They usually follow Gigi wherever she goes. They should be lounging on her queen-size bed right now.

Mark Antony meows loudly and walks to his bowl. There are still remnants of food at the bottom. Gigi must have been up to feed them this morning, but why shut the door and keep them out of her room? A prickling sensation grows at the back of my neck.

Cleo is doing figure eights around my ankles as I puzzle over this. I step to the side and turn toward the kitchen table so that she'll skitter away, and that's when I see it. A note placed in the center of the table. I grab it, and the prickling sensation spreads from my neck to my arms and stomach, continuing down to my feet.

Right away, I recognize Gigi's pink stationery, the elegant slope of her handwriting. Then I see my name written at the top of the page.

> Evie,
> I need to clear my head. I promise I won't be too far away.
>
> All my love,
> Gigi
>
> PS: Don't worry about feeding Mark Antony and Cleo. I've got that taken care of.

I read it one, two, three more times. The words begin to tremble, and I realize that my hands are shaking.

"No. No, no, no, no." I turn around and shout, "Gigi? Gigi!"

I suddenly hear a loud ruckus upstairs, like someone fell out of bed and landed on the floor. Mark Antony and Cleo hightail it out of the kitchen, and I race into the hallway, hoping and praying to see Gigi. Instead, I see Milo rushing out of his room. He struggles to run and put on a shirt at the same time. For a moment, I forgot he stayed here.

He looks at me with the wide, alert eyes of someone who just woke up and is trying to adjust to chaos. "What? What's wrong?"

I don't answer and dash upstairs, brushing past him with my sights set on Gigi's door. I push it open and walk into her empty room. It smells like Chanel No. 5, and her huge bed is neatly made, covered in a soft cream-colored comforter. Nothing looks out of place. Nothing, except for the fact that Gigi isn't here!

I groan. I lean against Gigi's dresser and try to catch my breath.

"What's wrong?" Milo repeats, coming to stand beside me.

"She's gone!"

"What?" he says, blinking. "*Who?*"

"Gigi! Who else?" I shove her note into his hands. "It says so right here."

Milo scrunches up his face and scans Gigi's letter. The seconds I stand there waiting for him to finish are agonizing. He reads so slowly!

I don't have time to wait. I walk around her huge bed to her nightstand and open her jewelry box, where she keeps her passport. It's still there, so at least now I know she hasn't left the country. She said she wouldn't be too far away, but "far away" could have a completely different meaning for Gigi. She could be anywhere! And when did she even leave? She must have written the note this morning. But how long before I woke up? Minutes? Hours? I insinuated that she needed to get out of the house, but I meant, like, take a walk around the neighborhood, not just disappear altogether! What am I supposed to do? I can't even call her because she doesn't own a cell phone.

This is like when she left LA after she and James divorced. She fell off the face of the earth for *weeks* and then suddenly reappeared in New York. At least this time she left a note.

This is all my fault. She couldn't stand to be around me anymore. I didn't even get a chance to tell her about the *Every Time We Meet* remake. I don't have the role if I can't get Gigi's blessing or convince her to agree to a meeting with James. How can I accomplish either of those things if she isn't here?

I think I'm going to be sick.

"So we can probably rule out that she's missing," Milo finally says, refolding the note and handing it back to me. He still has crust in his eyes and sleep lines on his cheeks.

"What do you mean?" I say. "Of course she's missing. You just took about three years to read her note."

He narrows his eyes and, with measured patience, says, "I did read the note, and what I read lets me know that she left on purpose. I think the better word is *disappeared*."

"Oh yeah, that's much better," I say sarcastically. I worry the note in my hands, but I stop because I'm afraid I might rip it. We might need this for evidence in the future. The last note that Gigi wrote before she went AWOL. The cops will have to keep it in a missing persons file. The story will break out everywhere. Gigi and I will be the subjects of yet another scandal.

Nobody can find out about this. *Nobody.*

"I talked to her this morning," Milo says, snapping me out of my downward spiral.

"What?" I ask, gripping his arm. He winces. "Sorry," I say, quickly pulling away. "You *talked* to her? Why didn't you lead with that?"

"You didn't give me a chance to!" he says, rubbing his arm where I grabbed him.

"What did she say? Tell me word for word."

"I got back mad late, like almost four A.M., because we spent a long time trying to figure out stuff for tonight's show. I walked inside, and your grandma was sitting in the living room with a suitcase next to her. I kind of just stood there because I didn't know what was going on. She told me that she'd been waiting for me, and she said that she had to go away for a bit to handle some things and that she needed me to take care of the cats. She said she wouldn't be too far away, just like she wrote in her note, and then she left."

"That's it?" I ask. "She didn't say where she was going? Or how long she'd be gone?"

He shakes his head. "Nah."

"And you didn't ask her?"

"No," he says, surprised. "It wasn't my business to ask."

"My grandmother, who is arguably one of the most famous people ever, hasn't bothered to truly take part in society for almost a decade, and when she suddenly decides to up and go, you don't think to ask *where she's going*?"

"No, because like I said, it's wasn't any of my business!"

"That's ridiculous!"

We both stand there fuming at each other.

"Yelling isn't going to solve anything," he finally says.

"Maybe not, but it makes me feel better," I mumble.

He lets out a short, surprised laugh and looks away, shaking his head. Before he can reply, the phone rings downstairs. Maybe it's Gigi calling. I hope to God that it's Gigi calling.

I run to the sound, and Milo is right on my heels.

Her answering machine picks up before I reach the phone.

"Peggy, hun, it's Candice. I'm following up on our phone call from last night. I found what you were looking for, and I'll

have it for you tonight. Don't worry; I promise to be discreet. It's been so long, friend. I can't wait to see you."

The message ends with a loud beep.

Now she's decided to go to the gala? I play it a second time to make sure I heard correctly. What was Gigi looking for? My wheels start turning.

"I have to go to the gala," I say.

"What, why?" Milo follows me out of the kitchen and into the living room.

I made that statement aloud more to myself than to him, actually.

I turn around, exasperated. "What do you mean, why? Gigi is going to be there, and I need to find her and convince her to come back. The last time she did something like this, she was gone for *weeks*. We don't have weeks right now. We have the ceremony on Sunday. She can't miss that."

"But she doesn't want to go to the ceremony," he says, frowning.

I ignore him and head upstairs. She doesn't want to go to the ceremony because getting the lifetime achievement award isn't important to her, but when I tell her how I need her to take a meeting with James, she'll change her mind to help me.

That's not any of Milo's business, though.

"And how do you even plan to find her?" he asks, still

following behind me. "Are you going to walk in, go up to the mic, and ask if Evelyn Conaway will please come to the stage?"

"Candice said she'd use discretion, which probably means no one else will know that Gigi will be there," I say. "Maybe they're going to meet in secret. I don't know! I just know that if Gigi's going to be there, I need to be there too."

Milo bites his lip. "I just don't think that will work."

"Well, it's a good thing I'm not basing this plan on your opinion," I say, and he frowns again.

We've reached my bedroom doorway. Now that I feel less frantic, I realize that Milo has watched me run around with my hair wrapped, wearing a big Mildred McKibben Performing Arts Academy T-shirt and plaid pajama shorts. If this were another day, I'd be embarrassed, but there's too much going on right now to care.

Well, that's not exactly true. I at least wish I weren't wearing my headscarf.

I step into my room, waiting for him to take the cue to walk away. When he doesn't, I grab my phone off my bed to Google the gala. It's at the Brooklyn Museum at 8:00 P.M., and it's black tie. Crap. Kerri is bringing all of my dress options on Sunday, so I don't have any black-tie clothes. Maybe I can borrow something from Gigi's closet.

When I look up, Milo is still standing in my doorway.

"Don't you have to work or something?" I ask.

"I don't clock in for another hour," he says. Then, determined, "I'm coming with you."

"What?"

"I'm coming with you to the gala."

I blink. "No, you're not."

"There's a better chance of finding her if two of us are looking," he says.

I narrow my eyes at him. He has a point. Suddenly, it doesn't seem so smart to turn down his help.

"It's black tie," I say. "Do you own a tuxedo?"

Ha. This is where I'll get him. What nineteen-year-old boy randomly owns a tuxedo?

"Yes," he says. "I do have one. I get off at four. What time should I be ready?"

"Seven thirty," I say reluctantly.

"Got it." He takes a step to walk away, then pauses. "Um, I'm gonna get ready for work . . . Will you be okay here by yourself?"

"Of course," I say, annoyed. "I'm perfectly capable of taking care of myself."

If only he knew just how much time I've spent alone.

"Okay, okay." He holds his hands up. "Well, if you need me, just call the store."

And with that, he turns and walks down the hall. I hear his door close, and I let out a deep breath.

Gigi is gone. That much is clear. But I still don't know *why*. What I do know is that she left around 4:00 A.M. after talking to Milo, and last night around midnight, she was wide-awake in her office. That's where I need to start looking for answers.

Chapter Seven

Gigi's office is only an office in the sense that there's a desk and a chair where she occasionally sits. The rest of the space is devoted to her personal Evelyn Conaway library. Bookshelves line the walls, containing every magazine with her on the cover, along with each of her movies in VHS, DVD, and Blu-ray format. Besides all her movies, she has footage of every appearance and performance, and she even owns cassette tapes, CDs, and vinyl records of each movie soundtrack she's ever recorded. Pictures from her various photo shoots over the years decorate the walls.

The champagne-colored carpet is made of expensive silk, and shoes aren't allowed, so I'm barefoot as I cross the room and look down at the envelopes covering her white marble desk. Last night she mentioned that she'd been overwhelmed by the amount of people who've reached out to her since the FCC Lifetime Achievement announcement. I sift through the envelopes and see that she's been invited to parties and screenings, most of which took place earlier this month or toward the end of July. There are at least thirty invitations on her desk alone. I'm sure there are more that she's thrown out.

Gigi wasn't always so antisocial. When I was little, she had parties at her house in Beverly Hills all the time. She'd walk me around, accepting hugs and kisses from her guests as she held my hand, glancing down every now and then with a reassuring wink. That was back when she was married to James Jenkins for the third time, years after my real grandfather, Freddy, had died from cancer. The parties were mostly James's idea, and Gigi always put on a good face to entertain everyone.

Some of my best memories took place at Gigi's house. I was homeschooled most of my childhood because I traveled around with my parents, depending on where they were filming their next documentary. But I spent my summers with Gigi, and it was always something I looked forward to because it meant I actually got to spend time with someone. My parents never ignored me, exactly. They were just understandably busy, which meant I was understandably lonely. I never felt that way when I was with Gigi.

Then she and James got divorced for the third and final time when I was ten, and everything changed. I didn't really understand what happened between them. Just that James had upset her so much she'd yelled at him on television.

After that, Gigi sold her house and moved to New York City without telling anyone, calling my parents weeks later to let them know she'd settled into a town house in Manhattan. She said she was tired of living in Hollywood, of paparazzi following her around, wanting to know what happened between her and James. So she got her peace and quiet, and New York was where I spent my summers. But as time went on, Gigi became more secluded, to the point that she barely left her house at all. Her constant companions were Esther, Frank, and me whenever I came to visit. My mom tried to get Gigi to move in with us back in California, but Gigi insisted she was fine and just wanted her own space.

Then I started at McKibben, and my parents took a break from filmmaking to settle in LA until I was old enough to be home alone. Once school got underway, I stopped spending every summer with Gigi because there were always acting intensives and shows I wanted to do. Our long summers were condensed to holidays, where we would travel to see Gigi. It was never the other way around. Now she's decided to finally leave at the worst time possible.

And what is it about Candice's gala that's so appealing to her? It's all the way in *Brooklyn*. It's hard to believe that Gigi would go that far when she doesn't even walk around the corner to the grocery store.

I need space. I need to be alone. Completely.

Brooklyn does, indeed, put a lot of space between us.

I take a step back from her desk and scan the room, pausing at the entrance to her walk-in closet, where she stores her vintage dresses and all the outfit pieces she's kept from movie sets.

Her closet is almost half the size of her bedroom, and when I step inside, I'm suddenly eleven again. It's my birthday, and Gigi's gift to me is a special photo shoot she's set up with Candice Tevin. She's helping me try on outfits.

"You should wear this, Evie Marie," she says, handing me a brown leather high-waisted miniskirt. It's the same skirt that Diane Tyler wears in Every Time We Meet.

I slip my skinny body into the skirt, and it falls down to my ankles.

Gigi laughs and pins the skirt so it stays in place. "You'll get the hips for it in a few years."

She lets me try on her designer stilettos, and I walk across the floor on wobbly legs. I stop and stand in front of the mirror and pose, pretending I'm on a red carpet. I smile serenely like I've seen Gigi do hundreds of times.

"Chin up," she says, coming to stand behind me. "When you hold up your chin, it elongates your neck. Remember that, all right? It's time to go."

She leads me downstairs to her living room, where Candice is waiting. A white backdrop and lights are already set up. Chaka Khan's "Sweet Thing" is playing on Gigi's record player.

Candice smiles at me. "You ready?"

I nod, starting to feel a little nervous. Gigi gives me an encouraging push, and Candice instructs me to stand in the middle of the backdrop.

"Okay, let's start with a few poses," Candice says. "Do whatever you want."

I stand there awkwardly, placing my hand on my hip like I've seen other girls my age do in magazines. It feels forced. Candice snaps a few photos and lowers her camera.

"Act a little more natural," she says. "Have some fun with it."

I shoot an anxious look at Gigi, and she saunters over to stand beside me. "Let's take a few together—how's that sound?"

"Okay," I say, relieved.

She puts her arm around me and smiles confidently at the camera, and when she starts swaying her hips along to the music, I copy her. Suddenly, we're dancing together and smiling at each other.

"Great!" Candice says. "Keep doing what you're doing."

After the song ends, Gigi wraps her arms around me and holds me close. She smells like Chanel No. 5.

"Happy birthday, Evie Marie," she says.

I look up at my grandmother, who is so regal and wise and beautiful.

"I want to be just like you when I grow up, Gigi," I say.

She's silent for a long moment, and I can't place her expression. Finally, she says, "You'll be better than me, surely."

"I'm heading out!" Milo shouts from the hallway.

I jump, coming back to reality. "Bye," I call over my shoulder.

I wait until I hear him jog down the steps and shut the door before I walk deeper into Gigi's closet. I find what I'm looking for all the way in the back. The brown leather high-waisted miniskirt and mustard-yellow turtleneck that Diane Tyler wore in *Every Time We Meet*. Part of me wants to try on the skirt now to see if it fits, but it doesn't feel the same without Gigi here, and I can't show her whether or not my hips actually grew into it.

But I do need to choose something to wear to the gala. Gigi never minded when I played dress-up in her clothes when I was younger, but I wonder how she'll feel when she sees me tonight, wearing one of her dresses without permission.

I run my fingers over the fabric of a short gold lamé dress. I love it, but it's definitely not right for tonight. Neither is the deep green strapless Alaïa. But I pause on a long black sleeveless silk Valentino gown with clusters of tiny pearls sewn into the bodice. A white faux-fur shawl is wrapped around the hanger. *This* is tonight's outfit.

I will find Gigi at the gala, and soon this nightmare will be over.

Chapter Eight

I step outside at seven thirty on the dot. While I was getting dressed, Milo shouted that he needed gum and ran around the corner to the bodega. That was ten minutes ago. How long does it take to grab gum from the corner store?

Eleven minutes, apparently, because a minute later, he's jogging down the street toward me . . . but he's not wearing a tuxedo.

He reaches the stoop, and I look at him, horrified, absorbing the fact that he's wearing a baggy brown suit. I'm so thrown by this, I don't even realize he's been staring at me with an appreciative smile on his face.

"Wow. Um, wow," he says. "You look great."

"Thank you." Gigi's black silk gown fits like a glove. I guess my hips did grow into something. I slowly walk down the steps and pause once I'm in front of him. "Milo . . . why are you wearing that?"

"This?" He casts a confused look down at his outfit. "It's for the event."

I shake my head. "You're supposed to be wearing a *tuxedo*. That's not a tuxedo." I bite my lip. "And I'm sorry, but it's also not very flattering."

"You don't think so?" he asks. "I wore it to all of my job interviews this summer. I got a compliment or two."

I find that a little hard to believe, but I keep from saying so. Sighing, I pull out my phone to call a car. "Thank you for trying to help tonight, but I'll have to go without you."

"What?" he says, blinking. "Why?"

"The event is black tie! Look at what you're wearing!"

He smooths a hand over his lapels and shakes his head. "What are you talking about? I *like* this suit."

"That's the problem," I point out. "It's a suit and not a tux."

"Well, you're wearing a wig. Why do you get to wear a wig, but I can't wear my suit?"

Frowning, I finger-comb my bangs. "I'm wearing this because I'm not supposed to be seen in public, and I don't want to be recognized. I told you that." Wait, why am I explaining myself to him? "I'm calling a car. You can't come with me. You'll stick out like a sore thumb. I'm sorry."

"No, no, wait," Milo says, covering my phone with his hand. "Vinny has a tux that he wears for school concerts. I'll ask if I can borrow it."

He starts texting at rapid speed, biting his lip as his fingers move. My eyes are drawn to his mouth and his gold nose ring. When he looks up, my cheeks get hot and I avert my gaze.

"Vinny said I can borrow his tux. We just need to go to my apartment so that I can change."

I start to protest, but Milo insists that it won't set us behind schedule because he doesn't live too far from the Brooklyn Museum.

"Okay," I finally say, remembering that two people looking for Gigi is better than one. "But I'm not taking the subway in six-inch heels."

On the ride to Crown Heights, Milo tells me that he, Ben, and Raf moved in together after they graduated from Brooklyn Tech last year and that Vinny stays with them on weekends when he wants space from his parents.

They live in a walk-up that's four stories high. I feel the burn in my thighs after climbing four flights of stairs, and I'm practically wheezing when we stop in front of his apartment door. I hear Bruno Mars's "24K Magic" blasting on the other side.

"Are they having a party?" I ask.

Milo shakes his head and winces a little. "Um, I apologize in advance for what you'll most likely witness once I open this door."

I raise an eyebrow, intrigued.

Milo turns the knob and pushes the door open. Raf is

standing in the middle of the living room, watching the "24K Magic" video on a small flat-screen TV, trying to replicate Bruno Mars's moves. The music is so loud he doesn't even hear us come inside.

The apartment is a small one-bedroom. The living room and tiny kitchen area are connected, and a short hallway to the right of the front door leads to a bathroom and a bedroom. A drum set is in the far right corner, taking up most of the available space. Clothes litter the couch, and a pile of dirty dishes sits untouched in the kitchen sink. No wonder Milo prefers staying at Gigi's. This place is a pigsty, and it's not nearly big enough for three people, let alone a fourth occasional roommate.

"Hi, Evie," Ben shouts over the music. He's sitting at the foldout kitchen table in the corner near the drums, holding the same thick dragon book from last night. He's wearing a T-shirt that says GREENLIGHT BOOKSTORE. I guess that must be where he works. I don't know how he can read with all this noise.

Raf spins around to face us and pauses the music video. Sweaty and out of breath, he says, "Evie Jones! Again! In our fucking apartment! I don't believe it."

"Shut up," Milo hisses. "Do you want the whole building to know she's here?"

"Yes, I actually do. Imagine how much clout that would give us."

"Who cares about clout in this building?" Ben asks. "Mrs. Carson next door, who sits inside and sews all day, or the tech bros below us, who stay up all night playing video games?"

Raf rolls his eyes. "I don't remember asking your opinion, Benjamin."

"Hi," I finally say, in hopes that they will stop talking about me as if I'm not standing here.

"So this is the apartment," Milo says to me, scratching the back of his neck. "It's usually a little cleaner."

"How would you know?" Raf says. "You're never here to clean. Anyway, I'm glad you're here now, because I've decided to call a last-minute meeting before tonight's show."

Ben puts down his paperback and groans.

"Sorry, I don't have time," Milo says. "Where's Vinny? He said he'd meet me here."

"What do you mean you don't have time?" Raf asks, incredulous.

"He's in the room," Ben says. "Why do you need his performance suit?"

"Performance suit?" I repeat, turning to Milo. "I thought you said it was a tux?"

Milo looks like he might pull his dreads clean out of his head. "It *is* a tux—just wait here, okay?"

He spins on his heels and walks down the short hallway into the bedroom. Vinny pops his head out of the room, waves at me, and then closes the door behind them.

Raf glances at Ben. "Why does Milo need Vinny's tux?"

Ben shrugs, nose deep in his book once again. "No clue."

Raf looks at me, slowly taking in my fancy gown. "Wait a minute. What's going on here? Where are you taking Milo?"

"I'm not *taking* him anywhere," I say. "He insisted on coming with me."

"To where?"

"A fundraiser."

"A *fundraiser*?" Raf glances at Ben again, who simply shrugs again. "What kind of fundraiser?"

"A fundraiser gala." I slowly make my way over to the black leather couch. "Okay if I sit down?"

"Of course," Ben says.

I gently push someone's sweatshirt aside and sit. Raf immediately slides next to me. "This is my bed. It pulls out into a king-size. Ben and Milo can have their little twins in their room. I've got all the space I need here." He spreads his arms wide and winks at me.

"Yeah, okay," Ben says. "You hate sleeping out here during the winter when the heat starts acting up. Evie, can I get you anything to drink? Water? Soda?"

"Oh shit. I just drank the last bit of soda," Raf says.

Ben frowns at him, and I quickly say, "I'm fine. Thank you, though."

"So is this fundraiser gala a date?" Raf asks.

"No!"

Like I said, I don't have anything against musicians as people, but that doesn't mean I want to date one, or anyone in the entertainment industry for that matter. I learned from Gigi and James's three failed marriages that relationships between entertainers just don't work. And I've learned from my own experience too. My first and only serious boyfriend was a boy named Devon, who I dated during my sophomore year at McKibben. That relationship lasted only two months. Turns out he just wanted to be introduced to Gigi and broke up with me once he found out she never visited.

But that's not any of Raf's business.

"Milo and I are *not* going on a date," I state plainly.

"Good." Raf looks visibly relieved. "I think you're great. I mean, truly, I do, but the band is about to take off, and we can't afford to have Milo mixed up in any gossip before that happens."

I wince. Of course. They don't want an attachment to my name bringing them down. "Got it," I mumble.

"Plus," he continues, "it would be long-distance, and we all know that never works out. You'd break up, and he'd be stuck writing sad, mopey songs for weeks, just like the last time he was dumped. Took him forever to get over that girl. Remember, Ben?"

Ben sighs and rolls his eyes. "It wasn't that long ago. Of course I remember."

To me, Raf says, "So have fun with Milo, but don't break his heart, okay? We're all nineteen, but he *just* turned nineteen. He's a whole baby. Our little church boy. We don't want him to have any distractions."

I stare at him, blinking. I am truly at a loss for words.

"You've got the wrong idea about Milo and me," I say slowly. "We're not going on a date tonight. We're not romantically involved at all."

"Okay, sure." He winks at me. Ben chuckles from behind his book.

"I'm serious," I say, frowning.

I'm saved from having to defend myself further when Vinny and Milo finally walk into the living room. Milo looks much sleeker now in Vinny's tux. It fits him nicely, except the pant legs stop at his ankles. I guess if anyone asks, we can just say he's going for a hipster look.

And *fine*, if I'm being honest, the first thing I notice is that he looks even more handsome, but I keep my expression neutral because Raf wolf-whistles and then glances at me to see my reaction.

"Hi again, Evie," Vinny says. "Milo, don't get any food on this tux. It's the only one I have, and my parents will kill me if it gets ruined."

"I promise I'll take care of it," Milo says, running his hands over the sleeves and picking a piece of lint off his shoulder. He looks at me, gaze direct and intent. "Is this okay?"

For some reason, my stomach clenches. Maybe it's because he actually seems concerned about what I think.

I swallow. *Get it together, Evie.*

"Better," I say.

"Cool." He smiles, relieved. "Ready?"

"Yes." I quickly hop up, eager to finally get going. To his roommates/bandmates/friends, I say, "It was nice to see you again."

"Have fun on your fancy non-date," Raf says as we leave. "Milo, try not to forget we have a show tonight."

Milo frowns at him. "You know I wouldn't forget."

"Are you coming tonight too, Evie?" Ben asks.

He looks so hopeful, peeking out from behind his book. It hurts my heart a little when I say, "No. I don't think I'll be able to." Tonight, I'll have to do damage control with Gigi. Even if I wanted to go to their show, I won't have time.

"Ah, okay. I'm sure you have much better things to do." But he doesn't say it in a sarcastic way. He smiles at me. "Have fun at your gala."

"But not too much fun," Raf whispers. "Remember what we talked about."

"What did you talk about?" Milo asks, still frowning at Raf. Is there a moment in time when someone *isn't* frowning at Raf?

"Nothing," I say, pulling on his arm. "Let's go. I don't want to be late."

Once Milo closes the door and we walk down the steps,

I whisper, "You didn't tell your friends anything about what we're doing, did you? About Gigi being gone?"

"No, of course not."

I look at him sideways. Gigi trusts him. And now I have no choice but to trust him too. We'll just have to put our differences aside and work together.

Chapter Nine

"Okay, so try not to talk to anyone if you can help it. But if for some reason you get tied up in conversation, just lie about who you are and why you're here."

"What?" Milo says.

We're standing in line outside the Brooklyn Museum, waiting to be admitted into the gala.

"Why can't we just be ourselves?" he asks.

I sigh. "Nobody is supposed to know that I'm here, remember? And do you actually plan on donating any money to this cause? Because if not, once Doves Have Pride blows up, you don't want to be remembered as the musician who walked around Candice Tevin's fundraiser and didn't give a dime."

"Okay, fair. But your plan would actually make sense if I had a disguise," he says, gesturing to me. "Unlike you, I'm not wearing a wig and sunglasses. People will remember my face."

I shrug. "That's why I said don't talk to anyone if you can help it."

"I'm not a good liar." He pulls uncomfortably at his collar.

"It's not that hard. You'll be fine." I use my phone's front-facing camera to check my smoky eye and red lip. I'm not the most skilled makeup artist, but I've learned a few simple tricks. Not that it matters, because I don't really plan on letting anyone see me. I'm going to go straight to Candice Tevin and ask her about Gigi.

"What would you say if you were me?" Milo asks.

"What?" I say. Are we still talking about lying? "Fine. You're Michael Barclay and I'm Karolina Ainsley. We're art collectors with a gallery adjoining my mansion on Long Island. The name of our gallery is Ainsley Barclay. Easy to remember, right? We particularly like to collect celebrity-themed art: statues, oil paintings, etc., and we're ecstatic that we might be able to purchase one of Candice Tevin's famous photographs. See? Easy."

We're inching closer to the entrance, and I watch as ticket takers stand at the door. We don't have tickets, but that's okay; I have a plan.

"Do I need an accent or something?" Milo asks, breaking my train of thought. "Michael Barclay sounds French."

"What? What are you talking about?"

"I don't know." He pulls on his collar again, casting a

nervous glance at his surroundings. "Are you sure about this? I think—"

I firmly plant my hands on his shoulders. "Yes, I'm sure about this. Listen to me, Milo. You cannot blow this for me, okay? I need to find Gigi, and I could use your help to do that, but if you think you won't be helpful, then you should go home right now and get ready for your show."

He stares wide-eyed, then shakes me away. "I've got this," he says, nodding confidently. "Just tell me if I need an accent or not."

"No," I sigh. "You don't need an accent. Better yet, you don't need to speak at all. I'll do all the talking, okay?"

It looks as if the time to do the talking has arrived, because we're at the front of the line.

"Good evening," a polite girl with blue hair says to me. "Tickets, please."

Milo makes a face as if he just swallowed a jawbreaker.

I lower my sunglasses just a teensy bit and flash a bright smile. "Yes, I have them, give me one second." I start sifting through my clutch. "Oh no. They were just here. I just had them. Didn't I, Michael, darling?"

Milo blinks at me as if I just spoke to him in another language.

I continue searching and hear some grumbles from the people behind me. The blue-haired girl raises an eyebrow. I drop into a crouch and pour everything out of my clutch and onto the ground.

"They're not here!" I cry. "And we spent so much money on these tickets!" I wipe at my eyes, careful not to smear my makeup. "Oh, this is just a nightmare! I promised Great-Aunt Belinda that I'd buy that framed photograph of Sidney Poitier for her! She's in the hospital, *dying*, and I won't be able to keep my promise!" I throw my clutch aside and burst into tears.

"Wow, um, okay, wow," Milo says under his breath. He drops down and scoops my clutch off the ground. He inches closer and rubs my back. "Evie, hey, maybe—ouch! Why'd you pinch me?"

"Miss, it's okay." The blue-haired girl steps forward and helps me up. "Just go inside, all right?"

I clasp her hands in mine. "Thank you. Thank you so much. You have no idea what this means to me."

She smiles and waves us on. Once we step through the doors, I check my makeup again and pat my cheeks. Taking a deep breath, I turn to Milo.

"Okay, how do I look?" I ask.

He stares at me. After a few blinks, he says, "Wow. That was . . . You're good."

I smile. "Thank you." At McKibben, my teachers loved that I could always cry on command during scene work. We were taught to think about the saddest moments in our lives and channel that grief. Conveniently, just now, I didn't have to think that far back.

Everyone stands in the large lobby, and servers maneuver through the thick crowd, holding drink trays. Signs hang from the ceiling that say THE CANDICE TEVIN FOUNDATION. I immediately scan the lobby for Gigi, even though I know she won't be out mingling with everyone else. If she's here, she'll be in a back room somewhere, and the only person who can lead me to her is Candice Tevin.

I loop my arm through Milo's and begin pushing through the crowd.

"Keep an eye out for Candice," I say to him.

"Wait, what does she look like?"

Before I can throw up my hands and call him useless, Candice Tevin herself walks onto the platform and welcomes everyone. She looks the same as I remember from my eleventh birthday, except now her long dreadlocks are gray. She wears a loose-fitting burnt-orange dress and matching dangling earrings.

"Thank you all so much for coming," she says, smiling at the audience. "Your support means so much to me and young artists all over the world who will benefit from your kindness. I wouldn't have been able to do any of this without you. The exhibit is on the first floor only, so please have a drink and make your way down the hallway directly to your right."

The crowd starts to move toward the exhibit, forcing Milo

and me in the same direction. I turn around, trying to keep my eyes on Candice, but I lose sight of her as she's surrounded by her team and led away.

"Oh shit," Milo whispers as we walk.

"What? Have you seen Gigi?" I angle my head this way and that.

"No," he says. "But that's Viola Davis *right there*. And Mahershala Ali is only a few feet in front of us! This is wild."

"They're just people," I say to him. "You know Evelyn Conaway personally. How are you starstruck by anyone else?"

"That's different," he says.

I tilt my head. "How so?"

"Your grandma doesn't act like a famous person," he says. "She has this warmth to her, you know? She makes you feel like you've been friends with her for years."

"Oh." Well, his answer was a lot more endearing than I expected. I agree with him about Gigi's warmth. I pat his arm. "Just relax. Okay, Michael Barclay?"

"Yes, Katrina Ashley."

"It was *Karolina Ains*—you know what, never mind. Those names don't even matter." I point to the left. "I'll go to this side of the exhibit, and you go to the right. We'll meet back here in half an hour if we don't see Candice or Gigi, okay?"

"Got it."

We quickly exchange numbers. Milo walks away and pauses, blinking as Shameik Moore passes him. Then, as if he knows I'm watching, Milo glances back at me and smiles sheepishly before continuing on.

I head to the left, glancing every now and then at the large photographs adorning the walls: Diana Ross, Beyoncé, Prince. She's even photographed Avery Johnson, the youngest Black man to start his own ballet company. Trying not to get distracted, I turn my attention back to the people around me, searching for Candice's orange dress. There *are* a lot of famous people here tonight. To be honest, I can see why Milo felt so overwhelmed, but I stay focused and walk slowly, tilting my sunglasses down just enough.

I move deeper and deeper into the exhibit, until I glance around and realize that the walls are now covered with photographs of Gigi. There's almost an entire section devoted to her. I pause in front of a photo that must have been taken on the set of *Every Time We Meet*. She and James Jenkins stand side by side, his arm casually thrown over her shoulder. They're both smiling widely for the camera, brown-skinned with bright-white teeth. Someone's already bought this one. There's a SOLD sticker in the corner of the photograph.

I move on to a photo of Gigi standing by a pool. She's wearing a white wrap dress, and my mom, who was a toddler at the time, has her arms around Gigi's legs. My grandfather stands a few feet behind them, watching with a smile. I step closer and examine every inch of the photograph. Gigi and my grandfather were friends for years before they fell in love.

I've always wondered how different Gigi's life would have been if my grandfather had never died. Maybe she wouldn't have married James Jenkins for a third time. Maybe her public blowout at the FCCs years later would never have happened. Maybe I could have grown up having her in LA.

Someone calls Candice's name, and I see a girl in all black rush past me down the hallway. Instinct takes over, and I hurry to follow her. A few feet ahead, the girl reaches Candice and whispers something to her. Candice nods, and they both make a sharp right down another hallway.

How suspicious is *that*? What are the chances that they're talking about Gigi?

I push through the crowd and try to catch them, but when I make the same sharp right, I find myself at a dead end in one of the quieter corners of the gallery. Candice is nowhere to be seen.

"Crap," I mutter, turning around in a circle to see if they somehow ended up behind me. Then I notice a door in the corner, painted to blend in with the wall. On the front of the door there's a tiny gold plaque that says PRIVATE: EMPLOYEES ONLY. Basically, a great potential hiding spot for Gigi.

There's only one other person in this section of the gallery, and she's staring at the photos on the wall, completely engrossed. Glancing over my shoulder, I try the doorknob, expecting it to be locked, but I'm surprised when it opens easily. I brace myself, expecting to come face-to-face with Gigi, but the room is pitch-black. I switch on the light and see that it's just a storage room filled with boxes that say Candice Tevin's name. A framed portrait of Stevie Wonder leans against the wall to my right.

Great, just great. I should've known it wouldn't be this easy to find her.

I turn to leave, but my foot bumps into a tower of boxes. The top box tips over, and I'm suddenly showered with dozens of sharp-edged Polaroid photos. Startled, I quickly jump to the side, but I knock right into the Stevie Wonder portrait, and it goes crashing to the floor.

"Oh no, Stevie!" I shout, struggling to stand. Mournfully, I pick up the cracked frame. *Crap. Am I going to have to pay for this?*

Instantly, a voice calls out, "Excuse me, what do you think you're doing in here?"

I spin around, and the same girl who rushed down the hallway with Candice is standing in front of me, holding the door wide open. Bewildered, her eyes dart between me and the cracked Stevie Wonder framed portrait.

"Um, hi," I say. From the corner of my eye, I see that the woman who had been engrossed in the photos on the wall just a few minutes ago has moved on to another section. She glances back at us and quickly looks away, clearly wanting nothing to do with my mess. I look down at Stevie. "I'm *really* sorry about this."

"You're not supposed to be back here," the girl says, stepping forward, taking Stevie out of my arms. "Candice is going to kill me! I was supposed to hang this up in the musicians section, and now it's broken." With frantic eyes, she looks up at me. "Who *are* you?"

"I'm Karolina Ainsley," I blurt out. "I own an art gallery on Long Island."

"Um, okay?"

Stupid, stupid, stupid.

I clear my throat. "Again, I'm really sorry. I'll just be going now—"

"Harper, did you find the Stevie Wonder portrait?" Candice Tevin herself appears in the doorway. Her eyes widen as she takes in the scene. "What's going on?"

Harper's voice is shaky. "Um, this Caroline woman found her way into the storage room. I think she was trying to steal the Stevie portrait."

"It's *Karolina*," I correct, because of course I would say this. "And I wasn't stealing!"

Candice blinks. Harper opens her mouth to say something else, and in a split second I make either the best or worst decision.

"That's actually not my name," I quickly say. "I'm Evie Jones, and I'm looking for my grandmother, Evelyn Conaway—Peggy, your friend."

This time Harper blinks as if I just said I'm here to see the aliens.

Candice looks me up and down from head to toe. "You don't look like Evie Marie. Why should I believe you?"

I take off my sunglasses and push my bangs to the side. "It's me, I swear."

Candice walks closer until she's standing right in front of me, and she peers at my face. "The last time I saw you in person was your—"

"Eleventh birthday," I finish. "We had a photo shoot."

Candice starts to smile. She opens her arms and pulls me in for a hug. "Well, just look at you. All grown up." After all I've been through today, this feels like the best hug I've received in years. Candice takes a step back. "Now, why are you dressed like this?"

"I'm not supposed to be here, and I don't want anyone to see me." She raises an eyebrow, so I add, "It's a long story."

She glances back at Harper. "I'll be out in a few minutes. Close the door behind you, please. If anyone asks for me, say I had to take a phone call."

"What about your wife?" Harper asks. "She'll be here in a few minutes."

"Tell her I'm on a *very important* phone call."

Harper nods, shooting a glance at me.

"Please don't tell anyone I'm here," I beg.

She nods again, quickly, like the thought of keeping my secret makes her nervous. She quietly closes the door behind her.

"Is my grandmother here?" I ask, now that we're alone. "She left this morning without much explanation, and I don't know when she'll be back. You said in your voice mail that you were looking forward to seeing her tonight, that you had something for her."

"She *was* here," Candice says. "She came by tonight before the gala started. She bought something that wasn't for regular sale."

"What was it?"

Candice shakes her head. "I'm afraid I can't share that with you." My eyes widen, and she quickly adds, "It's just a portrait she's wanted for a long time."

I guess I'll have to settle for this answer. "Around what time did she leave?"

"A little before eight," she says.

My stomach sinks. If we hadn't wasted time so that Milo could borrow an actual tux, I could have spotted her.

"She was in such a rush, she forgot to take this with her," Candice says, brushing past me and grabbing a small envelope from one of her boxes. She hands it to me. Inside, there are two old photos and a USB drive. The first photo is Gigi sitting on her front stoop in Brooklyn when she was a little girl. She's wearing a white-and-yellow church dress, with matching yellow ribbons tied at the ends of her pigtails. She's smiling at the camera in a slightly mischievous way, like even back then she had a plan to go far, far away. The words *Peggy, 1958* are written on the back.

"This is one of the first photos that I ever took," Candice says. "We spent so much time playing in front of that old apartment."

The other photograph is of Gigi when she was older, at least my age. She's standing in a bar with a waitress's apron tied around her waist, holding a microphone in her hand.

"I took that back when she worked at Don & Jake's, where she used to sing sometimes. This was a few nights before she met your grandfather. I told her she would be completely mad if she went with him to California, but she left anyway. She was restless living here, unsure of where to go or what came next. When the opportunity to move presented itself, she left without giving it a second thought or saying where she'd gone. She never listened to anybody."

I nod because I know this to be true.

"Weeks after she moved out there, she called and told me she was going by the name Evelyn Conaway," Candice continues. "She asked me to visit her and said I should bring my camera, so I did. Everything changed for us within a couple of years. Funny how life works, isn't it?"

"Yeah," I say softly, staring at the picture of Gigi. The expression on her face is serene yet flirty, as if she knew in just a matter of months her life was going to change majorly. "She's never cared what people think about her, not even when she was my age."

"Ha! Now what makes you think that?" Candice asks, raising an eyebrow.

I think of the photo shoot I had with Candice on my eleventh birthday, and a slideshow of Gigi's red-carpet photos flips through my mind.

"Well, you just said yourself that you've been taking her picture since you were kids," I say. "She's always been confident."

Candice laughs softly, shaking her head. "No, she hasn't. If you knew how many times she needed to be pep-talked before a photo shoot or an audition, you wouldn't think that at all. Everything isn't always as it seems. Peg got confident over time, but it took her years to not care about what other people thought."

And now her resolve is unshakable. So much so that she doesn't feel the need to accept a lifetime achievement award.

I place the photos back in the envelope. "What's on the USB?"

"Just some videos I found on an old camera. I thought she'd want to have them."

I look down at the items in my hand and feel more lost than ever. "Do you know where she went?" I ask. "If you do, please tell me."

"I'm afraid I don't." She has a weird look on her face. As if there's a lot more that she just isn't saying.

"This is really important," I stress.

"Truly, I don't know. I didn't have a reason to think she wasn't going home. I'm sorry."

"It's okay," I say, sighing. "It's not your fault."

What am I supposed to do now? This was the only lead I had. What will my parents say when they find out?

"If you're looking for her, why don't you get in touch with Esther?" Candice says, as if this should have been my first thought.

"But Esther isn't her assistant anymore—she retired. Why would she know?"

"Just because she's retired doesn't mean she doesn't know what your grandmother is up to. I'm pretty sure she still schedules all of Peggy's doctor appointments and such. Now she just does it from home. You should give her a call."

"I will," I say, feeling a new sense of hope. I hold the envelope close to my chest. "I'll make sure my grandma gets this."

Candice nods, eyeing me closely. "Even with the wig and all the makeup, I still see so much of her in you."

I wish I saw some of Gigi in me.

I wish this situation, and everything that caused it, wasn't happening at all.

The door suddenly opens, and Harper pokes her head inside. She looks a little frazzled. "Candice, I'm sorry to interrupt, but you're needed out front."

"Excuse me," Candice says to me, following Harper out into the hallway.

I walk a few paces behind them. I need to find Milo and get back to Gigi's, and I need to figure out a way to get in touch with Esther. Gigi probably has her address and phone number written down somewhere.

We reach the lobby, and a wave of whispers spreads through the crowd. People begin to part like the Red Sea. *Who the heck is here, Michelle Obama?*

I stand on tiptoe, tightly holding on to the envelope, straining to see what's going on. Then I see who all the fuss is over: James Jenkins.

He's in his early seventies, but he still has a dashingly handsome way about him. He walks confidently and upright, smiling and shaking hands with everyone. He's wearing an impeccable suit, and it reminds me of how stylish he was when I was younger. I wonder if Gigi would be annoyed to see the way he's swaggering through the lobby right now.

I knew I'd have to come face-to-face with him this week, but I'd hoped it would be under better circumstances. That our first time seeing each other again in eight years would be about me, him, and Gigi discussing my role in the *Every Time We Meet* remake. I didn't plan on running into him here.

He's not only in New York for the FCCs. A new Aliens Attack Earth movie comes out this weekend, and he's probably here for promotion. He's making his way toward Candice . . .

toward me. Oh no. Now isn't the time for a family-but-not-really-family reunion.

When we make eye contact, his walk slows, and he blinks. Can he see right through this silly disguise, unlike Candice? I take a step backward and search for an alternate route.

Quickly, I turn to Candice. "It was nice seeing you again."

"Likewise," she replies. "And don't forget to give her the envelope."

Nodding, I back away and turn in the opposite direction. I hurry to the meeting point, expecting to see Milo, but he's not there. I pull out my phone to text him, but I see that he's already texted me multiple times, and he's called twice.

Hey

Evie, which direction did you go in?

I'm so sorry! I had to leave early! Band emergency!

You okay?

Will you come to the show after?

The Goose's Egg in Williamsburg. Tell Adrian at the door that you know me

Wait a minute. He *left*? Just up and left when we had a whole mission? I knew I shouldn't have agreed to let him come with me! I'm definitely not going to his show now. What does he think this is?

I rush outside and down the museum steps, careful not to

slip and fall in my heels. Once I reach the sidewalk, I use an app to call an Uber and drop my phone back into my clutch. And that's when I come to the startling realization that I don't have any house keys. My makeup and phone are the only things I remembered to bring with me. Gigi's spare keys are in my other bag from last night.

How am I supposed to go back to Gigi's and look for Esther's number if I can't get into the house?

Okay, Evie, calm down. You are a smart, capable young woman. You can figure out what to do.

Should I call a locksmith? Would it be safe to call a locksmith to Gigi's house? I don't want anyone to know where she lives.

I squeeze my eyes closed and wait for the hysteria to fade away. An answer will come to me once I calm down.

"Excuse me, miss, do you need any help?"

I open my eyes, and an older, well-dressed Black man is standing in front of me. "I'm fine, thank you." I push my sunglasses farther up my nose and take a step back.

"I didn't mean to bother you," he says. "You just seemed a little upset. And maybe lost?"

I am both of those things. "I'm neither of those things."

"If you need a ride, I'd be glad to take you where you need to go," he says, smiling. It doesn't look creepy. Instead, it's oddly reassuring, like a smile from your grandfather. "My boss got here late, so he'll be in there for a while."

"I'm really okay, but thank you."

In a final moment of clarity, I realize the best option would be to go to Milo's show and get his house keys.

I cancel my ride and order a new one to drop me off at The Goose's Egg. What a terrible name for an establishment, by the way.

The man nods as he backs away. "Have a good night. Stay safe."

"Thanks," I say, watching as he walks toward his car.

That was weirdly kind of him. Or maybe it was a normal gesture and I'm just too jaded and unused to random acts of kindness.

My car arrives in two minutes, and then I'm on my way to Williamsburg to get keys to Gigi's house. And to see Milo and his band. This is *not* how I expected my night to go.

Chapter Ten

The line to get into The Goose's Egg is really long. This is the first surprise. Either it's a really popular bar, or everyone is here for the show. I can't figure out which one it is. And I keep getting weird stares because I'm dressed in my gown instead of a T-shirt and jeans like everybody else. I look as if I got lost on my way to Cinderella's ball. At least I can hide behind my sunglasses.

I wait impatiently as the line inches forward, and when I reach the door, I get carded. This is the second surprise. It's not like Simone and I were big partyers or anything, but when we did go out, all I had to do was name-drop my parents and we were let inside. I don't think I've ever been carded before.

"ID, please," a burly security guard says. He's young, no older than twenty at most. He has curly black hair, and he's wearing a tight black T-shirt that hugs his muscles.

I look around. "Um, how old do you have to be to get in?"

"Twenty-one."

I frown. "But the boys in the band aren't even twenty-one."

He rolls his eyes. "Doesn't matter. Look, either show your ID or get out of line."

"Wait! I know Milo. See, look." I pull out my phone and show him Milo's text messages. "You're Adrian, right? He told me to ask for you."

"Uh-huh," he says. He looks me up and down. "Have we met?"

"No." I clutch Gigi's envelope to my chest. "But can you let me in, please? I'm not even going to stay the whole time. I just need to get Milo's keys."

"Sorry, no can do. If I let you in without an ID, I'll have to do the same for everyone else." He shrugs and motions for me to move aside when people start complaining.

I want to point out that Doves Have Pride is composed of four nineteen-year-olds, which most likely means the majority of the people waiting in line have fake IDs. But I don't say that, because I want to be on Adrian's good side.

"Wait, you have to believe me," I say, grabbing on to his arm. He looks down like he might karate-chop my hand if I don't stop touching him.

I quickly pull away, and I'm all out of ideas when, miracle of miracles, Vinny steps outside.

"Did Michelle get here yet?" he asks Adrian.

"Nope." Adrian juts out his chin toward me. "But this girl claims to know Milo."

"I *do* know him." I shove myself in between them. "Vinny, please tell Adrian that I'm not lying."

Vinny blinks at me. "Hey, I thought you said you weren't coming." To Adrian, he says, "We know her."

Adrian frowns and crosses his arms. Finally, he says, "You can go inside, but I'd better not see you with a drink in your hand."

My stomach squeezes. Little does he know, I never want to even look at alcohol again. "Loud and clear."

Vinny is waiting for his girlfriend to bring a neck strap for his saxophone, so he doesn't come inside with me. My plan is to find Milo and get his house keys, but once I'm inside, I see that's not going to happen.

It's already loud and *packed.* It doesn't help that the venue isn't all that big. It's hot, and the floors are sticky. I find a semiclear spot to stand near the bar just as a guy appears and announces that Doves Have Pride will perform in five minutes. The crowd erupts into cheers. I have to watch whatever video of theirs went viral because, clearly, it's doing wonders for their popularity.

When the boys stroll onto the stage, the applause in the room is deafening. Raf eats it up, waving and smiling at the crowd. He even blows a few kisses. Vinny ambles behind Raf, and he has a wide-eyed, almost shocked look on his face, like he can't believe this many people showed up. He's carrying his saxophone, so I guess his girlfriend came through with his neck strap. Ben doesn't even bother to glance at the crowd as he makes a beeline for his drum set. He taps his drumsticks against his thighs, sighing as Raf continues to blow kisses. Milo brings up the rear, and Raf frowns as the crowd's attention shifts away from him to Milo.

Milo does not blow kisses. He smiles shyly and does a little wave before he hooks his guitar up to the amp. Several girls manage to push their way to the stage so that they're standing right where he can see them. Interesting.

The boys are wearing the black Doves Have Pride T-shirts along with matching leather pants. I guess Raf got what he wanted after all. I can't decide if they look ridiculous or charming.

Raf leans into the mic and clears his throat. The crowd gets quiet, and he starts singing a cappella. "My girl left me all by myself. She wouldn't give me another chance. Maybe I can change her mind if I put on these leather pantsssss."

Ben counts them off and Raf sings along to the beat. I thought that *funk and R&B mash-up* was a weird description, but it's actually the perfect way to describe their sound.

The crowd knows all the words to this song, and they know the words to the next one too. They sing at the top of their lungs as they dance and jump around. Even the bartender, who keeps glaring at me because I'm standing by the bar but not ordering any drinks, is moving her hips to the beat.

I find myself glancing again and again to the girls who are dancing in front of Milo. He's not looking at them. He's either staring down at his hands as he strums his guitar or glancing around at his bandmates, like he's making sure that everything is going smoothly, that they're all okay. Every now and then, he does a quick sweep of the crowd, but he never notices me all the way in the back. Which is fine. It's not like I came here for us to lock eyes across the room and for him to sing to me.

I didn't come to this smelly, crowded bar to notice how charismatic Milo looks with his guitar. Or that he almost seems like a different person onstage. He's not clamming up like when he was starstruck at the gala. He's totally in his element.

I also didn't come here to ogle him and his handsome face. Or to watch his arms flex as he pushes back his dreads.

No. I came here for house keys and to yell at him for leaving me at the gala.

It's a good thing he's not the lead singer, because then I might really be in some trouble.

Of course, the moment that I have this thought, they start a new song, and Milo is the one singing lead. It's slower, an R&B love ballad with hints of soul.

"When I see you, I feel like I'm home. Girl, I know we're

young, but this love is grown. You kiss me so softly when I sing. For you, I would do anything."

His voice is deep and raspy, and it makes my stomach clench. He sings with his eyes closed, and as I watch his lips move, I go completely still.

Now I see why those girls flocked to the stage. This is what they were waiting for.

Milo opens his eyes, and I suddenly have an absurd urge to push my way to the front of the crowd. I want him to see me, to know that I'm here. But I don't dare move, because, as I said, that urge is absurd.

This is the boy who is mooching off your grandma, Evie! Get ahold of yourself!

When they switch songs, Raf takes the lead again. It's more upbeat, and Raf, Milo, and Vinny do a funny synchronized dance routine, while Ben stays behind the drums. The crowd eats it up. After they finally wrap up their last song, Raf thanks everyone for coming, but he can barely be heard over the applause and shouting. People are still cheering when they walk offstage, and Raf lingers behind to grin and soak it all in.

Something about the smile on his face and the wonder in his eyes is so familiar. The way the crowd shouts his name with such enthusiasm. It takes a minute for me to realize this is the same way I looked during the film festival panel back in May. When I thought my career was about to take off. I thought the world was my oyster then too.

I envy him, and I'd give anything to trade places right now.

Raf finally leaves the stage, and I watch as the boys slip through a side door by the stage. I ease my way through the thick crowd until I'm standing at the same door. Adrian is guarding it, of course. He frowns at me.

"Not you again," he says.

"I need to talk to Milo. That's it, and then I'll be out of your hair."

He reaches back and turns the doorknob. "You his new girl or something?"

"*What?* No. Absolutely not." I shake my head so hard I'm worried that my wig might fly off.

"Okay." He chuckles and moves to let me inside the room, quickly closing the door behind me. Again, he's not that much older than I am. What's with all the authority? He's the perfect example of what happens when a person lets too much power go to their head.

The boys are sitting on a beat-up couch, and despite their great show, they don't look too happy. One by one, they glance in my direction.

"Evie," Milo says, standing up. "You came."

He walks toward me, and his smile is so genuine it almost makes me forget how annoyed I am that he left me at the gala. Almost.

"You left me there," I say, frowning. "You could have at least tried to find me first."

"I know; I'm sorry," he says quickly. "There was an emergency. Raf accidentally broke Vinny's neck strap." He pauses. "Was she there?"

I shake my head, not wanting to get into what's going on with Gigi in front of the other boys. I glance over to find them staring at us.

"Um, great show, guys." I look at Milo. "I mean, really. I didn't know you were a singer too. Why didn't you say anything?"

"I don't know." He does a little shrug.

"He's *shy*," Raf says mockingly. "Why is it that the girls always want the shy ones?"

"We have more important things to worry about than who the girls do and don't want," Vinny mumbles, his head down as he cleans his saxophone.

"That's why you think I'm upset?" Raf asks, suddenly jumping to his feet. "We played a damn good show like we promised we'd do, and that asshole A&R guy didn't even show up!" He whirls around and points a finger at Milo. "*You* said he'd be here."

A lot of the music majors at Mildred McKibben were always trying to get meetings with artists and repertoire executives from different record labels back in LA. The fact that an A&R person was supposed to see Doves Have Pride is pretty impressive.

Milo holds up his hands. "That's what I was told. I can't help it if he didn't come tonight. I already said I was sorry."

"Doves Have Pride does *not* get played," Raf says, fuming. "We play other people."

"We don't do that either," Ben says. "Our next show isn't for another two weeks. Your A&R guy won't wait that long, will he, Milo?"

Vinny sighs. "I'm sure he has better things to do."

"I'll fix this." Milo stands in front them and holds his palms up like he has an offering. "It will work out. I promise."

Raf huffs. "That's what you said last time. You know, I was always skeptical about this. Ever since you said—"

"Can we not do this right now?" Milo asks, shooting a glance at me. "Don't you want to go out there and talk to your fans?"

Raf runs a hand over his hair and smooths out his shirt. "Yeah, I guess so." He walks to the door and opens it with a flourish. "Ladies, ladies," he says, but the only person standing on the other side of the door is Adrian.

"The next band needs the greenroom," Adrian barks. "Time to scram. And remember what I said: If I catch any of you drinking alcohol, I'm throwing you out myself."

"Everyone except me, right, big cuz?" Raf says, leaning close.

Adrian snorts and puts his hand over Raf's face, pushing it away. "*Especially* you."

"Hey, Adrian," Ben says, his brown cheeks reddening a little.

"What's up, Ben?" Adrian's tough exterior softens somewhat, but he frowns again as Milo and I pass him, bringing up the rear.

The rest of the group grabs a table at the back of the bar, but I tug on Milo's arm to stop him from walking.

"I need your house keys," I say. "I'm locked out."

He fumbles around in his back pocket and drops his keys into my open palm. He starts talking, but I can't hear him over the music. I shake my head and point to the DJ, who's playing between bands. Milo leans down and says close to my ear, "The silver key is for the top lock, gold is for the bottom. What's with the envelope?"

Feeling his breath on my neck makes me shiver, but I try to cover it up. "Something for Gigi. Do you know how to get in touch with Esther?"

"Esther?" He takes a step forward and turns his ear toward my face so that he can hear me better. "Why do you need to talk to her?"

"Because Candice thinks Esther might know where Gigi is," I say. "I need to see her."

"I know where Esther lives."

"That's great! Can you give me her address?"

"Well, I don't know her address," he says, frowning. "I just know how to get to her house and what street she lives on. I have a good sense of direction. I can take you."

"I don't need you to take me," I say, annoyed. Does he think I'm incapable of going by myself? "Just tell me where it is."

"Why is it so hard for you to accept my help?" he suddenly grumbles, shocking me into silence. I realize how even-tempered he usually is now that something is clearly bothering him. "Sorry," he quickly adds. "I'm just mad because this exec from Vivid Music Group was supposed to come see us tonight, but he never showed. And then my parents called . . ." He abruptly stops and shakes his head. "It's just a lot." He blows out a heavy breath. "Have you ever loved something so much you'd give up anything to do it?"

The conversation has taken a turn, but I nod, thinking about how I love acting. Thinking about the choices I've made to save my career.

"That's how I feel about music," he says, glancing back at the empty stage. "I have to do what I can to see this through. I can't believe the A&R guy never showed."

"I'm sorry," I hear myself say. I've been where he is, deep in the pits of disappointment. It's the worst. Mostly because I don't want to argue anymore and I feel bad for him, I say, "So will you show me where Esther lives tomorrow morning?"

He nods, eyes still on the stage, watching as the next band arrives. When the lead singer speaks into the mic, there's a loud burst of feedback. I wince and cover my ears, and Milo does the same.

"I'm really surprised you came tonight," he says, turning to me and speaking directly in my ear over the noise. "Were you here the whole time?"

Him being so close is a little too much. If I don't move right now, I might be tempted to stay by his side for the rest of the night.

"Yeah, I was. I'll see you tomorrow." I start to push my way toward the door, but Milo is right behind me.

"I'll walk you out," he says, maneuvering in front of me so that he can clear a path. I don't argue. I mean, what's the point of having such broad shoulders if you can't use them to move people out of your way? *Stop thinking about his shoulders, Evie.*

Apparently, broad shoulders aren't enough to stop Raf.

"Whoa, whoa, leaving already?" he asks. He definitely did not listen to Adrian's strict no-drinking rule, because he's already buzzed. He looks back and forth between Milo and me and wiggles his eyebrows. "Going on another non-date?"

"You need some water," Milo says, attempting to steer him away. Is it just me, or does Milo look a little flustered by Raf's question?

"No, no, wait." Raf manages to avoid Milo's hands. "I just want to say something." He burps and then takes a deep breath. "What I want to say is that one day, Milo, you're gonna be in the songwriting hall of fame. While I will be one of *People* magazine's most beautiful people." He looks at me. "Hey, Evie, maybe we'll be in there together? Are you gonna be in a new movie soon?"

I force a smile and take a step back. "I should really go now."

"You're going?" Ben asks, suddenly appearing at my left. "Did you really like the set? Do you think we did okay?"

"Yeah, you really did." Another step back.

"Hey, Evie," Vinny shouts, appearing at my right. "I wanted to introduce you to my girlfriend, Michelle. She's a big fan of your parents."

A short girl with long black hair and round brown eyes is standing beside him. She leans forward and says very quietly, "I loved their documentary about the aftermath of Hurricane Katrina, and I really loved you in *Mind Games*, but that's all I'm going to say because I respect your privacy."

"Thank you," I say, shaking her hand. "It's nice to meet you."

"You know what, fuck that A&R guy," Raf says out of nowhere. "We don't need him; we don't need anybody! We only need each other. Right?"

The other boys laugh. "Right," Milo says.

Raf smiles wide and full of joy. "Come on, group hug." I edge away, but Raf says, "No, you too, Evie, or whatever it is you want us to call you in that wig."

"Shut up," Milo says, elbowing Raf in the side.

Milo shoots me an apologetic glance as I'm enveloped in a group hug with a boy band plus one girlfriend.

How did this happen? I only came here for house keys.

"I love y'all," Raf says, getting teary-eyed. "I mean it, I do."

Ben sighs. "Are you gonna start crying? Should I get Adrian?"

"No," Raf says, sniffling. "He'll know I've been drinking, and he'll kick me out!"

I look around at their smiling faces, the genuine love they have for one another, and it suddenly all feels like too much. I had this once, but it wasn't real. I'll never be able to open myself up the same way again.

My face feels hot, and my eyes well up. I have to get out of here.

"Come on," Milo says to me, grabbing my hand and leading me away from the group. His fingertips are calloused, I guess from all that guitar playing.

I wait until we're outside in the clear before I pull my hand away. My palms are a little clammy.

"Are you okay?" Milo asks once we're waiting for my ride. When I don't answer, he sighs. "I'll probably stay at my apartment tonight. But I'll see you tomorrow morning to go to Esther's. If you need me to come back tonight for any reason, just call me."

I can take care of myself is on the tip of my tongue, but I suddenly feel so exhausted. "Okay. I'll see you tomorrow," I say, facing forward.

The entire ride back to Manhattan, I can't shake how unsettled I feel.

It was just a silly group hug, but it left me feeling so empty. And so, so sorry for myself.

Is that what friendship is like when the people involved truly love and care about one another?

Once I'm back in bed at Gigi's, I go onto YouTube, fully intending to look up the viral Doves Have Pride video out of curiosity. But instead, I search for the video that I've banned myself from watching. The video loads and I see my flushed cheeks and the way I tightly hold on to the champagne bottle. I hear my wavering voice, the British accent and slurred speech. I hear Simone laugh in the background as she records.

Then I scroll through my phone, searching for the one video of us that I still have saved. We were at McKibben, standing backstage during our production of *The Crucible* sophomore year. I was Mary Warren and she was Ann Putnam. We couldn't stop giggling at how we looked in our white bonnets. I listen closely, trying to determine if Simone's laugh in this video is any different from her laugh in the video she recorded in May. But I can't tell. Both times, we look and sound so happy.

Friendship might be for Gigi and Candice and for Milo and his friends. But it isn't for me. I have a good reason not to be big on friends, and these videos are a great reminder.

I try to go to sleep, but I can't. My brain goes on a loop:

video, getting fired, backlash, how to make it better. Over and over. Finally, after too much tossing and turning, I get out of bed and go into Gigi's office, carrying Candice's USB. I watch the old videos until I feel myself dozing off at Gigi's desk.

Footage from homemade video—August 12, 1970

Evelyn Conaway and James Jenkins sit side by side in a limo on their way to the premiere for* **Every Time We Meet. *Evelyn is wearing a black sleeveless silk gown with clusters of tiny pearls sewn into the bodice. A white fur shawl is wrapped around her shoulders. James, with his arm resting on Evelyn's knee, has on clean-cut black slacks and a maroon blazer. Candice Tevin sits across from them, recording.**

Candice (off camera): How are you feeling about tonight? Are you nervous?

Evelyn looks away from the camera and shifts in her seat

Evelyn: No.

James chuckles

James: Yes, you are. You just told me—

Evelyn: I'm *not* nervous.

Candice: James, are you nervous?

James: Nothing to be nervous about. We worked our butts off and put out a good film. The way I see it, all we've gotta do now is smile for the cameras and look good.

Candice: Well, the reviews are positive so far. Everyone is talking about your chemistry.

James smiles and nudges Evelyn. She rolls her eyes but also smiles

Candice: The press doesn't know that you're officially

dating . . . Are you going to tell them tonight? You do make a lovely couple, I have to say.
Evelyn: Thank you, Candice. But no, we're not telling them. It's none of their business.
James turns to Evelyn, frowning
James: So, if they ask, you want me to lie?
Evelyn: We can tell them that we're friends. That's not a lie, technically. I just want to keep what we have between us for as long as we can. Before they start writing about us in the tabloids. You're too important to me. Is that such a bad thing?
James stares at Evelyn for a beat. Then he puts his arm around her shoulder, pulls her close, and kisses her on the mouth
James: No, it isn't.
James turns to Candice
James: I'm gonna marry this girl one day.
Evelyn laughs and shakes her head
Evelyn: You're mad. But I love you.
James: You hear that? Candice, did you get that on camera?
Candice: Absolutely did.
recording ends

Chapter Eleven

FRIDAY, AUGUST 14

There are a ton of videos on Candice's USB, so many that I was too tired to watch them all last night. There's a video of Gigi standing backstage at the 1970 Academy Awards, the year she was nominated for her role in *Every Time We Meet*. She's slowly swaying back and forth with her eyes closed and her head angled toward the floor. It almost looks like she's having a peaceful moment, but after what Candice told me about Gigi not always being so confident, I'm wondering if she was just trying to calm her nerves. There are videos of Gigi traveling to different countries or on the sets of her photo shoots. At one point, it looks like Gigi must have owned the camera, because James often recorded her around the house.

When I'm fully awake, I rewatch the footage from each of Gigi's weddings. The first time she and James got married, only a few months had passed since they'd filmed *Every Time*

We Meet. She wore a simple white dress, and her hair was big and curly. James wore a button-up and a pair of slacks. They stood in the living room of the house they shared in California. Apparently, lots of people were married in their homes back then. Gigi said they got divorced because they thought it was too hard to focus on their careers and their relationship at the same time. But that mind-set didn't last for too long, because in 1974 they remarried. Gigi wore a white gown that was clearly more expensive, and James actually wore a tuxedo. They shared the same wide, youthful smiles, almost naively hopeful, as if they expected everything to work the second time around. It turned out that Gigi wanted kids, but James didn't, so they divorced again.

The third wedding video was recorded in 1979, and Gigi stood across from my grandfather Freddy. This time her dress had an empire waist because she was five months pregnant with my mom. While my grandfather was known for being a producer, he acted as Gigi's manager as well. They'd always been close friends, but it turned into something more after her second divorce from James. From the way Gigi and my grandfather stared into each other's eyes during the ceremony, it's clear that their love was real.

My mom and Gigi always say life was really hard for them after my grandfather died. Somehow, James came back into the picture and helped Gigi when she needed him the most, and in 1990, to no one's surprise, they got married again for the last time. In that wedding video, Gigi is wearing a white suit, and James stands across from her, flashing a huge smile. My mom stands to Gigi's left, holding a bouquet of flowers. They were together for twenty-two years by the time they divorced in 2012. The reason behind their final separation is still a mystery.

Simone and I were friends for four years, and when she betrayed me, it felt like the worst sucker punch to the gut. I can't imagine how Gigi must have felt when James hurt her after all they'd been through. It's sad to think that a love like theirs can't last.

I don't really have time to dwell on that this morning, though. Milo texted that he'd meet me outside on Gigi's stoop at 10:00 A.M. I quickly get dressed, and my foot is almost out the door when my mom FaceTimes me.

"*Crap*," I mutter. I forgot to call her and Dad yesterday. Gigi is AWOL. What am I supposed to say to them?

I contemplate not answering, but I know that will only make things worse. I'm already on thin ice with my parents. I just need to pretend that everything is okay.

"Hi, Mom," I answer, smiling brightly.

As usual, her face is too close to the phone, so I get a nice view of her nose before she leans away. My dad is sitting right beside her.

"We've been waiting to hear from you since yesterday," Mom says, frowning.

"Sorry," I say. "I've been really busy."

"How is everything going?" she asks. "How's Gigi?"

"She's good. Everything's great."

"I tried calling her too, but she didn't answer." Mom raises an eyebrow. "That's unusual, don't you think?"

I shrug, sitting down on the couch in the living room beside Mark Antony and Cleo. They narrow their eyes and scoot a few inches away from me.

"I don't know," I say. My heart is beating a mile a minute. I really need to relax. "She didn't answer when I tried to call at the airport either. She's doing this thing where she screens all of her calls. But she's also been really busy getting ready for the ceremony. I'll tell her to call you when she has a chance."

My dad leans over into the camera. "I hope you're taking care of yourself out there. No partying or drinking, remember?"

"Yes, Dad." I hold back a sigh.

"Well, is Gigi busy at this very second?" Mom asks. "I'd like to talk to her if she isn't."

"She's asleep," I say quickly. "She isn't feeling well. I'll tell her to call you back once she's awake."

I watch my mom's face closely. She can smell a lie from a mile away. She says it's one of the skills she gained while growing up in Hollywood.

"How bad off is she?" Mom's eyebrows draw together. "Would you mind going to check on her while you have us on the phone?"

"Umm . . . well, actually, she . . ." *Oh God, Evie, think of something.*

"*Meowww.*" Cleo saunters across my lap and glares at me over her shoulder. Catspeak for "I'm hungry."

"Actually, Mom, I've gotta go. I promised Gigi I'd feed her cats. See." I flip the camera so that it's facing Cleo. "I'm helping out since she doesn't feel well. I have to call you back later. Love you! See you on Sunday!"

I hang up while they're in the middle of saying goodbye so that they can't find a way to continue the conversation. I don't know how much longer I can lie to them.

After feeding the cats, I finally step outside, and Milo is waiting for me on the bottom stoop, dressed in his work uniform.

"Is the wig-and-sunglasses combo going to be an everyday thing?" he asks as I walk down the steps toward him.

"Yep." I readjust my sunglasses for good measure.

"I thought we agreed on ten o'clock?"

"I know. I'm sorry. My parents FaceTimed me and wanted to talk to Gigi. I didn't know what to do."

He raises an eyebrow. "Wouldn't it be easier to just tell them what's going on?"

"*No.* They'd shut everything down and make me come back home. No FCC ceremony. No nothing." I sigh. "Our relationship has become . . . complicated during the last few months. I'm starting to think maybe it always was."

He nods. "I feel you on that."

"You do?"

"My parents agreed that I could take a year off before college to focus on music and that I'd have to start taking classes and move back home if nothing happened. Now my year is almost up, and they don't think the band is going anywhere, so they want to know which CUNY classes I'm signing up for in the fall. My mom wants me to rejoin the church choir because she thinks I've gone too long without God. It's like she's afraid I'm going to become the Antichrist of R&B. So, yeah. I think that our relationship is complicated too."

"Wow," I say, blinking.

We fall into a silence, like we're taking a moment to acknowledge that we understand each other a little better.

Milo speaks up first. "Can I have my keys back? I can get copies made for you if you want."

"I have my own keys," I say. I've had keys to Gigi's house since she moved here. What does he think this is? "I just forgot them last night."

As I hand over his keys, our fingers lightly brush, and we both quickly pull away.

"Sorry," I mumble, my cheeks heating up. Then I wonder why I'm apologizing.

Milo clears his throat, glancing away. "It's cool."

This time the silence between us is a little awkward. After a beat, we start walking toward the subway.

"Um, so where does Esther live?" I ask.

"Harlem." He looks at me. "You ever been there?"

"No." I start to tell him that I've never been higher up than Eighty-Seventh Street, but then I notice a black car idling a few houses down. Something about it unsettles me, but I can't figure out why.

I turn to Milo. "Didn't Gigi say there was a black car waiting outside a few days ago? She thought it was the paparazzi."

Milo squints at the car and nods slowly. "She did see one, but that's pretty common for this neighborhood. Everyone has drivers who take them to work."

"Hmm," I say, still not entirely convinced.

For good measure, I readjust my sunglasses and turn away. We continue on toward the subway, and I hope that each step brings me closer to Gigi. I'm still worried about missing the ceremony, but now I just want to know that she's okay.

Chapter Twelve

Harlem has a completely different feel from Gigi's Upper West Side neighborhood. I mean, there are definitely more Black people around. Maybe one day when I'm not in the middle of a crisis, I'll come back and see it properly.

We turn onto 123rd Street, and Milo continues to use his "memory" to find Esther's apartment.

"It's right . . . here," he says, stopping in front of a brownstone. There's a tidy little garden to the left of the stoop.

One thing I remember about Esther is that she loves plants. She had an office at Gigi's house in Beverly Hills, and when I visited during the summer, Esther would "hire" me as her assistant and pay me a dollar each morning that I watered her plants. After dinner, she and Gigi would take me to get ice cream, and I'd spend that money on two scoops of cookie dough. Frank used to drive us around, and Esther, me, and

Gigi would sit in the back seat together, Gigi dressed in whatever disguise she felt like wearing, and Esther dressed in her sensible button-up and knee-length skirt.

"Esther and Evelyn—we're a package deal," Gigi always said.

Milo rings the doorbell, and I hope that package deal is still true. Will Esther know where Gigi is? Is it possible that Gigi's here?

We wait for a few silent moments, and then a woman's voice calls, "I'm coming, I'm coming."

Esther opens the door, and her mouth breaks into a wide smile. She's wearing a bright-yellow sundress, and her hair is shorter now than it was the last time I saw her over Christmas. It's cut very close to her scalp, almost like mine. But, you know, her haircut was intentional and looks nice. Her brown skin is a little wrinkled, but she looks just as cheerful and energetic as I remember.

"Milo!" she says, ecstatic. She hugs him so tight it looks as if his eyeballs might pop out of his head. "I didn't know you were coming by today. How are you, sweetheart? And where have you been? You haven't stopped by to visit Ruby in weeks!"

I blink, surprised. This is a much warmer welcome than I was expecting.

"I'm sorry," Milo says. "I've been really busy with band stuff."

"Oh, that's all right. We aren't mad at you. We know you're

on your way to becoming a big star. Ruby will be happy to see you, either way." She finally turns to me and shoots Milo a coy glance. "And who is your lady friend?"

"Oh no," he quickly says. "It's nothing like that at all. She's—"

"Hi, Esther," I say, taking off my sunglasses. "It's me, Evie Marie."

Esther blinks a few times, taking a step back and holding a hand over her heart. "Evie Marie! Come here, girl!" And then I'm pulled into one of her eyeball-popping hugs. "Peg told me you'd be in the city this week, but I didn't expect to see you. Come in, come in."

We're ushered inside, and I find that Esther's brownstone is quaint and sweet, just like her. Shoes line the hallway, which opens into the wide space of her living room, and the kitchen connects to the right.

"How many times have you been here?" I whisper to Milo as Esther beckons for us to follow her into the living room.

He shrugs. "I don't know, a handful. Whenever your grandma wants to come by."

"You mean Gigi actually leaves her house to see Esther?"

"Yeah," he says, confused. "You know, she doesn't stay inside *all* the time."

Before I can ask him to further explain, Esther says, "Ruby, look who's here. Your favorite."

There's an older woman sitting on the living room couch, wearing a pink bathrobe and matching fuzzy slippers. She's watching *Every Time We Meet* on the huge flat-screen television in front of her. It's the fiftieth anniversary this year, so I'm not surprised that the movie is playing on cable right now. Some stations are running daylong marathons.

The woman—Ruby—slowly turns to face us, and her mouth forms into a smile.

"Milo," she says, grinning. "Hi, baby."

"Hey, Ruby." Milo walks over and plants a kiss on her cheek. He sits down on the couch beside her. "How've you been?"

"Good, good," she says, gently patting his knee. She speaks just as slowly as her movements. "Look at you. Always so handsome."

"That's my older sister, Ruby," Esther whispers to me. "You were so young the last time you saw her, maybe five or six. She was living in Houston, but she came up to live with me after her stroke. It's one of the reasons I retired. That and the fact that your grandmother basically forced me to. Said I needed to enjoy my life while I still had time left." She laughs and then says, "Ruby, you remember Evie Marie, Peg's granddaughter? She's all grown up now. Isn't she lovely?"

Ruby leans forward to look at me and blinks, offering the same slow smile she had for Milo. "Oh, yes. Lovely just like Peggy. How are you, baby? I hope you still aren't upset about what that evil British director did to you. Just like a white man to try and steal your joy."

"Oh, Ruby, don't start with that," Esther says. But she adds, "Not that I disagree, of course."

"You hold your head up high, you hear me?" Ruby says. Because she speaks a little slowly, her words feel more deliberate, weighted.

"I hear you," I say. Now everyone is staring at me, and I feel a little self-conscious. I need to remember why I came here in the first place. "Esther, I was wondering if I could talk to you about Gigi. It's important."

"Of course." Esther gestures for me to follow her into the kitchen. "I was just getting ready to give Ruby her breakfast, but you and Milo are welcome to eat too. I actually insist on it."

A sizzling pan of bacon and home fries sits on the stove next to a pan of scrambled eggs. Esther begins pouring glasses of orange juice, and I decide it's best to just be quick about this Gigi business.

"Okay, so Gigi left yesterday morning. I have no idea where she is or when she's coming back, and I'm worried about her."

Esther frowns and places the carton of orange juice back in the fridge. "What do you mean, she left?"

I pull Gigi's note out of my pocket and hand it to Esther. She shakes her head as she reads and *tsk*s under her breath.

"Do you have any idea where she might be?" I ask. "The FCC ceremony is on Sunday. I don't know if she plans to be back before then."

Esther shakes her head again and hands the note back to me. "I have no idea where she is. Have you told your parents?"

I consider lying, but I don't want to add Esther's name to the list of people I'm deceiving. "No, I don't want them to worry. I just want to find Gigi before this all blows up. When's the last time you talked to her?"

"Wednesday night," Esther says, piling food onto three plates. "She was a little upset, but that didn't seem too unusual. She's been in a bit of a bad mood since she found out she was being honored at the FCCs. I didn't think that she was *this* upset, though."

I inwardly wince, knowing Gigi was most likely upset because of our argument.

"So you have no idea where she might be?"

"None at all," Esther says. She picks up the plates and hands one to me. "This is for you. Eat. Who else knows about this?"

"Me, you, Milo, and Candice Tevin," I say. "Gigi went to Candice's gala last night because she needed to buy something, but Candice wouldn't tell me what it was. Candice is the one who suggested that I ask you about Gigi."

Esther frowns again. "I wish I could tell you more, Evie Marie, but I really have no idea what's going on with Peg. Nothing is ever simple with her, but I'm sure you know that by now. Disappearing is how she deals with stress. I can't tell you how many times she went off the grid after finding out that she didn't get a role or after she became overwhelmed by one thing or another—once, in 1982, she called me from Mexico two days before the Academy Awards. Two days! And you know what her explanation was? She needed some fresh air to think, like there wasn't enough fresh air back in California. You should call your parents and tell them what's going on."

I start to feel a little nauseous. Calling my parents is the last thing I want to do. But I don't want Esther to worry or, worse, take it upon herself to call my parents instead. "I'll tell them," I say. So much for not lying to her.

Esther brings the plates into the living room for Milo and Ruby, and I follow behind, carrying my own plate. Their eyes are glued to the television screen, but every now and then, Ruby glances at Milo and smiles at him like a schoolgirl with a crush.

"Milo, honey, will you get three trays for me?" Esther asks. "You know where they are."

Milo goes and grabs trays from across the room, and he unfolds them side by side in front of the couch. He walks over to me once he's finished and whispers, "What did Esther say?"

I start to tell him that Esther doesn't have any answers about Gigi, but Esther herself interrupts me.

"Sit down and eat, Evie Marie," she says, before hustling back into the kitchen.

"Oh, no, Esther, we can't stay," I call, but she doesn't hear me. To Milo, I whisper, "Gigi hasn't been here. Esther doesn't know anything."

"I'm not surprised," he says. "Do you think maybe you should just let your grandmother come home when she's ready?"

I shake my head, irritated. "You wouldn't understand. She's not your grandmother."

He pauses and takes a deep breath, like he's thinking hard about how to respond.

I start to say that I'm sorry. That it's not his fault I'm so frustrated. But then he says, "You're right. She's not my grandmother, but I care about her too."

"I can't hear the movie over your whispering," Ruby says.

Milo and I apologize and take a few steps back toward the hallway. "Just stay for breakfast," he says. "They enjoy the company."

I look at Esther's hopeful face as she walks back into the living room, and then I look at Ruby, who is waiting for Milo to return to her side. I don't want to disappoint them.

"Okay," I say, sighing.

Milo and I sit down on the couch, with him in between Ruby and me.

Esther stands by and watches until I put some eggs on my fork and lift it to my mouth. When she's satisfied that I'm actually eating, she flops onto the love seat and lets out a deep breath.

"Ah, watching your favorite movie, huh, Ruby?" Esther says.

Ruby nods, taking slow bites of her home fries. "I love Diane and Henry. Even though I can't stand James Jenkins."

Esther shakes her head and shoots me a look that says, *Don't even get her started.*

Disappointment has ruined my appetite, but Milo is busy stuffing his face. Ruby catches me watching him, and her eyes sparkle as she glances back and forth between us.

"You make such a lovely couple," she says.

Midchew, Milo coughs in surprise.

"No, it's not like that," I say quickly. I start to add that we're just friends, not even that, but then I catch Esther's eye.

"Just go with it," Esther whispers. "Ruby's memory isn't so good."

"So lovely," Ruby says, still smiling at us. "Milo, I'm glad you finally found a nice girl."

It takes all of my energy to keep from rolling my eyes. If only they saw all the girls who came to his show. They wouldn't be so worried about him finding someone then.

Milo flashes a huge grin as I glare at him. "Thanks, Ruby."

"That last girl was bad news," Esther says. "We don't want another girl like that." It's unclear if Esther is playing along or if this is actually how she feels.

"That's what I keep saying!" Ruby chimes in with more energy than she's shown all morning.

"Hey, look, Ruby, it's your favorite part," Milo says, nodding at the TV, smoothly managing to change the subject. He isn't smiling anymore. I guess Esther was being truthful. Who is this ex-girlfriend that everyone keeps bringing up, and what in the world did she do to Milo?

He's staring at the television with such focus, and I know it's because he's trying to avoid eye contact with me. Whatever, that's fine. I give up and turn to look at the TV too.

Every Time We Meet is my favorite movie of all time, and it's not just because Gigi is the star. It was one of the first high-profile romantic movies about a Black couple, and it was an instant success when it premiered.

Diane is the young daughter of a wealthy shoe-factory owner in Harlem. She falls in love with Henry, a Southern boy with no connections, who gets a job working at her father's factory. Various circumstances keep them apart, namely that Henry is poor and that Diane is already engaged to a man she doesn't love but of whom her parents approve. When Henry, who has been working and saving, proposes to Diane, she refuses him. She knows her parents will never accept Henry, and although she loves him, she is afraid to live in a world where she doesn't have her parents' approval. Heartbroken, Henry decides to leave New York and start over in Chicago. He wants to forget all about Diane and the pain she's caused him. Diane is equally heartbroken and ashamed of breaking things off with Henry simply because of what her parents might think. When they push Diane to move forward with her wedding to the other man, she tells them the truth about Henry. Unsurprisingly, they aren't supportive, but Diane realizes she no longer cares what they think. She just wants to be with Henry.

In the final scene, Henry is at Penn Station waiting to board a train to Chicago. He's staring at the train schedule with his hands stuffed in his pockets, his small, shabby suitcase by his side. He looks heartbroken, thinking he's lost Diane forever. But then Diane appears, running through Penn Station, calling Henry's name. He turns around to face her. She's winded, her cheeks flushed. She sputters at first, knowing she has so much to say but unsure of where to begin.

"Henry," she simply says, placing her hand in his.

Henry stares down at their entwined fingers and looks up into her pleading eyes.

"Well, darling," he says, "I'm sure glad you showed up."

Diane laughs and wipes her eyes. They leave for Chicago together.

Gigi and James Jenkins had *a lot* of chemistry. So much so that at the time, people believed they were actually dating. Spoiler alert: They were. Gigi says they tried to keep it a secret for a while, but people eventually found out.

Over the years, there have been talks of a remake, but

nothing ever happened. It was like everyone knew you couldn't top the original. But James Jenkins seems to think differently. How am I supposed to fill Gigi's shoes and play Diane? Especially when Gigi herself might not even approve of me taking the role? What if everyone just hates me even more and blames me for ruining a beloved classic?

"You okay?" Milo whispers about halfway through the movie.

I nod, facing forward.

"You sure?"

I nod again. This time I glance at him.

His eyes drift to my plate. "You haven't eaten anything."

"I'm not hungry," I whisper back.

He reaches with his fork and starts eating some of my eggs.

I gasp. "I didn't say you could do that!"

"Sorry." He laughs. "You might not be hungry, but I still am."

"Shh," Ruby hisses. But before she turns away, she smiles at us slyly.

I sigh and put my plate on Milo's tray; he might as well eat the food if I'm not going to.

I focus on the movie again and find myself wrapped up in it, just like Ruby and Esther, who I'm sure have seen it as many times as me, if not more. It's hard not to swoon when Henry first appears on-screen, smiling like a charming country boy. And when he and Diane kiss for the first time, you have no choice but to sigh aloud. They really do make you believe that they're in love.

During the final scene, when Diane runs through Penn Station, we're all sitting on the edges of our seats. Even Milo. With tear-filled eyes, Diane searches for the right words to say to Henry, and he delivers his iconic last line. If someone said that to me in real life, I'd swoon for days.

The movie ends, and Ruby claps slowly but enthusiastically.

"This one will always be my favorite," Esther says, standing up and gathering our plates. "Peg gets so annoyed when I say that. She always says, 'It was my first movie! I got so much better later on!'" Esther chuckles on her way into the kitchen. Once she returns, she adds, "We'll be watching as Peg receives her award on Sunday night. It's long overdue. To think James received the award almost a decade ago! To think he *called* her. As if she wanted to speak to him!"

"Wait, what?" Now she has my full attention. "James Jenkins called her? When?"

"Wednesday night," Esther says. "Now that I think about it, that might have been why she was so upset when she called me. She'd just finished her phone call with James. I didn't think much of it because you know how she feels about him. They haven't spoken in years, and suddenly he calls her out of the blue."

He wasn't supposed to be in contact with Gigi. *I* was supposed to be the one to reunite them. Did he already tell Gigi about our deal? Did she know all along?

Oh no.

I gulp. "What did they talk about?"

Esther shakes her head again. "She wouldn't say. She just kept going on about how he had so much nerve to even dial her number."

"So that means James was the last person she talked to before you?" I ask.

"Well, yes, I guess so," Esther says. "I don't even know how he got her number."

"He's a rascal, that's how!" Ruby says.

I quickly stand up. I need to find a way to get in touch with James, and I can't do that here. "I really have to go now. Thank you so much for breakfast, Esther. It was nice to see you, Ruby."

Milo stands too. I edge away toward the hallway, and Esther rushes over to me.

"It was so good to see you again," she says, hugging me tightly. She pulls away and studies my face. "You look *just* like her. You always have, ever since you were a little girl."

"I wish I had more in common with her than just my looks." I meant to only say that in my head, not out loud.

"I know you've been hard on yourself after what happened with that director, but if you think your grandmother didn't make mistakes too, you're wrong. Her career wasn't perfect. You should ask her about the pitfalls."

Maybe Gigi would have told me the stories of her pitfalls after the video leak, if only I'd actually had the heart to talk to her. Now she's gone, and I can't ask her anything.

"I'll do that," I promise Esther.

I turn around to see where Milo's gone, and he's crouched down in front of Ruby.

She pinches his cheek. "You know, you're charming, just like Henry."

"You think so?" he asks, grinning at her. "That's a lot to live up to."

She gives him a warm smile. "Oh, I'm sure." She glances at me, then turns back to Milo and winks. "And I know what's what. Thanks for indulging a little old hopeless romantic for a morning."

Wait a minute. She knows we aren't actually dating? She tricked us!

Ruby laughs at my shocked expression and pats Milo's shoulder as he wishes her goodbye.

Esther basically forces us to take containers of extra food when we leave, and I feel bad when I promise her that I'll call my parents if I don't hear from Gigi by the end of the day. What I actually plan to do is find a way to get in touch with James Jenkins. He's one of the last people Gigi talked to before she left. He has to know something.

"Esther and Ruby are big fans of yours," I say to Milo as we walk back to the subway.

He shrugs, smiling a little. "They're sweet."

"According to Ruby, you're charming, just like Henry."

He chokes out a laugh and looks away, embarrassed. "You heard that?"

I try to hold back my laughter. His embarrassment intrigues me. "Let's see just how charming you really are. Can you say Henry's famous line for me?"

He stops walking, so I stop too. He leans down so that his face is level with mine. My silly little heart goes *thump*, *thump*, *thump*. He blinks at me, and I hold my breath, waiting. Then, just as he opens his mouth and I expect to hear those swoony words, he laughs and simply says, "Nope."

I blink as he starts walking away. "Nope?"

"I'm not Henry," he says. "I won't even pretend to be."

But then, as we wait for the subway, he reminds me to put my sunglasses back on and uses his MetroCard to swipe me through the turnstile. He's not Henry, but I can begrudgingly admit that he is something.

As we ride the train for the third time this week, I think about the conversation from our first subway ride and how it went unfinished.

"Do you really think that Gigi is lonely?" I ask.

He glances down at me, and I'm wondering if he's going to evade the question like he did before. But he says, "The day I first brought groceries to your grandma, I was nervous, of course, because she's Evelyn Conaway, you know? Mr. Gabriel was all like, *Don't stay too long or annoy her. Just drop off the food and go.* But as soon as your grandma let me in, she just kept talking to me. She asked what I did other than deliver groceries, so I told her about the band. She told me she worked at a speakeasy when she was around my age."

"Don & Jake's," I say.

Milo nods. "Yeah, Don & Jake's. She asked if I wanted to listen to some records, and I thought I should say no because Mr. Gabriel told me not to stay longer than necessary, but I just had this feeling that she wanted to spend time with someone, that she was tired of spending so much time alone. So I stayed, and we listened to Curtis Mayfield. Every time I dropped off her groceries, we'd listen to a new record. I guess we bonded over music."

"Okay," I say, absorbing this. I imagine Gigi, sitting at home alone, just waiting for someone to come along and talk to her. My heart aches. "But how did that turn into you staying with her?"

"She was just trying to help me out."

Again with the vagueness. "And you said she doesn't stay

inside all the time. I could have sworn that Gigi hadn't left her house in eight years. Where does she go?"

"Nowhere too far," he says. "Sometimes she brings me with her to Esther's, and every now and then she'll want to go for a walk in Central Park. But she always wears these weird outfits so that no one recognizes her. Big hats and glasses." He pauses. "Kind of like what you're doing now."

"Yeah," I say, sighing. "I've put that together too."

All this time, I thought that Gigi never went anywhere unless Frank was around to drive her. But why did I just assume that this was true? It's not like she ever said so herself. She'd just been adamant for so long about not coming back to LA; I thought that meant she never went anywhere.

When we get off the subway and walk up Gigi's street, the same black car is idling a few houses down.

"That car is still here, hours later!" I hiss, pointing.

Milo shrugs. "I really think you're reading too deep into this."

But then, as if the universe wants to help prove me right, the driver-side door opens and the same older man who approached me outside the museum last night walks toward us.

Alarm bells sound off in my head again, and for some reason, I doubt that this man is a friend of Gigi's like Mr. Gabriel. Did he follow me here? Has he been waiting for me since last night?

"Milo . . ." I stop walking.

He follows my line of sight and stops too, shifting to stand in front of me.

The man continues to approach, smiling widely. He stops when he's a few feet away.

"Can I help you?" Milo asks.

"Yes, good afternoon," the man says. "I was hoping *you* might be able to help *me* with something." He lowers his voice a little. "Does Ms. Evelyn Conaway live here?"

I gasp. So much for thinking he was a harmless and kind old man! He's a stalker!

"Why?" Milo asks, his voice serious. "Who are you?"

"Forgive my manners. My name is George. I'm an employee of Mr. James Jenkins," he says. "I was instructed—"

"Wait, *James Jenkins* is your boss?" I interrupt.

"Yes." He looks at me and blinks. "You're the young lady from last night. Lovely to see you again."

Milo's head jerks back in surprise. He glances at me and raises an eyebrow.

George continues, "I was instructed by Mr. Jenkins to give this invitation to Ms. Conaway the moment she surfaced from her home, but I haven't had any luck so far today."

He pulls a small white envelope out of his pocket. Slowly, Milo takes it from him.

I stand on tiptoe and peek over Milo's shoulder as he

opens the envelope. Inside, there's an invitation to the premiere party for *Aliens Attack Earth 4*, including a personal note from James.

> Peg,
> I know your feelings haven't changed since the last time we spoke, but given the recent circumstances, I hope there is a chance you will reconsider. Please come tonight. I would love to see you.
> J

Um, excuse me?!

"What recent circumstances?" I ask, swiping the note out of Milo's hand. I look at George. "What is James talking about?"

"I'm afraid I don't know," George says. "I'm just a driver and occasional errand runner. I don't involve myself in Mr. Jenkins's personal affairs."

My head is spinning. Her feelings haven't changed since the last time they spoke? Her feelings about what, exactly? This has to be in reference to that phone call they had.

"Sounds like it will be a great party," I say to George. "I'll make sure she gets this."

Milo says, "Um." I give him a pointed look, and he gives one right back.

"Great!" George says. "Mr. Jenkins will be thrilled." He nods goodbye and smoothly walks back to his car.

"You're not thinking of going, are you?" Milo asks, although his tone says he knows that's exactly what I'm going to do.

"James obviously knows something," I say. I guess it's time for the not-exactly-family reunion I've been avoiding.

"I thought you weren't making any public appearances before Sunday."

"I'm not. That's why I have my wig." I look over the invitation again. "It's at The Copacabana on Forty-Eighth Street."

Milo frowns. "I don't think your grandma would want you to go to his party."

"Of course she wouldn't. But I also didn't want her to up and leave without telling me if she'd be back before what is quite possibly the biggest night of both of our lives, so I guess we'll have to call this even. And she never has to find out that I was there if you don't tell her."

He narrows his eyes, and I narrow mine too. We're in a standoff on Gigi's front stoop.

He breaks the silence first. "You shouldn't go by yourself. I'll go with you."

He braces himself, like he's ready for me to argue. I take in his long and lanky limbs, and when I look up at his face, I fixate on his nose ring and full lips. But only for a moment.

"Just in case anything happens," he adds quickly, "I want to go with you as a friend. Or I guess I should say *acquaintance*, since you're allergic to friendships."

"*Ha*," I deadpan. "At least you won't need a suit for this."

His apprehensive expression changes to a smirk. "Good."

Chapter Thirteen

Back during my brief time in the spotlight, I had a stylist and we created an Evie Jones aesthetic: bright and flirty, yet classic. There is nothing bright or flirty about the black silk sleeveless dress and white patent leather platform boots I took from Gigi's closet. But that's the whole point. I don't need to call attention to myself tonight. The plan is to blend in, find James, ask about Gigi, and then get out of there.

I finish the look with my bob wig and sunglasses and take a car to the venue. I'm not surprised there's a line outside. Paparazzi are snapping pictures of the celebrities who skip the line and walk right through the door.

Milo is already standing in line, and he waves when he sees me coming. He's wearing a denim jacket, a striped white button-up, black jeans with rips in the knees, and classic black Vans.

"Hi," I say.

He takes in my whole look, and then he smiles. "You look really nice."

"Thank you. So do you."

He blinks. "You mean you're not going to make me go home and change this time?"

"Of course not," I say, surprised. I feel prickly all over with guilt. "Your suit wasn't that bad, really. It just wasn't appropriate for the setting. I'm sorry if I offended you."

He laughs. "I was only joking, Evie. But thanks for two compliments in a row." He gives my shoulder a friendly little pat and removes his hand before I can react.

"And here I thought you didn't like to lie," I say.

"Jokes and lies aren't the same thing."

"Mm-hmm," I hum. I turn away to pull out my invitation and so I can stop looking at his smile. As we inch closer to the door, I prepare myself to smoothly explain that Milo is my plus-one, but it turns out I won't have to do any explaining at all.

"*Adrian?*" Milo says, looking up at the bouncer, who is apparently employed by every nightclub between Manhattan and Brooklyn. "What are you doing here?"

"I'm working," Adrian says. "What the hell are *you* doing here?"

"We're here for the party." Milo points at the door, and Adrian quirks an eyebrow.

"How did you score an invitation?" he asks.

Milo, who clearly wants to give Honest Abe a run for his money, just stands there and gulps.

"We know people," I say, stepping forward and showing my invitation.

Adrian looks at me carefully with his huge brown eyes. "Oh, look, it's the girl from last night."

"I told you I wasn't lying about knowing Milo," I say triumphantly.

"Uh-huh." He squints at the invitation like he thinks it's fake. "Who do you know?"

I blink. "What?"

"You said you know people. What people do you know?"

I bet I could name at least fifteen people who are inside this establishment right now, but none of them would recognize me looking like this. And I doubt that any of them would come to my aid.

"I don't see why that's important," I say, crossing my arms, trying my best not to pout like a little kid. "You have our invitation. Now can you please let us inside?"

He stamps a little green alien on the backs of our hands. "Go ahead, but let me remind you, *no alcohol.* If I find out you were drinking—"

"You'll pull us out yourself," Milo finishes. "We know, bro. Thanks."

It's clear once we're inside that Adrian didn't spout his no-drinking rule to every person who looks under twenty-one. Two guys, who are already drunk, amble in our direction, and when one trips, Milo grabs my hand and pulls me out of the way. As we continue on, the crowd gets thicker, so I don't let go. My sunglasses make everything darker, but I don't dare take them off. The music is crazy loud, and the bass vibrates so hard it's throwing off my equilibrium.

There are people in alien costumes, taking pictures with guests, and they look cartoonishly evil. On principle, I've never actually seen any of the Aliens Attack Earth movies, but I hear they're entertaining. Tonight, the aliens are like little specks in a sea of partygoers. Too many people in one place. That was always my least favorite part about going out, but Simone never minded it so much.

When I think about it—and trust me, I've had plenty of time to think about it—I realize Simone only wanted to be my friend because she thought it would give her some kind of connection. The first time we met, I was sitting at the lunch table alone. It was the second day of freshman year. The majority of my classmates had already decided I'd been given enough handouts and that I didn't need their friendship too. But Simone sat down right across from me.

"Hey, I'm Simone," she said, tossing her long braids over her shoulder. "What's your concentration?"

"Acting," I said, relieved to have someone to talk to. "I'm Evie."

I thought it was a Black thing, you know? Like how Black people always seem to find one another and congregate, regardless of where they are. We were two of the few Black girls at McKibben. But now I see how she would find ways to ask about my parents, to ask about Gigi.

Like on my fifteenth birthday, when Simone came to my house and was surprised to see that it was just a dinner for the two of us and my parents. "Where's your grandma?" were the first words out of her mouth, instead of "happy birthday."

I was just so desperate and grateful to finally have a friend that I ignored all the signs. And it cost me my career.

"You okay?" Milo shouts over the music, angling his face toward mine.

I didn't realize that I zoned out. And we're still holding hands. I should probably let go, but then I might lose him. This place is really packed.

I nod, then shout back, "Yeah!"

We stop at a corner of the room, near one of the bars. It's a great vantage point to scope out the entire club. All the way to the right, there are roped-off sections with tables, and that's where James Jenkins is sitting. It looks like he's only surrounded by his team. There aren't any other actors up there with him.

Do men in their seventies usually go to after-parties for their films? I don't know. But I guess most men in their seventies aren't like James Jenkins. I have to find a way to get up there and talk to him.

Beside me, Milo sings along to the song that's playing. It's not one I recognize. I pull on his arm to get his attention, and that's when I realize there are three boys standing a few feet away and they're staring at us. They don't stop staring when I make eye contact with them either. They whisper to one another, and then, as if gathering confidence, they start to walk over.

Crap. They know who I am. The wig and sunglasses aren't enough. Are they Paul Christopher superfans, coming to get revenge?

"Milo," I say, pulling harder on his sleeve, nodding my head at the boys.

They approach, and I ready myself. *No, I'm not who you think I am*, I'll say.

But they don't even look at me. One boy says to Milo, "Yo, are you in that group Doves Have Pride?"

Milo blinks, then his mouth splits into a huge grin. "Yeah, that's me."

"That EP you dropped over the summer was lit," another boy says. The others nod enthusiastically.

I stare at them in complete silence. My jaw is on the floor.

The boys turn around and beckon over more friends. Like

bees to honey, they flock to Milo until a small crowd has surrounded us, and they all want to know more about Doves Have Pride. When is their next show? Why is Milo here? Were they included on the *Aliens Attack Earth 4* soundtrack? Answers: Two weeks. He's chilling with his friend (me). No, but he wishes they were.

After all the questions are answered and Milo autographs one girl's hand, the small crowd disperses. Milo has a dreamy-eyed look on his face. Meanwhile, I'm astounded. I mean, from the amount of people at their show last night, I could tell they had a following, but I didn't realize it went past Brooklyn.

I guess this is what happens when you avoid social media. You miss everything.

Milo is practically glowing.

"I really need to see your music video," I say.

He turns to me, shocked. "You haven't seen it yet?"

"No," I say sheepishly.

"*Wowww*, that's messed up."

I start to tell him about my social media hiatus, but two of his fans return and excitedly ask if Milo will take a picture with them. As he pulls out his phone, he moves his arm wide, and his drink splashes down the front of my dress.

"*Oh no*," I groan. Gigi is going to kill me. This dress is vintage silk!

"I'm so sorry," the boy says. He reaches out to, I don't

know, attempt to help me or something, but I shake my head.

"It's okay." I turn to Milo. "I'm gonna go to the bathroom and rinse this off."

"I'll walk with you," he says, but I shake my head at this too.

"No, no, stay and take your pictures. I'll be fine."

He doesn't look happy about it, but he also doesn't want to disappoint his new fans either. "I'll wait for you here."

I nod and make my way to the bathroom, which is really hard to do while wearing these sunglasses and without having Milo's height or broad shoulders to push through the crowd. I don't understand how there are celebrities who wear sunglasses 24/7.

Several groups of girls are taking pictures in the bathroom mirror, and I bypass them for the sink at the end of the row, farthest away from everyone. They eventually clear out as I struggle to rinse the spot from my dress. When the door shuts behind them and I'm finally alone, I take off my sunglasses so that I can see better. As soon as I get the alcohol smell out of Gigi's dress, I'm going to find a way to talk to James and then be out of here.

"This is the most boring party I've ever been to."

My head snaps up as the bathroom door pushes open and I hear a familiar voice.

Almost as if it's happening in slow motion, I watch as

Simone Davis walks into the bathroom, her phone pressed to her ear.

You've *got* to be kidding me.

Her braids hang long and loose down to her waist, and she's wearing a tight-fitted fuchsia minidress. She looks amazing. Somehow that makes everything much worse.

Her eyes widen when she sees me. "Oh shit," she whispers into her phone. "Celia, let me call you back."

She hangs up, and we stare at each other across the room. My heart is hammering in my chest, like it wants to climb its way up my throat and escape.

"Evie?" she says in disbelief. "What are you doing here? Why are you dressed like that?" She looks me up and down, scrunching her eyebrows together.

I always imagined what I would do or say if we saw each other again. I'd scream and shout, make her feel horrible, bring her down as low as she brought me. But I can't say anything. I'm too shocked, frozen to the spot. I feel like all the blood is rushing to my face, as if I've been on one of those spinning rides at an amusement park. I didn't expect to run into her here, although I should have. Everyone is in the city for the FCCs. Why didn't I guess that she'd be here too?

"Were you invited?" she asks, walking closer. She narrows her eyes. "I can't believe you somehow found your way here, at a James Jenkins party, of all places. Your grandma can't be too happy."

"Don't you dare speak of my grandmother," I say, finally finding my voice, and it's laced with venom. "How can you talk to me like you didn't ruin my life? Why did you leak the video, Simone? How could you do something like that to me?"

She sighs. "Not everything is about you, Evie," she says. "That was your problem to begin with. When it came down to supporting you or helping myself, I chose me. You got that role in Paul Christopher's movie because he's an Evelyn Conaway fanatic and you know it. I have the role now because I deserve it. Not everyone has the whole world handed to them on a silver platter, like you. Some of us have to do what's necessary to get what we want. I was always going to choose me. Don't act like you wouldn't have done the same."

"I wouldn't have," I say. Now I'm crying. "I never would have done what you did."

I can't believe I used to think she was my best friend. How could I have been so naive?

"Were you always pretending to be my friend?" I manage to say, wiping my face. "Was any of it real?"

She stares at me, her mouth set in a tight line. I hold my breath as I wait for her response because I need to know the truth. For some reason, her answer means everything in this moment. If she says that our friendship was real, could I find it in myself to forgive her? I've been so *lonely*. As much as I hate her, I miss her even more.

In the end, it doesn't matter, because she doesn't answer my question. She blinks and tilts her head as if she's just come to a realization.

"Oh my God," she says slowly. "Is this a disguise? Are you wearing a disguise right now, Evie?"

I push past her, and she grabs on to my arm. I yank away with a hard tug.

"And Celia Reyes, really?" I say, spinning around to face her. "That's who you were on the phone with? The same girl who dumped you a million times? The girl you cried on my shoulder about? Great! That's just great!"

"What do you care?" she yells, following after me out into the empty hallway. Now I see why no one came into the bathroom to disturb us. One of the *Aliens Attack Earth 4* cast members is giving a drunken speech onstage, and everyone has their phones out to record him. "The only reason you never liked Celia is because when I was with her, it meant that I was spending time away from you. Do you know how exhausting it was being your only friend? To watch you get cast in lead roles at McKibben and have to pretend to be happy for you, like I wasn't jealous?"

Now she's crying too. The two of us standing in the hallway, sobbing in front of each other.

I don't have time for my messed-up past with Simone. I have to find James Jenkins.

"I can't do this right now." *Or ever.* I turn away and head back toward the dance floor.

"I don't know why you're here, but you obviously don't want people to know that you are," Simone calls. "Imagine what people would say if they heard Evelyn Conaway's granddaughter was out supporting James Jenkins. That Evie Jones finally made a public appearance again."

I freeze and then spin around. I slowly breathe in and out, trying to keep my voice level. "You wouldn't."

"There you are."

A warm hand smoothly slides around my shoulders. I look up to find Milo by my side.

"What's wrong? What happened?" He takes in the expression on my face, the tears rolling down my cheeks. He looks from me to Simone, who is now staring at us, openmouthed.

"You're in that band," she says, pointing at him. "I've seen that video of you singing to the tourists in Times Square."

Milo smiles tightly, nodding. "That's us."

"What are you, her boyfriend or something?" She stares at his hand on my shoulder. To me, she says, "I thought you had a rule about dating people in the entertainment industry."

Milo makes a little noise and looks down at me. While his

face remains impassive, I can tell that he's thinking, *So* that's *what it is.*

"We're not dating," I say, even though she doesn't deserve an answer and has no right or place to bring up something I told her in confidence.

I pull on Milo's arm. "Come on, let's go."

"But I don't get it," Simone continues, looking at Milo. "No one wants to work with her anymore. She's basically a pariah. Why would you hang out with her?"

Milo frowns hard at Simone, and his fingers spread and tighten on my shoulder.

"It's not worth it," I say, continuing to pull him away, focused on getting to James's VIP section.

"What the hell is wrong with that girl?" Milo asks, glancing over his shoulder. "And why were you crying? What happened?"

I don't even have a chance to answer him before I hear Simone yell my name.

"Evie, wait!" she shouts. "Let's take a picture together! You and me and your new friend!"

She's shouting on purpose. She knows I don't want to be recognized. Milo and I haven't even made it out of the bathroom alcove when Simone grabs a nearby party photographer and points directly at me.

Loudly, she says, "That's Evie Jones, Evelyn Conaway's granddaughter. Remember, from *Mind Games*, the one Paul

Christopher fired? I want to get a picture with her. Come on, Evie, let's take a picture together for old times' sake!"

The party photographer turns to me, confused. But just the mention of my name is enough bait. Slowly, he grins at me and lifts his camera.

I turn to Milo and say one word: "Run!"

Chapter Fourteen

We run to the exit, and the party photographer is right on us.

"Wait, wait! Just one picture, Ms. Jones!"

Milo bursts through the door, grabs my hand, and pulls me outside with him. A bunch of paparazzi are standing on the sidewalk, smoking cigarettes and waiting for grand celebrity exits. They startle at the sight of us.

"Who are they?" one confused photographer asks, but we keep running before they even have a chance to figure it out.

Behind us, I hear the party photographer say, "Apparently, that's Evie Jones, the one Paul Christopher fired."

Then all chaos breaks loose. And of course at the moment we need him, Adrian is nowhere to be found.

"Ms. Jones! Ms. Jones! Evie, can you tell us where you've been all these months?! Who's the guy?"

I run faster than I've ever run in my entire life. But I'm no match for Milo and his long legs. Especially not while wearing these platform boots. The only reason I'm moving so quickly is that he's basically pulling me down Forty-Sixth Street.

We make a sharp right onto Seventh Avenue, and I've never been so thankful for Times Square tourists to help us blend in. Most paparazzi gave up after a block or two, but there are a few persistent ones who are still running after us.

I tighten my grip on Milo's hand as he quickly pushes his way through the crowd.

"Evie!" I hear a photographer shout. "Just one picture!"

Seriously, are they so desperate that they'd brave tourist central? I have to do something, and fast.

I spot a diner called The Red Flame to my right, and I call Milo's name, urging him along toward the diner. We're panting as we rush inside, and the hostess backs away, holding up her hands in surprise. I spin around and glimpse one of the photographers who's still searching for us in the crowd. Thinking quickly, I start pulling Milo's jacket off his arms so that they won't recognize him, and so that he's blocking me.

"What are you doing?" he asks as I continue tugging on his sleeves. I take his jacket and throw it over my shoulders. Behind him, a photographer is right in front of the door, looking in the opposite direction. When he starts to turn his head toward us, I pull Milo down so that his face is right in front of mine.

And I swear it wasn't supposed to be a real kiss. We were

just supposed to pretend to kiss so that the photographer wouldn't see our faces and move on.

But it's like our mouths have ideas of their own, because once Milo's face is level with mine, our lips come together like magnets. I wait a fraction of a second, giving him a chance to pull away if he wants to. But he doesn't. He pulls me closer and deepens the kiss, wrapping his arms around my waist.

I've been kissed before, during performances and in real life. But I've never been kissed like *this*. So slowly and deeply, as if it's the only thing that matters. His lips are soft, and his mouth tastes like spearmint. I reach up, placing my hands on his firm shoulders. His skin is warm, radiating through his shirt.

Our kiss feels like it lasts a century, when, in reality, only a few minutes pass. I finally pull away, lifting my fingers to my swollen mouth. Milo blinks at me, looking completely dazed. I glance behind him. No more paparazzi. The kiss worked. In more ways than one, if I'm being honest.

"They're gone," I say breathlessly. Calmly. But on the inside, I'm thinking, *Oh my God. We just kissed. We just kissed!*

"We just kissed," Milo says, like he can't believe it. "You just kissed me."

"It—it was for the paparazzi," I stammer. "I didn't want them to see our faces."

"You just kissed me," he repeats, smiling this time. He has nice teeth. Nice lips. Nice everything.

Ugh! What have I done?

I shake my head. "It wasn't even real! It was just for the paparazzi!"

"Was it, though?" he says, shaking his head too. "I think you kissed me because you wanted to."

"No! Well . . . no. No." I'm a broken record.

"Um, excuse me, do you guys want a table, or what?" The hostess is staring at us impatiently. "I know we're open twenty-four hours, but that doesn't mean you get to stand by the door all night."

She raises an eyebrow. I imagine how we must look to her: a sweaty, winded couple who just ran through Times Square, holding hands, making out as soon as we got through the door. She probably thinks we're tourists who are madly in love or something.

"Table for two, please," Milo says. When I look at him, he adds, "What? We're here. We might as well eat."

I don't agree with that logic, but I do think it's best to hide out and lie low until we can trust that all the paparazzi have left the area.

"Um, can we sit in the back, please?" I ask. "Like, as far from the door as possible?"

The hostess frowns, clearly done with us. "Um, okay. Sure."

She seats us at a booth in the back, right near the loud kitchen, where we can hear the cooks and servers bustling on the other side of the swinging door.

I focus on the menu in front of me, avoiding eye contact

with Milo. I can't believe I just kissed him. Fast thinking on my part, yes, but I did not bother to think about the repercussions! And my lips are still tingling.

Okay, get it together, Evie. Fries, you like fries. Get some fries. And a milkshake. You love those, remember?

But I can't stop picturing the way our mouths melded together, the thrill I felt when his tongue bumped into mine.

What is wrong with you? Stop it!

When I glance up, I find that Milo is watching me. He starts to smile and opens his mouth, but I'm quick to cut him off.

"Don't say anything else about the kiss," I warn.

He laughs. "Okay, fine. It was a good kiss. That's it. I've said my piece."

My stomach does a little flip, and my cheeks suddenly feel like they're covered in lava. I take a sip of my water and clear my throat, turning my attention back to my menu.

"We just ran from the paparazzi," he says. "Like, straight-up just ran from them."

And then the hysteria from tonight finally catches up with me because I burst out laughing, and I can't stop. "I've *never* done that before!"

Milo sits forward, laughing too. "Me neither! That was nuts. I don't know how anyone can live like that, being followed every day. Now I see why you have the wig."

"Well, the wig is pointless now," I say once I stop laughing.

"They might have gotten a few pictures of me like this, and who knows what Simone is going to tell people." I shake my head, angry all over again. "I can't believe she ruined my chance to talk to James. I have to figure out something else before Sunday."

A waitress comes over to take our orders, and I realize I never actually decided on a meal. Milo waits for me to order first, but when I stare at him blankly, he orders a burger and fries and a root beer. Then the waitress looks at me, smiling patiently, unlike our hostess. There's so much food on this menu. I don't even remember the last time I ate a meal at a public place. Sometime in early May, I guess. It's as if I've forgotten how to order food.

"Um," I say. "Um . . ."

"Pancakes?" Milo suggests, raising an eyebrow.

"Yes!" Pancakes sound amazing right now. "I'll have the blueberry pancakes, please, with extra whipped cream." I push the menu away but quickly pull it back. "I'll also have a black-and-white shake and french fries."

"Coming right up," the waitress says. Once she walks away, I finally take off my sunglasses and lean back against the booth cushion. I let out a deep breath.

Milo gulps down his water and then steeples his fingers. He has the look of someone who is about to ask A Question.

"So . . . that girl," he says carefully, "is she the reason you aren't big on friends?"

I stare at him, trying to decide if this is something I even want to talk about. When he found Simone and me, I was crying and angry. I don't have to explain myself, but I don't want to keep everything bottled up either.

"Yes," I finally answer.

"What happened? If you don't mind me asking?"

I look down and start folding my napkin into squares because I need something to do with my hands. "Her name is Simone. We went to the same performing arts school in LA. She used to be my best friend."

Milo waits as if he knows that there's more to the story.

"She was my only friend, actually," I continue. "For our senior showcase, everyone performs monologues, and it's a big deal because lots of directors and producers in the industry come looking for new talent. Paul Christopher came to see us my junior year, and that's how I got the role in *Mind Games*. When we found out he was coming back for our senior year, we all freaked out, of course. And after the showcase, he invited a few of us to audition for his new movie. Simone and I both auditioned for the lead. I got the role, and she didn't."

"That must have been awkward," he says.

I nod. "It was, but after a while, I thought everything was fine." I sigh and finally look up at him. "You know the video of me speaking in a British accent like Paul Christopher, the one that got me fired?"

"Yeah," he says.

"Well, I was with Simone that night, and she was the one who leaked it. I thought she was recording me as a joke, something we could rewatch and laugh about later. But the next morning, she sent it to media outlets. And then I was fired, and she was hired in my place. And now she's the face of Beautiful You. I almost had that campaign."

"That's so fucked up," Milo says, his voice low. "Damn, Evie. I'm sorry."

I look away, because the last thing I want is for him to feel sorry for me. "It's partially my fault too. I should have seen it coming."

He blinks and shakes his head. "Why would anyone expect a friend to turn on them like that?"

I laugh bitterly. "You are going to be in for a rude awakening once your band makes it big. You guys have something really special. You need to stick together and watch out for people who try to break into your circle."

"Don't you have any childhood friends you can trust like that?"

"No. I never had any close friends before Simone." I place my hands flat on the table and stare at my fingers. Talking about this is embarrassing. "I used to travel a lot with my parents while they filmed their documentaries, so I was never in one place long enough to make friendships that lasted. I guess Gigi has always been my real best friend."

I glance up, expecting pity. Instead, he smiles. "Yeah, she feels like a best friend to me too."

For the first time, Milo talking about his closeness to Gigi doesn't annoy me. Maybe it's because he says this with such genuine affection. Still, I can't return his bright smile. Gigi is my best friend, and for the first time ever, she doesn't want to talk to me. She doesn't even want to see me. What if she never speaks to me again?

Our food arrives, and once our server walks away, Milo asks, "What's next for you as far as projects go? I mean, only if you're willing to talk about them."

I take a long slurp of my milkshake before I answer. "Nothing right now." I'm definitely not telling him about the possible *Every Time We Meet* remake. "I guess you could say that my current project is getting everyone to stop hating me."

"I don't think *everyone* hates you," he says, taking a big bite of his burger.

"Have you seen what people have said about me online? You saw the way the paparazzi chased me. They can't wait to print my picture and write a caption about how I'm a horrible person who has no respect for Paul Christopher or for real cinema."

Milo shrugs. "I don't know. I think that's a stretch. I didn't even know who Simone was until you told me just now. All that stuff happened months ago. I bet a lot of people have moved on and would be happy to see you in something else."

"Really?" I say, surprised. Suddenly, I *do* have the urge to tell him about the remake, just to see what he might think. But I know better than to do that.

He nods. "Sure. If 'the legendary' Paul Christopher made the decision to cast you in one of his movies, it's obvious that you can act. You've already got the beauty part down."

He says it so easily I'm not sure if he's flirting or speaking matter-of-factly. Our kiss has changed things.

"Thank you," I say either way. There goes the lava over my cheeks again.

Our eyes lock across the table for longer than necessary. I'm the first to look away.

"Enough about me," I say. "You're the one who's so famous. Show me this YouTube video everyone keeps talking about."

He shakes his head, smiling. "Right, because you still haven't seen it."

He pulls out his phone and cues up the video. It begins with the camera focusing on Raf, standing in crowded Times Square. He's wearing a bright-red T-shirt and shiny black leather pants. They look ridiculous and tight. In the next shot, Milo appears beside him, strumming on his guitar, wearing the same leather pants, and my stomach flutters at the sight of him. I'm not the only one who's affected this way, obviously. In the background, a bunch of tourists are staring at Milo specifically. The next shot has Ben with his drum set, and then Vinny runs in, playing his saxophone. And yes, both are wearing leather pants. They perform a little dance routine each time they sing the chorus, and they encourage tourists to dance with them. The video ends as the police run up, ready to ticket them for not having a recording permit, and I'm laughing so hard Milo has to shush me.

"I can see why that went viral," I say. "It's good. The song's good too. But why leather pants? Where did that come from?"

He shrugs and puts his phone back in his pocket. "I went through a breakup last year, and I was writing a bunch of sad songs. The guys got tired of it and told me to write something happy. One day Raf found these ridiculous leather pants at a thrift store, and I started to write a song about them as a joke. But then we put music to it, and it sounded good. It kind of just took on a life of its own."

"Raf mentioned the sad songs to me," I say. I am really curious about this breakup and this ex-girlfriend, but I don't want to ask; it's his business, not mine. And I know how guarded I can be, so I don't want to push it. But finally, curiosity wins. "Who was she?"

He takes another bite of his burger. For a second, I think he's avoiding the question, and I start to feel bad for asking, but then he clears his throat.

"Her name was Imani—*is* Imani," he says. "There's not really much to tell you, to be honest. We went to Brooklyn

Tech together. She left for Texas A&M after graduation and didn't want to do the long-distance thing, so we ended it. Or she ended it, I guess."

I wince. "That's rough. I'm sorry."

"And she was mad that I was taking a year off to focus on music instead of going straight to college," he adds. "So there's that."

"It's hard to be in love and be a creative," I say automatically. He blinks, so I explain. "It's something Gigi always says."

He nods. "I know. That's where I first heard it. Your grandma really helped me out during those first couple of months, when I was really down. I moved out of my parents' apartment in Bed-Stuy because I have three little sisters and there wasn't enough space in our two-bedroom apartment. That, and my parents can be kind of . . . overbearing sometimes, you know? They think I'm wasting my time on music, and they never come to our shows. And then I moved in with the guys. But after a while, I thought that maybe I should just quit the band and go to college and major in something that will make a lot of money, and then I could help my parents financially, at least. I didn't want to give up on my dream, but not everybody has the luxury to be impractical." He pauses and looks down at the table. "The day I'd decided to tell the guys that I was quitting and moving out, I came by your grandma's to drop off her groceries, and she could tell there was something off about me. Eventually, I told her my plan to give up on music, and she convinced me not to. She said it would be pointless to waste so much talent."

I smile a little. "That sounds like something Gigi would say."

"She told me I could stay with her sometimes if that made my commute a little easier," he continues. "That changed everything for me. I've never had someone like her in my life before. I feel like she genuinely cares about what happens to me. She believes in me. That's why we got so close."

He leans forward, looking at me. Earnestly, he says, "I know that she's *your* grandmother. You have a place in her heart that I'll never be able to take, and I don't want to. I just want you to know that I care about her a lot, and I feel protective of her. That's why I was so suspicious of you coming to visit this week."

"I was suspicious of you too," I say, narrowing my eyes. "I still am."

He smirks, leaning back. "Glad to know we're still on the same page."

I take another sip of my milkshake to hide my smile. "So you really want to make it big with the band, huh?"

"I hope so," he says. "It's all I've ever wanted. I almost feel like I'd do anything to just get signed."

"Well, once that day comes and you record an album, maybe you can write a song about me and how we ran from the paparazzi. With the way things are going for you, I'm sure there will be even more paparazzi-dodging in your future."

He laughs. "Maybe. But what if I've already written a song about you? Do you really think you need two songs?"

I freeze. My mouth goes slack-jawed. "You wrote a song about me?"

"Maybe. Maybe not." He picks up a fry and holds it above my shake. "Can I?"

I blink, thrown off. "Can you what?"

"Dip my fry in your shake?"

"What? No! How gross. Why would you ever do that?"

His eyes bug out. "Evie . . . are you telling me you've never dipped a french fry in a milkshake before?"

"Of course not. This can't be a thing that people actually do."

His mouth is hanging open. "People do it all the time!" He pushes his plate toward me. "Take one. You try."

I hesitate, wondering if he's playing a trick on me or if this is just one of the many things I missed out on during childhood.

I take a fry and slowly dip it in my shake. When I take a bite, it's soggy, but salty and sweet. I try another one.

"Oh my God, this is delicious."

He grins, triumphant. "Told you."

We both start eating milkshake-dipped french fries, and something about this feels like déjà vu, which is strange, because I've never sat in a diner and eaten french fries with a boy before.

But then I realize it's not *my* memory. I'm thinking about Diane and Henry from *Every Time We Meet*. Their first date is at a restaurant in East Harlem, and they stay so late into the night that the staff begins cleaning up while Diane and Henry are still busy talking. I almost bring this up to Milo, but I don't want him reading too deep into the comparison.

When the waitress returns with the check, I wonder again how we must look to her. A boy and a girl—who inexplicably wears sunglasses at night—laughing over french fries and a milkshake.

"I can pay," I quickly say as Milo takes out his wallet.

"Let me."

"No, seriously, I can—"

"I *know* you can, Evie," he says. "But it's Friday, and I got paid today. So just let me buy your dinner, okay?"

"Okay," I say, only because I have a feeling we'll just keep going back and forth. Plus, it's not as if we're really on a date or anything.

Then, because I can't seem to help myself, I suddenly blurt out, "Raf thought we were going on a date last night. And he told me not to break your heart. Isn't that ridiculous?"

Seriously. *What* is wrong with me?

"Not really," Milo says, shrugging. "I tend to like girls who are unavailable and/or unattainable. You fall into both of those categories, so I can see why Raf would make that assumption."

"Oh." My heart starts to beat a little faster, and my palms get clammy. I look down and smooth out my dress just to have something to do other than stare at him. But when I look up, I find that he's studying me in that careful way again, like he's trying to read my mind.

"What?" I say.

"Nothing. I'm just thinking about the first time I saw you in person—last Christmas, when your grandmother had us come over and sing Christmas carols for you and your parents. We were all really nervous to meet you, especially me, since your grandma talked about you so much, but then you were on your phone the whole time we were there, and you didn't even look up at us once. I remember thinking that you were nothing like the kind and funny girl that your grandmother had described. You just seemed really stuck-up."

"Excuse me—"

"Wait, let me finish," he says. "Now that I know you better, I can see what your grandmother means. What she didn't say is that you're spontaneous and clever and headstrong to a fault. And that you like to kiss people out of nowhere."

The lava on my cheeks spreads down to my neck and chest. Pretty soon, my whole body is probably going to catch on fire. Flustered, I hiss, "I don't just go around kissing people! That won't ever happen again."

He grins. "Really? That's too bad."

I glare at him, but he continues to grin. Then his expression turns into something a little more serious, and we're staring at each other in silence. My heart gallops in my chest. I take measured breaths to slow it down, but there's no use.

"Y'all have a good night," the waitress says, giving Milo his change and a receipt.

We snap out of our staring trance and stand up awkwardly.

As we ride the subway to Gigi's, we sit side by side, and I try my best not to think of that kiss, or the way he looked at me over dinner, or how we had our very own Diane-and-Henry moment.

Because none of it really matters. Gigi was right. Falling in love isn't meant for creatives. I should be concerned about finding Gigi above anything else.

Once we're back at Gigi's, Milo goes into the kitchen to feed the cats and I head upstairs to my room. As I'm taking off Gigi's boots, Milo comes to stand in my doorway.

"Today was fun," he says.

Fun. I wouldn't have thought to use that word, but he isn't wrong. Aside from the Simone run-in and not actually getting a chance to talk to James, today was more fun than I've had in a really long time. I almost felt normal again.

Milo really isn't so bad.

I look at him now, leaning against the doorjamb, all tall and handsome. I bet he'll make his next girlfriend really happy. In another world, one where I could bring myself to let someone in again, maybe that girl could be me.

But in this world, I'm unwilling to give my heart to someone just so they can inevitably break it.

"Good night, Milo," I say.

He nods and taps the doorjamb. "Night, Evie."

Footage from homemade video—May 17, 1974
Evelyn Conaway and James Jenkins are at the home that they share in Los Angeles. They've just been married for a second time and are standing in their bedroom. Evelyn stands at the entrance to her closet, and James stands in the doorway, recording.

James (off camera): So how does it feel to be Mrs. Jenkins again?
Evelyn pauses in the act of taking off her heels, turns around to look at him, and covers her face
Evelyn: I can't believe Candice let you borrow that thing. Is it too much to ask that a camera not follow me around at home too?
James chuckles
James: Aww, come on. I'm just trying to capture the moment. Can you answer the question, please? How does it feel to be Mrs. Jenkins again?
Evelyn: Wonderful.
Evelyn walks over and stands directly in James's line of sight
Evelyn: It feels absolutely wonderful.
James: You look like you have something else you want to tell me.
Evelyn smiles and reaches for the camera, turning it on James, who is leaning against the doorjamb, smirking
Evelyn: How do *you* feel to be married to me again?
James: It's indescribable, babe.

******James reaches out and wraps his arm around Evelyn's waist, bringing his face right up to the camera lens******

James: What do you want to do to celebrate?

Evelyn: I want you to take me to the movies.

James: If that's what my lady wants, that's what my lady gets.

recording ends

Chapter Fifteen

SATURDAY, AUGUST 15

"Evie, is there something you want to tell me?" Kerri asks as I hold my phone to my ear.

I sit up in bed, groggy and half awake. Milo and I didn't get back until almost 3:00 A.M. last night. I fell asleep without even taking off my makeup. Now, five hours later, I can barely open my eyes.

"What do you mean?" I clear my throat and fight off a yawn.

"Just ten minutes ago, I received this Google alert from *Us Weekly*: 'Evie Jones Is in New York, and She's Got a New Look and a New Guy.'"

I'm definitely awake now. "Oh no."

"Oh yes." Kerri continues to read, "'After avoiding public appearances for months, last night Jones was first spotted at the *Aliens Attack Earth 4* after-party, revealing a new short bob cut and a new beau, whom we've identified as Milo Williams from the indie band Doves Have Pride. They were later seen kissing at a diner in Times Square.'" Kerri pauses. "I just sent the article to you."

I pull my phone away from my ear to open the link. Sure enough, there's Milo and me, running down the street, hand in hand. I'm facing forward, and you can only see the back of my head, but Milo is looking at the paparazzi with wide eyes. Then there's the photo of us kissing at the diner. Even with Milo's back to the door and his jacket covering me, you can still see my face angled toward his as we kiss. His arms are wrapped around my waist and mine are looped around his neck. It was supposed to be a quick kiss where neither of us moved. Obviously, we got *way* too into it.

"Oh no," I repeat. It seems to be all that I can say.

"I'm already trying my best to do damage control and get these pictures down from other sites. And I just had a lengthy phone call with your parents, assuring them that everything was fine." Kerri sighs deeply. "Evie, didn't we agree on no public appearances? And a James Jenkins party, no less! I know you're tired of being cooped up, but you're really not doing us any favors here."

"I know. I'm sorry, Kerri. Really." *Please don't quit.*

She sighs again, deeper this time, if that's even possible. "What does your grandmother think about all this?"

"Nothing! She's not upset." She doesn't know I was there, so at least I can assume this is true.

"And what's the deal with this musician? How long has this been going on? And when, exactly, did you plan on telling me?"

"There's nothing going on, Kerri. He's just a friend." I wince. A *friend*?

"Well, he'd better be a squeaky-clean little Boy Scout," Kerri advises. "We don't have time for playboys or partyers who can't seem to keep themselves out of jail or rehab."

"He's not like that," I say, more defensive than I mean to be. I think back to last night and how long Milo and I talked at the diner. How I opened up to him in a way that I haven't opened up to anybody in a long time, and I'm not even sure why I did so. Maybe it's because all he wanted to do was listen. "He's decent, I think."

"Decent," Kerri repeats. "Hmph. And I've never even heard of his band. I watched that YouTube video, though. 'Leather Pants.' Cute. Who represents them?"

"No one yet."

There's a knock on my bedroom door, and then Milo pops his head inside. He holds up his phone, showing the *Us Weekly* article. Eyes wide, he asks, "Have you seen this?"

"Who is that?" Kerri asks, alert. "Is that boy with you right now?"

"Um, yes," I say as Milo walks farther into the room until he's standing at the foot of my bed. He's dressed for work. He glances up at the canopy draping and smiles.

I pull my knees up to my chest, suddenly feeling embarrassed for him to see me wearing pajamas with my hair wrapped. But he's already seen me this way, and I didn't care before. Why do I care now?

"I thought you were staying at your grandmother's house," Kerri says. "Is that where you are?"

I hesitate. "Yes . . ."

"I don't like the sound of this, Evie! Do I need to fly out there tonight?"

"That's really not necessary," I say quickly. The last thing I need is for Kerri to come to New York and discover that Gigi is nowhere to be found. I still have a chance at handling this on my own before everything blows up. I just need to find a way to get in touch with James Jenkins. "Sunday morning still works. I'm fine. Everything is fine."

"We had an agreement, Evie. Please, no more traipsing around the city, okay?" She sounds frustrated. "I know these past few months haven't been the best, but things are going to change for you soon. You are an intelligent young woman. I trust you to make intelligent young woman decisions."

"I will. I'm sorry." I turn away from Milo so that he won't see the guilt on my face. I hate disappointing people in general, but I particularly hate disappointing Kerri because she always goes to bat for me. My stomach sinks.

"No need to be sorry; just remember what I said." She

pauses again. "Are you sure you don't need me to fly out today? Because I will be on the next flight if you need me."

"I'm okay," I say, hoping that it sounds true.

After a long beat: "All right. I'll see you tomorrow. Call me if you change your mind."

When we hang up, the notifications I missed early this morning start rolling in. Four missed calls from my dad, seven from my mom. Great. Kerri said she talked to them, but I know they're expecting an explanation from me as well. I turn my phone over, and Milo sits quietly at the edge of my bed.

"Are you in trouble?" he asks.

"Kind of." I scoot a little closer to him, then wonder why I'm scooting closer. I haven't even brushed my teeth yet! But if I scoot back, it will look weird, so I freeze where I am, not too close but not too far away either.

If Milo notices my weird behavior, he doesn't mention it. He slides his phone across the bed to me. "Have you seen the comments?"

"No." I close my eyes and shake my head. "I don't want to see them either."

Sensing my anxiety, he retrieves his phone and says, "Well, I'll read you two of my favorites. Here's the first one: 'Is that even Evie? Doesn't look like her. Either way, her hair is cute. Love the bob.' And here's the second: 'He's hot. Good for Evie!'" He looks at me and grins. "Good for you."

I roll my eyes and fight the urge to smile. Then I bite my lip and add, "I'm sorry they name-dropped you in the article."

"It's kind of helped," he says, shrugging. "The band's Instagram page has over five hundred new followers already."

"Wow," I say. "Good for *you*. I'm sure Raf is thrilled."

"Oh, definitely. He keeps joking that's the reason the A&R guy called back this morning and said he'll see us play tonight."

"Tonight?"

He nods. "Adrian helped me convince the owner of The Goose's Egg to fit us in, so all we need is for the A&R guy to actually show up this time." He sighs and adds, "I think my parents will be there too."

"Really?" Now my eyes are bugging out.

"Yeah. Checking in to see if it's time to lay down the law. Summer's almost over. They're gonna want me to sign up for some classes. At least three. Which means less time for work and, more important, less time for music."

"I'll keep my fingers crossed for you," I say.

Clearly, my positivity shocks us both, because Milo blinks. "Thanks. That means a lot."

I wait for him to get up and leave for work, but he doesn't. He spreads his palm over my comforter and relaxes a little.

"Will you come to the show tonight?" he asks.

"Probably not," I say. I'm more focused on getting in touch

with James. Speaking of that, I should probably call Kerri back because I bet she'll be able to find out James's schedule today.

Milo looks down and nods. Is he disappointed? I'm a little surprised. I can't remember the last time someone wanted me to be somewhere for them.

"I have to find a way to get in touch with James," I say. "That's all I can really think about right now."

"Yeah, of course. Let me know if your plans change. We all want you there."

"Okay," I say.

His gaze drifts down to my lips, and I wonder if he's thinking about our kiss from last night just like I am. He leans forward, and I don't move, because I'm curious to see what he'll do. That curiosity lasts for a good two seconds before the sirens go off in my head.

Too close! Retreat! Retreat!

Abruptly, I scooch back so that I'm basically glued to my headboard. "I have to call Kerri."

He blinks and moves away just as quickly. "Right. I, uh, have to go to work."

"Okay," I say, clearing my throat. "Did you feed the cats?"

"Yep, all fed." His movements are jerky and awkward as he makes his way out of my room. He pauses in the doorway. "See you later?"

I nod, and then he disappears, followed by the sound of his feet pounding down the stairs.

That was close. Literally. I've decided Milo is an okay human being, but I can't let myself get distracted like last night.

I grab my phone to call Kerri and see what she can tell me about where James will be today. Because the only thing that matters is finding Gigi.

Chapter Sixteen

It took some finessing, but Kerri, who can do anything she puts her mind to, learned that there's an outdoor screening of *Every Time We Meet* later tonight at Bryant Park and that James is scheduled to do a Q&A beforehand. Of course, when Kerri asked why I needed this information, I told her that it was for Gigi. She didn't ask any more questions after that.

Gigi loved going to outdoor movies when I was a kid. It was her favorite summer pastime. She'd wrap a silk scarf around her head, tie it underneath her chin, and complete the look with a hat and sunglasses. She'd also let me wear one of her scarves, and then she'd make James wear a hat, just so that he wasn't left out. We'd go to the drive-in and park way in the back. It didn't really matter what movie was playing, because Gigi barely paid attention. She was more interested in watching the people around her, how the audience reacted to the actors on-screen. She said she felt like she was jumping out of the fishbowl and into the ocean.

James would buy me all the snacks I wanted, and I'd sit in the back seat of his Cadillac, stuffing my face with popcorn and licorice. He had a way of being everywhere and nowhere at the same time. Back when he and Gigi were married, I'd go days without seeing him, even though I knew he was in the house, and then he'd randomly show up in the kitchen one morning, pouring himself a bowl of cereal.

"Evie Marie," he'd say, smiling at me. "Long time no see."

Or he'd show up at the perfect moment, like when Gigi was ready to go to the movies. If the situation were different, I'm sure she would have enjoyed sneaking out to see *Every Time We Meet* in the park today.

It's dusk now, and I'm ready to leave, just wearing my baseball cap and sunglasses this time. After *Us Weekly* posted those pictures, there's no point in wearing the wig anymore. But I wonder if there might be some truth to what Milo said this morning. Not all of the comments underneath the article were terrible. Maybe everyone doesn't hate me anymore?

Milo already fed Mark Antony and Cleo, but I'm standing in the kitchen wondering if I should give them a little extra before I go. That's when the doorbell rings.

Gigi wouldn't ring her own doorbell. And Milo has keys . . . Who could that be?

Hesitantly, I walk to the door, with Mark Antony and Cleo

following behind at a safe and curious distance. When I peek through the peephole, I gasp so loudly both cats scurry back down the hallway.

In disbelief, I open the door.

"Evie Marie," James Jenkins says, his smile full of charm. "Long time no see."

All I can do is stare at him as he slides past me into the foyer. He's dressed in a tan suit, and he looks cool even though it's sweltering outside. He still has a full head of hair, but it's mostly gray now. I haven't seen him up close and in person since I was ten years old. This is so bizarre.

He takes in his surroundings and finally focuses on me.

"What are you doing here?" I ask, still not sure that this is actually happening. Suddenly, I'm afraid that he's here to take back his offer. I couldn't coordinate the meeting with Gigi, so he's handling it himself. And I didn't hold up my end of the deal, so I don't have the role.

He takes a step back and looks me over. His smile is a little sad. "It's been some years, hasn't it?"

I'm eighteen, but standing here now, I feel like a little kid again, running into James in the hallway at Gigi's old house.

"I saw you at Candice's event," he says. "You were wearing your grandmother's dress."

When I blink in surprise, he adds, "I was married to her three times. I know her wardrobe. And last night, you came to my party and ran from photographers."

I don't even try to deny it. "I wanted to talk to you because I thought you might know where Gigi went."

"What do you mean?" He tilts his head, looking at me thoughtfully. Then he pauses. "Well, she hasn't appeared to yell at me, so I'm going to guess she's not here?"

"She hasn't been here since Thursday," I say. "So you don't know where she is, then?"

He raises an eyebrow and shakes his head. "Why would I?"

"Because you were one of the last people she talked to before she left. And you wrote her a note." I pull his note to Gigi out of my back pocket and hand it to him. "You said you knew her feelings hadn't changed since the last time you spoke, which I'm guessing was Wednesday night when you called her. Did you tell her about the remake?"

He blinks. "Of course not. I thought we agreed it was a conversation that you would handle?"

"We did," I say, sighing in relief. "I am handling it. But if you didn't talk to Gigi about the remake, then why'd you call her?"

Slowly, James places the note in his jacket pocket. He starts to answer my question, then pauses as if he's thought better of it. "Some things are just better left between an ex-husband and wife."

I don't know what to say to that. The conversation lulls for a moment. Then he turns and opens the front door, holding out his hand. "Come with me. Let's take a little drive."

"Wait, what?" I say, but he's already walking down the

steps toward his car. His driver, George, waves at me as he opens the door for James. "A drive to where?"

James glances back at me. "We're just going to Bryant Park. They're showing *Every Time We Meet* tonight. I'd like to continue our conversation, and as much as I enjoy standing in Peg's hallway, I am running a little late to my Q&A."

He doesn't know where Gigi is. I don't need to go with him. But now I'm intrigued that he wants to be in my company, so I hurry to sit beside him in the back seat of his car.

Once George begins driving, James turns to me and asks, "How are you, Evie Marie? Really?"

I shrug a little, glancing out the window as we drive through the city. I'm unsure of how to answer his question. "I'm trying my best."

"I hope you haven't let all that Paul Christopher stuff truly get you down."

"My career was about to take off, really take off," I say, frustrated, "and then that stupid video leaked, and suddenly I became public enemy number one. I'm Evelyn Conaway's granddaughter. The daughter of Andrew and Marie Jones. I can't go down in history as the bad egg who screwed with the legacy. My parents are disappointed, and Gigi seems like she's not bothered by what happened, but how could she not be? Now she's gone, and I have no idea where to find her. I just want to make everything right again."

"Is that why you finally decided to accept my call?" he asks.

Again, I don't try to deny the truth. I nod. "But I think the better question is why you offered the role to me in the first place."

"What do you mean?" He genuinely looks confused. "I'm a producer too. I have talent scouts on my roster just like everyone else. I specifically sent a few to your school, and they confirmed that you were quite special. I've had this remake in the works for a few years, and it only made sense that you'd play Diane. It just wasn't easy to get ahold of you."

I look away, thinking about how I'd purposely told Kerri not to accept any meetings from James or his team. It took me being desperate with no other options to finally answer.

"I don't blame you, of course," he says, and I turn to him again. "Your loyalty is to Peg. I understand that."

"She doesn't know about our deal," I say. "We don't have her blessing. She left before I could even tell her, all because we had a stupid argument." I look down at my hands and bite my lip. "Are you going to give the role to someone else now?"

He's quiet for a beat. "Let's just wait and see" is all he says, which isn't that reassuring. "It might take Peg some time to come around to the idea of it, but she'll support you."

His words should make me feel better, but Gigi's disapproval isn't the only thing eating away at me. "What if no one else wants to see me play Diane?" I say. "What if you make a mistake by casting me?"

"Why do you want to act?" he asks suddenly. "It's not just

because you want to be like your grandmother or because you want to be a part of some legacy. What is it that's making you fight so hard right now?"

I blink and try to think of an eloquent, profound answer. But I decide to go with the basic truth. "I love performing," I say. "I love turning into someone else and entertaining people. It makes me happy, more than anything else."

He gets that thoughtful look on his face again and doesn't say anything for such a long time that I wonder if he's going to respond at all.

"Let me tell you something," he finally says, "and I want you to listen good. I've thought that my career was over plenty of times. When I was addicted to drugs. When I went to rehab and thought I couldn't trust myself to be around people in this industry ever again. I thought I should just give up and try something else. What was the point? Everyone already had their opinions about me, and I didn't have the strength to prove them wrong. But underneath all that, I still wanted to act. It's what I love and what I've always loved. I had to realize my own worth. Nobody else could do that for me. And nobody else can do that for you, you understand?"

"Yes," I say quietly.

"Good." He looks me over again. "I'm sure you hear this all the time, but you look just like her. Especially with all of your disguises."

People have been comparing me to Gigi my whole life, but

for the first time, hearing James say this, I feel like one day maybe I'll actually live up to the comparison.

We arrive at Bryant Park, and a team of people who must be the event organizers approach the car. James leans forward and says to George, "Tell them to give me a minute, will you, please?"

"Yes, sir." George smoothly gets out of the car and intercepts the crew.

To me, James says, "Your grandmother loved going to outdoor movies, remember?" I nod. "I came by to invite her to the Q&A because I thought there might be a small chance she'd put our differences aside and enjoy watching our first movie together, fifty years later."

I stare at his open yet solemn expression. It's the same expression Henry wears while standing in Penn Station, when he thinks he's lost Diane forever.

Unable to help myself, I ask, "What did you do that hurt her so badly? Why did you even have to do it?"

I feel like I'm repeating myself, and I realize it's because I just had a very similar conversation with Simone last night about my own life.

"I was a selfish man," he says. "Your grandmother helped me through the toughest years of my life, and I owe everything to her. I made a decision because I wanted to be back on top, and that decision broke her heart. There's no excuse." More quietly, almost to himself, he adds, "We all deserve a little forgiveness."

I'm not really sure what to say, because I honestly don't know if I agree with him. Maybe everyone doesn't deserve to be forgiven. But I don't have to respond because he's already getting out of the car.

"Now come and listen in on this Q&A," he says, holding open the door for me. "See how an old pro does it."

The field is covered with people camped out on blankets, ready to watch the movie. James and I are flanked by security as we walk through the crowd, and I hide behind my baseball cap and sunglasses, careful not to make eye contact with anyone. But then a girl passes us, wearing a T-shirt with an old picture of Gigi when she was younger, at least in her early twenties. EVELYN CONAWAY FOREVER is written at the bottom in bright-white letters. I figure the girl probably made the shirt herself, but as we approach the stage, I see that more people in the crowd are wearing the shirt too. If only Gigi could be here to witness this.

James walks onto the stage to begin the Q&A with a writer from FilmBuzz.com. Most of the Q&A consists of James answering questions about what it was like to film *Every Time We Meet* and to see the cult following it's garnered over the last fifty years. When the Q&A is wrapping up, the interviewer tells James how excited she is for Gigi to receive the lifetime achievement award tomorrow night at the FCC ceremony.

Little does she know, there's a chance that Gigi might not show up at all. Kerri and my parents will be here tomorrow morning, and they'll want answers. Just like the thousands of people who will watch the FCCs and question Gigi's whereabouts.

"I'm excited for Evelyn to be honored as well," James says. Then, somehow, he glances back, finding me among his team, and smiles.

After the Q&A, they dim the park lights before the movie starts. I turn to George, ready to tell him that I'm not staying for the movie and won't need a ride, and that's when I spot her.

A woman who is making her way through the front of the crowd, near the screen. She's wearing a floppy, wide-brimmed white hat, a white T-shirt, and blue jeans. She walks just like Gigi, that easy, confident stride.

Frantically, I run off the stage and down to the field, trying to catch her. I knew I'd find her. I just knew it. People start throwing popcorn at me for getting in the way of the screen. One guy shouts, "Sit the hell down!" And then I trip over someone's outstretched foot and fall forward onto my face.

"Sorry," a girl says, helping me back up.

I stand quickly, brushing off my clothes, but it's too late. The wide-brimmed hat is gone, and I've lost Gigi.

Crap. Of course, the *one time* I don't have Milo with me is when I could've used him and his ridiculous height the most.

Maybe there's a chance it wasn't her. But who else could that have been? I have to find out for sure.

Chapter Seventeen

When I burst through Gigi's front door, I hear the sweetest sound I've heard in days: Gigi's voice.

"Gigi!" I shout. But as I move farther into the house, I don't see her.

". . . call you back as soon as I'm able." Her voice is followed by a loud beep. And then it hits me: Gigi isn't actually here; that's just the sound of her answering machine. Whoever called doesn't bother to leave a message.

I slump against the wall, feeling tired to my core. The brief euphoria of thinking that Gigi had finally come home leaves me with an aching heart. Once again I wonder if I've messed up so badly that Gigi may never want to speak to me again. The silence in this house is so overwhelming I can't stand it.

Then Mark Antony and Cleo appear at the bottom of the staircase, and Cleo meows long and loud. It lets me know that she misses Gigi just as much as I do. When I walk toward them and reach down to pet their heads, they don't move away like usual. Sheesh. They must really miss her if they're letting me pet them.

They follow me as I walk upstairs, pausing in the doorway to Milo's room. I step inside, looking around at the few things he has here. A basket of folded clothes on the floor, a pair of sneakers by his bed, and coconut oil on his nightstand. His Doves Have Pride T-shirt is at the top of the basket, which confuses me. Doesn't he need it for his show?

I picture the boys now. I bet they're nervous and jittery because the A&R guy will be watching. And I bet Raf will throw a fit about Milo not having his shirt. I wonder if I should call him or bring the shirt to their show tonight, but I decide against it and force myself to leave his room.

I go and sit down on my bed. Tomorrow, everything is going to go to crap. I have to think about what I'm going to tell my parents and Kerri. They're going to ask why I didn't say anything sooner, why I thought I could handle any of this on my own, and I won't have any answers. Flopping back onto my pillow, I let out a deep sigh.

The thought of sitting here alone in Gigi's quiet house until I have to face my doom is unbearable. I *know* I saw Gigi tonight. I wish I could tell someone about it. Milo is the only person who knows what's happening, but I don't want to distract him on such a big night.

Then, as if I thought him up, he texts me. **Is there any chance you're at your grandma's? I forgot my band shirt and I *really* need it. Can you please please bring it here? I'd owe you forever.**

I text back right away, **I'll bring it.**

Without a second thought, I sit upright, go into his room, and grab his Doves Have Pride T-shirt. Then I'm on my way out the door.

Adrian doesn't bother carding me when I get to The Goose's Egg. He just sighs. "Oh, look. It's Milo's friend who is not his girlfriend. New haircut?"

I reach up to touch my head and remember I'm only wearing my baseball cap. I'm not even wearing my sunglasses anymore. If I can walk through Bryant Park and not be recognized, I think the chances of me being recognized here are pretty slim. The disguise Kerri and I created is starting to feel a little silly now.

"Hi, Adrian," I say, holding up Milo's shirt. "Milo needs this."

He narrows his eyes and then nods. "Go on in. No drinking, or—"

"I *know*," I say, and he actually cracks a smile.

The show hasn't started yet, but the crowd is here, and they're ready. I keep my head down as I walk straight to the back room. I knock twice, and Milo opens the door. We stand face-to-face for the first time since our awkward morning. My heart rate quickens as I fumble for something to say.

"Hey" is what I end up with. I shove his shirt into his hands. "Here you go."

"Thank you so much, seriously," he says, smiling, clearly relieved. He wraps me in a quick, tight hug. I'm caught off guard but immediately relax in his arms. He pulls away too soon and glances behind me, biting his lip and looking anxious.

"What?" I say.

He nods his head. "Just spotted the A&R guy."

I turn around and find a tall white man wearing an orange baseball cap sitting at the bar, nursing a beer. He looks bored, like he'd rather be doing a million other things right now.

But to Milo, I say, "He seems excited."

He nods quickly, as if he's trying to convince himself that this is true.

"Are your parents here too?" I ask.

"Yep. They promised they'd be standing front and center." He steps aside and holds the door open for me. The other boys are sitting on the couch side by side, looking incredibly anxious, just like Milo.

"Evie found my shirt," Milo says. He whips off his current plain black T-shirt and switches it for his band shirt.

Wow. Half-naked Milo. *Look away. Look away!*

"Thank God!" Raf says, hopping up. "Or, I guess, thank

Evie." He starts pacing like a caged tiger. "Can you imagine the immediate rejection we would have faced if we went out there and only three of us matched?"

Vinny groans, clutching his saxophone to his chest. "Yeah, I'm sure that would have lowered our chances."

"My shirt still stinks from the other night," Ben says, sniffing his underarms. "I didn't have a chance to wash it."

"Just try not to lift your arms around the A&R guy, okay?" Raf says.

"He's out there now," Milo adds. "We're past the first battle. He's here, so we can relax a little."

"Yeah, nothing big riding on this night at all," Raf says, sitting down once again, bouncing his knees. "It's not like our entire lives could change or anything."

"Shut it, Raf." Vinny closes his eyes and pinches the bridge of his nose. "What we need now is positivity, not your sass."

Raf blinks, dubious. "My *sass*?"

"Can we not do this right now?" Milo begs. "We don't need to be nervous. We're good. We *know* that. Other people will see it too. *We're good*."

I'm struck by Milo's conviction, how he knows the group's value. The rest of the boys stare at him in silence. Ben is the first to stand up. He taps his drumsticks together once, twice. "Well, guess we'd better go, then."

Milo, Raf, and Vinny stand too. The boys share one determined look and then put all their hands into a circle, bumping fists before they break apart. They're like the Doves Have Pride Power Rangers. It's kind of adorable.

"You'll be fine. You'll be great," I whisper to Milo as we leave the room. I want to tell him about seeing Gigi, but now seems like the wrong time. He's already so nervous. I don't want to throw him off even more. I'll just wait until they're done. "Good luck."

"Thanks." He squeezes my hand before we separate.

Eager fans burst into cheers as the boys step onto the small stage, and I notice a middle-aged Black couple standing up front, watching the crowd with bemused expressions. They must be Milo's mom and dad. Even if they want him to give up music and go to school full-time, it's nice that they're here supporting him anyway.

I make my way to the back, standing near the bar again. I'm only a few feet away from the A&R rep. He glances down at his watch as one of the bar employees introduces the band. They take their positions, and the A&R guy lifts his head.

"What's up, y'all?" Raf says into the mic. There's a loud burst of feedback, and then the mic cuts off.

Oh no.

Milo leans into his mic and tests it, his eyes widening when there's no sound. He looks off to the side of the stage and waves someone up for help. A collective groan erupts from the crowd. The A&R rep frowns and places his drink on the bar. He calls over the bartender. *Crap. Is he asking to pay his tab?*

One of the employees is still trying to figure out what's going on with the microphones. Meanwhile, the crowd is only getting more and more antsy. The A&R rep stands up to leave, and I glance at Milo up onstage, who looks panicked. All his hard work to get this record-label guy to see them is going right down the drain.

I know how terrible it feels to lose out on the chance of a lifetime. I wouldn't wish that on anyone, especially not Milo, after all the sacrifices he's made for his music. I'm standing right here. I have to do *something.*

I take a couple of steps forward and place my hand on the A&R rep's shoulder. He turns around and quirks an eyebrow.

"Hey, do I know you?" I ask. "You look familiar."

He looks me up and down. "I don't think so."

"Are you sure? Weren't you at Yara Shahidi's birthday party last February?" *I* wasn't even at Yara Shahidi's birthday party, but I heard about it.

"Nope," he says. "Wasn't me."

I spare a quick glance past him toward the stage. Raf leans into the microphone again, but it's still not working.

The A&R rep shoves his wallet into his pocket.

"Maybe you just have one of those faces," I say, coming around to stand in front of him. I lift my baseball cap so that it's no longer so low on my face. "I'm Evie Jones. You might not know me, but my parents—"

"Are Marie and Andrew Jones," he finishes. "I know your

grandmother. You were involved in that Paul Christopher drama a couple of months ago."

"All water under the bridge," I say smoothly, flashing a bright smile. Although on the inside I'm wondering if I've made things infinitely worse. He could be one of Paul Christopher's superfans.

"I've never seen a Paul Christopher movie," he says. He grabs the beer that I thought he was trying to abandon. "Thrillers aren't my thing. I like classic movies. Like your grandmother's. They have them all on Netflix." He peers at my face. "You look different."

I shrug easily. "I cut my hair."

He makes a *hmph* sound and looks around. "What are *you* doing here?"

"Oh, I'm a big fan of the band. They're really good." Insert dramatic pause. "I hope you weren't planning to leave before you even heard them play. Were you . . . Sorry, I don't think I got your name."

"Adam Griffin. Vivid Music Group." He finishes scoping the room and returns his attention to me. "So you like this band?"

I nod quickly, glancing once again over his shoulder. Milo says something into the mic. "Testing, testing." And it works! Thank God. The crowd starts clapping as Milo strums on his guitar.

"They're the best," I finish. "Hottest thing out right now."

"You're not the first person to say that," he says. "I hope you're right."

Adam turns around, observing the crowd's enthusiasm. Slowly, he sits back down. I let out a relieved breath.

The good news is that the boys don't disappoint. Aside from the mic mishap, and Raf forgetting a lyric or two from nerves, their performance is mostly flawless. Raf hops around on the stage, leaning down to sing to the audience, and Milo does that thing where he focuses intensely on his fingers while he plays. Ben's drum solo elicits a few whistles, and Vinny makes playing the saxophone look effortless.

Adam nods his head along throughout, and when the band finishes with "Leather Pants," he even smiles.

Their set wraps up, and the crowd's cheers are thunderous. Up in the front, Milo's parents aren't jumping around like everyone else, but they are clapping.

Adam looks over at me, a hint of a smile still on his face.

"You were right," he says. "Thanks for the tip."

"No problem."

I watch as Adam makes his way to the stage. The boys huddle together to meet him. When I see smiles break out on their faces, the knot in my stomach loosens. I was able to use my name for good. Go figure.

I sit at an unoccupied table in the corner to wait for Milo to finish talking. A few more minutes pass before the boys finish their conversation with Adam. He shakes each of their hands and makes his way out the door.

Milo stands on tiptoe, looking around, and after a beat, I realize that's he searching for *me*. My stomach is a butterfly nest.

He spots me and lifts a hand, beckoning me over. I'm halfway to him when his parents beat me there. They're both tall with dark-brown skin, just like Milo. They're dressed as if they were on their way to a church picnic but were accidentally detoured. When I reach them, I hang back a few feet, trying to give them space. But Milo waves me forward again.

"Evie, these are my parents," he says. "Mom, Dad, this is my friend, Evie, Ms. Conaway's granddaughter."

His mom, who has beautiful, thick eyebrows just like her son, looks a little uncomfortable in the setting, but she smiles at me and shakes my hand. "It's nice to meet you, Evie. Your grandmother is wonderful."

"Thank you," I say.

Milo's dad has a bald head and a thick goatee. "Let me ask you something, Evie, do you think it's too loud in here? I said that to Milo, and he thinks I'm overreacting."

Milo sighs, smiling. "Dad, come on."

"I'm just asking a question," he says, looking at me like he genuinely wants to know my opinion.

"It is a little loud," I say honestly, laughing. Beside me,

Milo makes a noise of protest. "But I think that's just the nature of these shows."

Just as I say that, of course, the next band walks onto the stage and the crowd starts shouting again. Milo's mom actually jumps.

"I think we'd better go," she says, kissing Milo on the cheek. "You did good tonight, and I know you don't want to hear it, but take a look at the CUNY schedule I sent you, okay? Humor your mother."

"I will, Mom, I promise," he says, hugging her. His dad gives him a hearty pat on the back, and then they gingerly maneuver their way to the door.

"They're going to pray for me at church tomorrow," Milo says.

I watch as his mom clutches her purse to her chest and his dad holds the door open for her. I think about my own parents and their sullen expressions during our last breakfast together. "You're lucky to have them."

He stares at me for a moment, once again trying to look deeper into what it is that I'm not saying. "Yeah, you're right."

We walk toward the back of the bar and sit down at an empty table. Now that we're alone, I say to Milo, "I'm pretty sure I saw Gigi at Bryant Park today."

His eyes go wide. "Really?"

Quickly, I explain James Jenkins's random visit and how we ended up at Bryant Park.

"I can't believe the one time I wasn't there, James Jenkins decided to show up," he says. "So what are you going to do now?"

"I'm going to go back home and hope that she's there," I say.

I can't think of the alternative, that she'll never show up and miss the ceremony entirely. That she won't sit in for a meeting with James and I'll lose out on my role in his movie, the only chance I have to make a comeback. That I'll have to explain all this to Kerri and to my parents.

Then we're interrupted when the rest of the boys appear.

"Adam wants us to come to the office tomorrow and play for the rest of the Vivid team," Raf says, practically bouncing up and down on his toes. "He likes us so much he wants us to come in on a Sunday! Can you *believe* that?"

I nod. "Yeah, I can. You guys were great."

They all beam at me. Milo softly taps my arm. "I saw what you did," he whispers in my ear. "You stalled him. Thank you."

"It was nothing," I whisper back. And really, it wasn't. After how he's helped me try to look for Gigi, it's really the least I could have done.

"Party at our apartment right now," Raf says. "We're going to invite everyone. Let's tell the masses."

"The masses," Ben repeats, rolling his eyes, but doesn't argue, following Raf into the crowd. Vinny goes off to find Michelle.

"Are you coming with us?" Milo asks. Did he scoot closer to me? His face is, like, right here.

"No," I say, gulping. "I should get back to Gigi's."

Raf pops up at the table again, flushed and excited. Ben, Vinny, and Michelle flank him.

"It's official," he says to Milo and me. "Everyone's coming back to the apartment."

Milo raises an eyebrow. "*Everyone?*"

"Well, a few people, if you want to be technical, but whatever. It's going to be a party. Let's go."

"You sure you're not coming?" Milo asks, looking at me.

"Yeah." But I'm really not sure.

"Aww, come on," Raf says. "Adam wouldn't have stayed if it weren't for you, Evie. You have to come. It wouldn't be the same without you."

"For the first time, I actually agree with Raf," Vinny says, smiling at me.

Ben says, "If it makes you feel any better, I don't want to party either, but I'm still going. Well, I guess I have to because I live there, but you know what I mean."

"Join us! Join us! Join us!" Raf begins to chant, and they all follow suit.

Milo leans over and whispers, "You can pretend to be our friend. Just for one night?"

I look around at their smiling faces, and I hear myself say, "All right, I'll come."

"Yes!" Raf says. "Let's move out, troops."

"It'll be fun," Milo assures me. "And when you're ready to

go, I'll take you back home. Our friends are chill. No one will take pictures of you or be weird."

I nod, suddenly feeling so strongly that I don't want to go back to Gigi's and be alone all night. I want to be around the boys, to be accepted into their fold. I do want to pretend that we're all friends and that everything is okay.

Chapter Eighteen

Raf really did invite everyone. Within a matter of twenty minutes, their tiny apartment is brimming with people. Even Adrian is here, hanging out by the door with a scowl, like he's still working. Raf directs everyone to the kitchen, promising food and drinks. Really, they just have three bags of family-size potato chips and two six-packs of beer. But no one seems to mind. Music is playing, and everyone is in a good mood since the boys performed so well.

I'm sitting next to Milo on the couch, and I'm sweating. That's what happens when lots of people are in small places and there's no AC. I lift up my baseball cap and scratch my scalp, and it feels so good I close my eyes and sigh.

"It'll be cooler if you sit by the window," Milo suggests.

I almost get up, but I feel a little silly moving from where I'm comfortable just because I don't want to take off my stupid hat.

Slowly, I remove it and smooth back my hair, feeling my short curls spring through my fingers.

"What?" I say when I look over at Milo and see he's watching me.

"Nothing," he says, not breaking eye contact.

Then Vinny calls his name.

"Milo," he says, standing in a group of three other boys, "come settle this argument, please. Dante here seems to think he knows everything there is to know about songwriting."

"Be right back," Milo says, rolling his eyes and walking over to Vinny.

There's no reason for me to stay seated on the couch, talking to no one. And I'm hot and thirsty. I walk to the kitchen, where Raf is in the middle of telling a story to a boy and a girl. Every time Raf moves his arms, beer sloshes out of his cup onto the floor. The boy is tall with light-brown skin, and his curly hair is cut into a fade. He leans back against the kitchen counter, with his arm leisurely draped around the girl's shoulders. She's short and pretty, her hair pulled back in a tight bun. She's wearing a purple leotard with cutoff shorts pulled over pink tights. She smiles at me when I enter the kitchen. She's focusing so intently on my face that I wait for her to say something about knowing who I am.

"I love your hair" is what she says.

"Really?" I blink. "Thank you."

She nods, still smiling. "I've been thinking about cutting mine, but I'm too chicken."

The boy smirks and nudges her. "Imagine what your mom would say."

"Evie," Raf says, linking his arm through mine. "Meet my new friends Chloe and Eli. Eli is the one who designed the band logo. When he said he was in the city, I said, *Bro, you've gotta come to the show.*"

"Do you live in the city too?" I ask them.

"I do," Chloe says. "I'm a student at the Avery Johnson Dance Conservatory." She gestures at her outfit. "Eli's just here visiting."

"I go to school in San Francisco," Eli says. "A much cooler city."

Chloe narrows her eyes at him. "Oh, so we're going to have this debate again?"

"You didn't let me finish," he says. "It's only a cooler city when you're there. See, look at you jumping to conclusions."

She rolls her eyes, and he pulls her close, kissing her cheek.

"Dammit," Raf says, watching them. "I need a girlfriend."

I reach past him and grab a cup, filling it with tap water. "I don't know, what if the band takes off? You don't want any *distractions*, do you?" I say, smirking, leveling my eyes at him.

"Ha, well played, Jones." He knocks his cup into mine.

"It was really nice to meet you," I say to Chloe and Eli as I leave the kitchen.

"Same," Chloe says, smiling. Eli just nods his head, too cool.

Milo is still deep in conversation with Vinny when I walk back into the living room. For a moment, I feel a little self-conscious that I won't have him beside me as a shield, but I realize I don't actually need him. No one cares that I'm here. If they've recognized me, they haven't said anything.

Feeling as if a weight has been lifted from my shoulders, I go to stand by the window because it's still really hot. Michelle and Ben are already huddling there, whispering to each other. Ben's eyes are bugging out, and Michelle places her hand on his arm like she's trying to placate him.

"Just go talk to him," she says quietly.

"I *can't*," Ben insists. "I don't even know what to say."

He glances up and catches my eye. Then Michelle turns around to follow his line of sight.

"Oh, good, Evie, you're here," she says. "You can weigh in on this."

"Weigh in on what?" I ask as she grabs my arm and pulls me closer.

"Ben has a crush on Adrian," she whispers.

"What?" I almost choke. "*Adrian?*"

"Don't be so loud," Ben hisses.

"But . . . but . . . he's so mean! And you're so nice!"

"He's nice to *me*." Ben glances across the room at Adrian,

who is leaning against the wall, brooding per usual. When his eyes find Ben, he smiles a little and nods. Ben smiles back, but he looks as if he might pass out from that small interaction. He grabs my hand and Michelle's. Then he pulls us toward the hallway and into the bedroom that he shares with Milo.

The two twin-size mattresses on the floor make an L shape and barely fit in the room. There's one wooden dresser that's covered in nicks. Milo's acoustic guitar sits in the corner, and there's a poster of Jimi Hendrix taped above the bed on the right. I guess that must be Milo's bed.

Ben sits down on the other bed, and Michelle plops beside him. They both look up at me, waiting for me to sit as well.

I rock back on my heels and bite my lip. "Are you sure you want me to be here too?"

"Yes," Ben says. "You're our friend, right?"

I blink. He asks the question so easily, like my answer should be an obvious yes. I realize in this moment how much I wish I could be friends with all of them. "Oh, um . . ."

Michelle doesn't wait for me to answer. "I say he should tell Adrian how he feels, straight-up."

Ben shakes his head and sighs. "You would say that, Michelle. You've been with Vinny since the seventh grade. I can't rely on the two of you for advice. And girls throw themselves at Milo, and Raf has no game. I can't rely on them either." He looks at me again. "Evie, you're cool and from LA and probably have lots of experience with this kind of thing, so can you tell me how to ask out Adrian?"

I smart a little at the idea of girls throwing themselves at Milo but shake it off. I've never really given advice before, especially not on dating. I'm not sure if I'm the person he should be asking.

"Well—" I start.

Then Vinny pops his head into the room. "Michelle, can I borrow you for a sec?"

Michelle nods and leans over to hug Ben. "You've got this," she says before hopping up and joining Vinny in the hallway, closing the door behind her.

Ben looks at me hopelessly.

"Just be yourself," I say, taking Michelle's place beside him. "You're so sweet and talented, and like I already said, you're nice. Maybe you don't need to tell Adrian how you feel right away, but you could ask if he wants to hang out sometime one-on-one and go from there. How could he say no to you?"

"You really think that will work?" he asks, looking deep into my eyes.

"Yes." I nod. "I really do."

I register that this moment is important. If he takes my advice, he really does think of me as a friend, because he trusts me.

Suddenly, he stands up, a determined expression on his face. "Okay. I'm gonna do it."

"Of course. You've got this." I give him a thumbs-up, stealing Kerri's signature move.

"Thanks, Evie," he says, smiling. Then he's gone. A boy on a mission.

I lean back on Ben's bed, not ready to rejoin the party just yet. My eyes find their way to the Jimi Hendrix poster again. I get up, stepping around the sneakers on the floor to get a better look at it. Milo's room here has way more character than his room at Gigi's. There's a stack of vinyl records right by his bed, and tickets from the shows he's been to are taped up on his wall. When I see a ticket from a Janelle Monáe concert, I get butterflies. He likes Janelle Monáe too?

I sit on his bed. It's soft and smells just like him. I lean down and take a big whiff of his pillow.

Oh my God. What is *wrong* with me? I need to get out of here before I'm completely in over my head with this boy.

I start to sit up, but then my eyes snag on something stuffed between Milo's bed and the wall. I bend down and lean closer. It's a notebook. A notebook that says SONG LYRICS.

Oh?

I glance over my shoulder, making sure no one is watching me, and then I open the notebook. A black guitar pick that's covered in little nick marks falls out, and I place it on the bed beside me. I'm, of course, expecting to see angst-filled songs about all of Milo's deepest, darkest feelings. Or maybe to find that song he allegedly wrote about me. It very well might be in here, but I can't read his handwriting. Like, at all. It's tiny and bunched up. Maybe he writes this way because he somehow knew a nosy girl like me would find her way into his room to do exactly what I'm doing right now.

"There you are."

I slam the notebook shut and look up. Milo, the lyricist in question, is standing in the doorway.

Smoothly, as if I weren't just caught red-handed, I say, "Here I am."

He glances at the notebook and raises an eyebrow. I shove it away as if it's cursed and I have no idea how it got into my hands.

"Did you help Vinny settle that argument?" I ask, trying to change the subject.

"Not really. Dante knows his stuff." He walks over and stands in front of me. He smirks. "If you wanted to read through my journal, all you had to do was ask."

"I wasn't reading it," I say.

He tilts his head and gives me a look that says, *Yeah right.*

"Okay, okay, I was," I admit. "I *tried* to, but you have poor penmanship."

He laughs and sits next to me, grabbing his guitar pick. "My dad bought this for me when I was eleven and first started playing the guitar for the church choir. Before I begin writing a song, I hold on to it and feel the good vibes." He hands it to me. "You try."

Feeling silly, I squeeze the pick in my palm. "I don't feel anything."

"That's because you're not thinking right," he says, tapping the side of his head. "You have to close your eyes and imagine that your good luck is already here, not that you're waiting for it."

I try to do as he says, but I only picture Gigi's face when we argued the night before she left. I open my eyes and give the pick back to Milo.

"Maybe it will work for me some other time," I say. Then I blurt, "Did you really write me a song?"

"No." He reaches past me to grab his notebook.

"Oh." Wow. All that snooping for nothing.

He flips his notebook open to a page that's halfway covered in his handwriting. "I wrote *pieces* of a song about you."

"Really?" There go those butterflies again. "Well, the least you can do is play it for me."

I say this jokingly, but I'm shocked as he leans over me and grabs his guitar from the corner. "I can do that."

He shifts the notebook so that he can read the lyrics. He begins to strum, then pauses.

"I've never played it before, so don't judge me," he says, narrowing his eyes.

"I won't. Go ahead," I urge, then feel embarrassed by my own eagerness.

He starts strumming again. "I wanna tell y'all about this

girl I know. She's really pretty from her head to her toes. Cool chick from LA with no time for me. She's never been on the subway; she's not from NYC."

I laugh, and he glances up at me and smiles before continuing on.

"That's because she's a movie star. Maybe I could impress her if I had a car. But all I have is my guitar and my words. Maybe that's all I need to impress this girl."

I've witnessed a lot of magical things in my life, but I've never sat mere inches away from a boy as he played a song about *me*.

It's a really simple tune, but his voice is so low and smooth. Rich, like honey. He closes his eyes and stops singing but continues to strum, nodding along.

I mean, is he even real? Where did he come from? Allegedly, he's Brooklyn born and raised, but I'm halfway convinced he's from outer space.

He stops singing and sets down his guitar. Blinking, I sit up straight, trying to hide the fact that I was practically drooling.

"You like it?" he asks. "Tell the truth."

"I do. I love it," I answer quickly, with complete honesty. "You're so talented, Milo. You all are. They'll probably sign you at that meeting tomorrow."

"I hope so," he says. "And thanks. That means a lot."

"You're welcome."

We fall quiet. I consider getting up and suggesting we go

back to the party before the silence turns awkward, but I don't want to leave his room yet either.

"Can I ask you something?" he suddenly says. Curious, I look at him and nod. "Did you really cut your hair because you wanted to try something new?"

"No," I admit. "I cut it because I was sad."

I think back to that day when I rushed to find the scissors, how I chopped and chopped at my hair until there was barely anything left. The numbness I felt as I stared down at the chunks surrounding me on the floor.

"I wanted to be somebody else," I say. "Have you ever felt that way?"

"Of course," he says. "I wish I had more money and wasn't living in this tiny apartment. I wish that our band was more successful and that my parents didn't feel like I was breaking their hearts and God's heart too."

"That's not you wishing to be someone else," I point out. "That's you wishing to improve the life you already have."

He nods, thinking this over. "I guess you're right."

"Gigi would've never cut her hair," I hear myself say. "She would've held her head high and ignored the gossip. People always say we look alike, but that's where the similarities end."

"You actually have a lot in common," Milo says, leaning back on his elbows. "For starters, you're both really stubborn. And intimidating."

I snort. "I'm not intimidating."

"Most intimidating people don't think they are intimidating," he says, smirking.

He leans closer and continues to stare at my hair. "It's not that bad. I kind of like it, actually. You get to see your whole face in a way that you couldn't with all the curls."

I start to say that it's in a weird growing-out stage, but I decide to shut up and accept the compliment.

"You should hear the way your grandma talks about you," he says. "You make her so proud. I don't think she cares about how different the two of you are. Maybe being different isn't so bad."

"Yeah, maybe," I say. Then, "Before Gigi left, I had something really important to tell her." My gut clenches up, and I stop. I've spent so long trying to push Milo away, but now I'm terrified that spilling this secret might make him hate me. I take a deep breath. "James Jenkins wants me to star in his remake of *Every Time We Meet*. But only if I have Gigi's blessing, and only if I can get her to meet with him."

I expect him to back away, but he doesn't. Suddenly, the words are spilling out of me. "I hate that I've struck a deal with the person my grandmother despises the most, but no one else was willing to give me a chance. I feel like I don't have any other options, and I wonder if that makes me a terrible person." I pause. "I can't believe I just told you all that."

"I don't think you're terrible," he says quietly. "I think you're making a tough decision under tough circumstances."

I nod, looking away. I feel exposed after telling this secret, but I won't lie, it feels good to finally tell someone the truth. Or more specifically, it feels good to tell this truth to Milo because he knows Gigi so well.

"What are you thinking?" he asks.

I turn to look at him again. I'm thinking that I never thought I'd find myself here with him in his room. That I like the feeling of being here, and I don't know what that means. And I'm wondering when we moved closer to each other.

"Milo!" Raf yells right before he comes crashing into the room. We jerk apart, and Raf freezes, slapping his hands over his eyes. "Sorry, sorry! Milo, I just wanted to let you know that we're playing beer pong on the table and that Ben said to tell you first because we all paid for the table and you should know how it's being used. I can't see anything. I'm definitely not watching the two of you kissing."

"We're not kissing," Milo says. He wipes a hand over his face, embarrassed. "You don't have to cover your eyes."

Raf separates two fingers and peeks at us. "Okay, cool. Like I said, we're playing beer pong if you want to join. You can even be on a team together! Or you could just stay in here . . ." He removes his hand and shoots me a pointed look before he closes the door.

Milo sighs. "He's . . . a lot."

"He thinks I'm going to seduce you and break up the band like Yoko Ono."

"Why would Raf think that?" He smirks a little. "You and I aren't even friends."

"I know. That's what I said."

He scoots closer. "Then what would you call us?"

I stare at the lack of space between our bodies, the way his chest rises and falls with each breath. I look up at his handsome face, at his lips, and my pulse goes into overdrive.

Breathlessly, I say, "I have no idea what to call this."

We stare at each other. My eyes roam his face. His full lips, which I've already kissed, the hoop nose ring. His dark-brown eyes, looking intensely back at me.

"What are you thinking?" he asks again.

I'm thinking that if it weren't for Gigi disappearing, I wouldn't be here right now. I'm thinking that Gigi's disappearance has turned my life upside down, another surprise in a long string of unwanted surprises. I'm thinking that I'm not sure how many more surprises I can take.

What I end up saying is "I think I'm scared."

He smiles a little. "Aren't we all scared of something?"

"What scares you?" I ask.

He doesn't answer right away. Instead, he continues to stare at me intently, searching my face. Finally, he says, "Hurting the people I care about scares me. That's why I don't like to lie." He takes another long pause. "What scares you?"

My answer is convoluted. A lot of things scare me. Failure.

Never booking another job. Never being able to place trust in another person again.

But in this immediate moment, my answer is simple.

"You," I say.

He blinks. "Why?"

"You're just so . . . so . . ." I find myself unable to describe him in one word. I'm equally unable to describe the warm feeling in my chest. I trail off, not even attempting to finish my sentence. I've purposely closed myself off to people, and somehow without even realizing it, I let down the drawbridge for Milo. It's too late to pull it back up now; he's already marching across.

I can't say that I'm surprised. Somehow, he's found a way to earn the trust of Gigi, the queen of grudges and privacy. It was only a matter of time before he wore me down too. And as much as I've resisted it, it's a relief to finally let someone else in.

"You don't have to be afraid of me, Evie." His voice is soft and low.

He slides closer, and I let him. He reaches forward and carefully holds my face in his hands, and I let him do that too. When he leans closer, closer, closer, until our lips are a breath apart, I don't stop him. I don't want to. My heart is pounding. It feels so loud to me. I'm surprised he can't hear it too.

"Are you afraid now?" he whispers.

Because I want to be honest, I nod. Quickly, I add, "But I still want you to kiss me."

Our lips meet somewhere in the middle. His mouth is soft and warm, and his kiss is gentle. Then the kiss deepens, and he snakes his arm around my waist, pulling me closer, right up against his chest. I lower my hands so that they rest on either side of his neck. I feel his pulse beating wildly.

We kiss like we've been waiting to do this forever, and maybe we have. Now that we're here, I don't know why we waited this long.

Oh yeah, I have myself to blame for that.

Breathlessly, I finally pull away and stare at him. He looks dazed, still gazing at my mouth. I can't seem to form a clear thought in my head.

"Overwhelming," I manage to say.

He chuckles, surprised. "What?"

"You're so overwhelming. In a good way. That's what I wanted to say before."

This makes him smile. He kisses me again until I feel as if our mouths might become permanently attached.

We pull away again. He lies back on his bed and leaves an open space for me beside him. I cuddle closely, resting my head on his shoulder. I touch my lips. They feel alive and warm.

When I glance at Milo, I find him staring up at the ceiling, frowning.

I start to shift away. "What's wrong?"

He looks down and notices the distance I've put between us. He takes in a breath. "Evie, I . . ." He stops, and my stomach tightens as I wait for him to continue. He shakes his head and pulls me closer. His weird expression slowly disappears. "Nothing's wrong. Come here. You okay?"

"I'm okay," I say.

It feels really nice that I don't have to lie. Maybe this is a good sign for me. Maybe it's a sign that everything else will be okay too.

Footage from homemade video—February 7, 1991

Evelyn and James are at home in Los Angeles. James has planned a huge surprise party for Evelyn's birthday. After saying hello to their guests, Evelyn sneaks into the kitchen alcove to have a moment alone. James soon appears, recording.

James (off camera): Happy birthday, baby! Were you surprised?

Evelyn frowns at him and turns away, slowly breathing in and out. James sets the camera down on the kitchen table. He and Evelyn can be seen standing face-to-face. He reaches for her, but she pushes him away

James: Peggy, what's wrong?

Evelyn: The last thing I wanted to do was spend my birthday around people who've become strangers. You know how I feel about keeping our house as private as possible. I just don't understand how you can hurt me so easily when you claim that you care about me more than anyone else.

James: Peg, babe, I'm *sorry*. It was just a little surprise party! I thought it would make you happy.

Evelyn: It doesn't feel like just a *little surprise*. Instead, it's like you kept this big secret from me because you wanted to throw a party even though you knew I wouldn't like it.

James: That's not what I was thinking at all. Hey, where are you going?

Evelyn brushes past James and out of the camera's line of sight

Evelyn (off camera): Just leave me alone, please.

James: Peg, hey. Wait a minute.

recording ends

Chapter Nineteen

SUNDAY, AUGUST 16

A text from Kerri wakes me up in the morning.

Today's the big day! Just landed at LaGuardia, on my way to the hotel. Your parents are on a later flight and they'll get in a few hours before the ceremony. Meet me at my hotel in an hour for hair and makeup? I'll send a car for you. See you soon!

I bolt upright and stare at my unfamiliar surroundings. A guitar on the floor by the bed. A Jimi Hendrix poster on the wall. Milo snoring quietly beside me.

I check the time. It's almost 10:00 A.M.

Crap. How the heck did I manage to fall asleep here?

My mind flashes back to our kiss and how I cuddled up to Milo like a caterpillar in a cocoon.

Oh yeah. *That's* how.

Last night was a nice distraction, but now it's time to face the music. I have to tell everyone the truth about Gigi. My stomach sinks at the thought of it, but what else am I supposed to do? I have to come to terms with the fact that this movie role is not going to happen for me.

I throw myself out of the bed, and Milo doesn't even stir. It's a good thing he's a heavy sleeper, because that makes this ten times less awkward. I grab his notebook, open it to a new page, and write him a note.

> *Sorry to leave without saying goodbye. I'm going to the Mark Hotel to meet my agent before the ceremony. See you later? –Evie*

I slide on my shoes and tiptoe out into the hallway. Then I hear Raf and Ben talking in the living room. I really don't want them to see me sneaking out. I can only imagine what they'll say. I hover in the hallway, trying to quickly figure out the best way to slip by without them noticing. I peek around the corner and watch them.

"Last night was the best night of my life," Raf says, sprawled out on the pullout couch. "Did you see me making out with Charisse? I knew she'd come over at some point."

Ben nods, sitting at the table, eating a bowl of cereal. Most of his attention is focused on the paperback novel in front of him.

"And I saw you with Adrian." Raf wiggles his eyebrows. "Why didn't you tell me you had a crush on my cousin? I could have helped you out."

Ben snorts. "Yeah, sure."

Raf lowers his voice to a whisper. "But did you see Milo and Evie? As much as I'm against dating celebrities or whatever, I like her."

I roll my eyes and try not to laugh. Now I can die happy knowing that I have Raf's approval.

"I like her too," Ben says, finally looking up from his book. He smiles at Raf. "She's cool."

"Imagine how Milo will tell *that* story," Raf continues. He deepens his voice so that he sounds like Milo. "I used to deliver groceries for Evelyn Conaway, and then one day she said she'd hook my band up with a music connect if I hung out with her granddaughter for a few days and made sure she didn't do anything out of control."

"Wait . . . what?" I go completely still, but somehow my mouth manages to move. I'm sure I've misheard him. But I start to feel nauseous as Raf and Ben turn to look in my direction, shocked.

"What did you just say?" I ask, slowly walking into the living room.

Ben's eyes widen, and he closes his book.

Raf's mouth falls open. "Evie, uh, hey, good morning! I

thought you were asleep." He starts to get up. "Do you want some cereal? We have Lucky Charms and Cheerios and—"

"Please repeat what you just said." I shake my head, trying to make sense of this. "Please."

Raf catches his breath, and his smile finally fades. "Your grandma," he says. "She said she'd help Milo out if he kept an eye on you . . . I thought you knew. I thought that's why you always looked like you didn't really want to be around."

"No." There's a dull buzzing sound in my ears, like static on a television. "I didn't know."

Raf sits there, blinking. "I'm so sorry."

All those times Milo insisted on coming places with me because he didn't want me to go alone, because he wanted to make sure I was okay. Because he was concerned about Gigi too. He said he just wanted to help. Those were lies.

And before the gala, I asked if his roommates knew anything about Gigi being gone. He said no. Another lie. Gigi asked him to keep an eye on me, like I'm a child who can't be trusted.

I'm not a liar. That's something you should know about me now.

But that was the biggest lie of all.

Oh my God.

The sympathetic look on Ben's face make me want to break into a run.

"I have to go," I say, abruptly turning and walking toward the door. I need to get out of here.

"Evie," Ben says faintly, "don't leave yet."

"Hey, hey, wait," Raf calls.

I'm pounding down the hallway steps, but I feel like I'm moving in slow motion, trying to run underwater. I burst through the door and inhale the muggy air. I lean back against the brick wall, squeezing my eyes closed. I think I'm going to be sick.

I won't cry here. With shaky hands, I pull out my phone to call a car to take me back to Gigi's, but I drop my phone right away. I bend down, fighting back sobs.

It happened again. I let someone get close to me just to be used. When will I learn? How stupid can I be? Apparently, very. Very, very stupid.

The door swings open, and Milo steps outside. He's not wearing any shoes.

"What are you doing out here?" he asks, moving toward me. Instinctively, I take a step back, and he freezes. "What's wrong?"

"You can drop the act, Milo." My hands continue to shake as I fumble around with my phone. "No need to babysit anymore."

"What are you talking about?" he asks. This time he does move forward, ignoring my iciness.

"You were using me!" I burst. "*That's* what's going on." I think of how he kissed me, how right it felt. But none of it was real. I swipe angrily at the tears sliding down my cheeks. "You kept insisting that you just wanted to help me out of the kindness of your heart, but really you were only keeping an eye on me because Gigi said she'd hook you up with that music guy. Why'd you kiss me? Because you figured it would distract me? Well, bravo, Milo. You're a pretty good liar after all."

He shakes his head, agonized, but I don't believe it. Not for one minute. "I almost told you last night, but I knew you'd be too angry to let me explain," he says. "I thought it would be better if I told you the truth once your grandma came back and we could put it behind us."

"You're right. I don't want to hear your explanation." I don't even bother with wiping my tears away anymore. "Do you know where she is? Have you known this whole time?"

"No! I don't know where she is," he says, holding out his hand for me. "I swear. She wouldn't say."

"You're probably lying right now." I turn away from him. "Go back inside, Milo. Leave me alone."

We look ridiculous, arguing like this in broad daylight. Milo's neighbors walk by, barely sparing us a glance. It's probably a normal Sunday morning in Brooklyn to them.

Milo moves to stand right in front of me. "It's not what you think. She'd already been in touch with the A&R guy before she asked me to watch out for you. And I agreed to it because I wanted to return the favor for all the times she's helped me. At first, I was just hanging out with you because your grandma asked, but I kept coming back because I *wanted* to see you." He shifts into my line of sight, desperate to meet my eyes. "It was so obvious to me that you were lonely. Every day I just wanted to know that you were okay."

"Ah, I see. So you felt sorry for me."

"No, that's not it," he says, frustrated. "I care about you, Evie. Please, you have to believe me."

Hurting the people I care about scares me. That's why I don't like to lie.

Ha, I've finally caught him in a lie. This is the most bittersweet triumph. I almost laugh.

"You used me because you didn't want your parents to force you to give up music and go to college," I say. "You sat there and listened to my story about Simone, but you're no better than her."

"I'm like Simone? Really?" He sounds like I just punched him in the gut, but I refuse to feel sorry. "That's how you feel?"

"*Yes.* That's exactly how I feel."

He laughs, but it's a tight, angry sound. "Well, isn't that the pot calling the kettle black? All this from the girl who went behind her grandmother's back to work with James Jenkins, the one man she hates most in the world. What makes what you've done any different, Evie?"

I glare at him, breathing hard. I hate that I shared my

secret with him last night only for him to throw it in my face. "It's not the same thing at all."

"Can we just go back inside and talk about this?" He glances around. "Please."

I shake my head. I'm not going anywhere with him. I'll never believe another word he says.

I look down at my phone, swiping forcefully. The stupid car app won't load. Of course this is the time it chooses to malfunction.

Then a lone green taxi turns onto Milo's street. Finally, the universe has decided to throw me a bone.

"Goodbye, Milo." I push past him and hail the taxi. "Good luck with your music. I'm sure your career will take off soon. Don't bother coming by to feed the cats. I'll take care of it myself."

"Evie, wait . . ."

He makes a grab for my arm, but I swivel and evade him, dashing for the taxi as soon as it pulls over. He's right behind me, but I shut the door on him.

He pounds on the window once. "Evie! Just let me talk to you."

I turn away and give Gigi's address to the taxi driver.

I refuse to look back at Milo as we drive down the block. So what if he lied to me? So what if Gigi had something to do with it? I've been through worse than this.

Heartbreak is nothing compared to being betrayed by a

best friend, to basically losing my career. It's nothing compared to disappointing your parents and making them stop their work because they don't trust you anymore. It's nothing compared to a grandmother who'd rather fall off the face of the earth and keep her own secrets than talk to me.

I barely even knew Milo. He means nothing.

Chapter Twenty

"Evie, what's the matter?" Kerri asks, ushering me into her hotel suite. A team of people that she hired for hair, makeup, and wardrobe is waiting for me in the living room, and when they see my swollen eyes and puffy face, Kerri pivots us into the bathroom.

"Just give us one minute," she says smoothly.

I sit down on the toilet seat with my face in my hands, and Kerri softly closes the door behind us. She crouches down in front of me and places her hand on my knee.

"Evie, honey, I need you to tell me what's wrong," she says. "You're scaring me."

She must really be afraid because she hasn't even asked about my wig or hat or sunglasses. I'm just regular me. And I feel like dirt. Less than that.

I sniffle and wipe my eyes, taking a few deep breaths. I look into Kerri's calm face. She's been my rock. The one who always told me the truth, no matter what, for the short amount of time that she's been in my life.

"Do you think we'd be friends if you didn't work for me?" I ask, knowing how pathetic I sound. "Would you want to be friends with someone like me?"

"Someone like you?" she repeats. "Of course I would. What, you don't think we're friends now?" She smiles at me, but it fades when I don't smile in return.

"Why are we doing this?" I ask quietly. "It's not worth it."

"What's not worth it?" she says, confused.

"*Me.* I'm not worth it. I should never put myself in a position where people have to decide whether or not they like me. I already know the answer."

"Of course you're worth it. Why are you talking like this?" She leans back, analyzing me. "You weren't happy before you left, but at least you were hopeful. Something's happened to you. Talk to me, Evie."

Well, here it is. The moment of truth. Literally.

Just as I'm about to tell Kerri that I have no idea where Gigi is and that she most likely will not be at the ceremony or meet with James Jenkins for any *Every Time We Meet* remake, someone knocks on the bathroom door.

"Uh, Kerri," a glam team member says, "there's a boy here to see Evie. He says he has her hat."

Milo? How did he know where to find me? Then I remember

that I wrote down the name of the hotel on the note I left him. And I left behind my baseball cap. Stupid.

Kerri looks at me and raises an eyebrow. "Please tell me this meltdown isn't about the musician."

"It's not," I say, shaking my head. "Not completely."

She frowns, doubtful. "Do you want to talk to him?"

"No." Of this I'm sure.

Kerri stands and goes to the door, opening it slightly. "Can you send him away? Evie doesn't want to see him."

Then I hear Milo call out my name. The next thing I know, he's pushing open the bathroom door in a frenzy.

"Excuse me," Kerri says, affronted. "What do you think you're doing?"

"Sorry," Milo says. "Evie left her hat at my house, and I came to give it back."

"I can't believe you followed me here," I say, standing up. "Go home, Milo."

He looks directly at me, undeterred. "Evie, just hear me out."

I stand there silently and cross my arms over my chest.

Kerri glances back and forth between us, and when I don't say anything, she nods. "I'm going to give you five minutes. *Five.* That's it. And then you've gotta go, and Evie, we have to get started on hair and makeup." She takes my baseball cap from Milo and narrows her eyes at him. "I'm watching you, kid."

She closes the door behind her, and the five-minute countdown commences.

Milo stares at me, a slightly wild look in his eyes. I still can't believe he came all the way here. "I'm sorry, Evie."

I shrug. "It doesn't matter. You got what you wanted. I'm not looking for my grandmother anymore, and I'm going back to LA tomorrow. The way I see it, we don't have anything to talk about."

"I didn't get what I wanted," he says, frowning.

I lift my hands and cover my eyes. I don't want to cry again. This entire week has been so melodramatic! I didn't ask for any of these feelings. I wish I could go back to Thursday, when I let him come with me to the gala. No—I wish I could go back to May, when Paul Christopher offered me the chance to audition for his film. I'd say no, and eventually something else would have come my way. My whole life would be different.

"Don't cry," Milo says, stepping toward me.

I hold up a hand to stop him. "*Don't.*" He freezes.

I hate that I let him hurt me, and I hate that I like him so much, even still. I have no one to blame but myself.

Milo sighs, still staring at me intensely.

"After you left, I kept thinking about where your grandmother could be," he says. "I thought about all the places I've been with her before, the places we didn't go this week." He pauses. "Do you remember the brownstone where she lived with her family in Brooklyn? She bought it a while ago, and I think she might be there now." Every bone in my body is telling me that I shouldn't believe him, that I should send him away. But I think back to the photo Candice gave me of young Gigi in her white-and-yellow dress, sitting on her front stoop. And I think about the sad look on Gigi's face when she took me to that same place five years ago. I don't know *why* she would be at her old apartment, but something about it makes sense.

"She's only brought me there once, but I think I remember where it is," Milo says.

"The same way you remembered where Esther lived," I say, annoyed. I shouldn't trust him, but what if he's right? I need to see for myself if it's true. "Can you take me?"

"Of course."

Kerri is in the middle of talking to the glam team when Milo and I step out of the bathroom. She turns around to face us.

"Everything okay?" she says, looking at me.

I contemplate lying, telling her that everything is fine and that I'm just walking Milo down to the lobby, when I really plan to leave and find Gigi. But I don't want to lie to Kerri anymore. She deserves the truth.

"Can I talk to you for a second?" I ask, motioning for her to follow me back into the bathroom.

"What's going on?" she asks, frowning once again. She closes the bathroom door.

I tell Kerri everything. How Gigi left, how I've been looking for her. And finally, how Milo thinks he might know where she is.

"Evie, this is *ridiculous*." She runs a frantic hand through her long hair. "I can't believe you waited until now to tell me!"

"I'm so sorry," I say, feeling sick to my stomach.

She shakes her head. "I can't allow you to go with Milo on a fool's errand. We don't have time. We can worry about James Jenkins and his team later, but right now, we need to get you ready to accept the award on your grandmother's behalf. I'll have someone call the FCC committee and let them know she won't make it." She reaches to open the bathroom door, and suddenly the idea of going to the ceremony when Gigi is so close feels impossible. I need to talk to Gigi, but more than anything, I just want to make sure she's okay. I want to see her and hug her and hear her tell me that she doesn't hate me.

"Wait!" I reach out and squeeze Kerri's hands. "Please, Kerri, just give me a chance to bring her home. If Gigi isn't where Milo thinks she is, we can call everyone and tell them the truth. But please, I just need to know if she's there."

Kerri is still shaking her head, blinking like she can't understand what she's hearing. "I'm going to come with you."

"I need to handle this on my own," I say. "I'll be okay. I swear."

She looks skeptical, and I know the last thing she wants to do is let me go. But she says, "At least have the driver who is waiting downstairs take you. And come *right back*. Please come right back."

"I will," I promise, and then Milo and I are out the door.

I hate that I've given Kerri a reason to distrust me.

And I hate that I'm depending on Milo again, but this will be the last time I ask for his help.

Chapter Twenty-One

There's a SOLD sign hanging in front of Gigi's old brownstone. Or new brownstone, I guess. I don't know what to call it. Milo tells me that this part of Brooklyn is Fort Greene. There are lots of babies and dogs and coffee shops. I bet it wasn't like this when Gigi was growing up.

Work has been done on the exterior of the brownstone. It's modern and new, and there aren't any cracks on the front stoop. But other than that, it looks the same as when Gigi posed here for a photo when she was a little girl.

In Gigi's note, she said she wouldn't be too far away. I just never thought to look here. This place is cemented in my mind as something from the past, falling apart and waiting to be torn down. But here's Gigi's childhood home, gleaming in the summer sun.

I walk up the steps, and Milo follows close behind. Should I knock first? What if the SOLD sign is because Gigi fixed up the brownstone and sold it to another family but never said anything? When I reach the door, I see that it's slightly ajar, as if someone thought they'd closed it but actually didn't. That's weird.

Slowly, I push the door open. I glance back at Milo, and he shrugs. We quietly step into the hallway. It's empty and smells like Lysol. There's a room at the end of the hall and a staircase leading up to the second floor.

Right away, I learn that we're not alone. There are people here, and they're arguing.

In shock, I register the sound of Gigi's voice. Gigi, who is usually calm and collected, is shouting. And a quieter voice—a man's voice—is trying to appease her.

Without another thought, I stealthily climb the staircase. Milo hesitates in the hallway, but I don't turn around to ask if he's coming.

The staircase leads to an open living room. It's empty save for a folding chair. And there, placed on the seat, is a big floppy white hat. Ha. I knew I saw Gigi at Bryant Park. At least at this I can feel vindicated.

The walls in the room are pastel blue, just like the walls of my bedroom, and it smells as if they were recently painted. Propped up in the corner is the blown-up portrait from the photo shoot I did with Candice Tevin on my eleventh birthday. Gigi and I are standing side by side. I'm smiling up at her, all big curly hair and scrawny limbs. And Gigi is looking right back at me, one hand on her hip, her other hand placed on my cheek. Is this what Gigi secretly bought from Candice?

I creep toward the sound of Gigi's voice coming from down the hall.

"I knew you were behind this," she says angrily. "There was no other reason why they would decide to honor me out of the blue."

"It isn't out of the blue," the man argues. "You've deserved this for years. *Decades.*"

His voice sounds familiar. So familiar that it makes my stomach twist. I pause by the doorway to the room in which they're standing. I peek my head inside, and the first things I notice are portraits I saw at Candice's gala. The portrait of Gigi with James Jenkins on the set of *Every Time We Meet* and another portrait of Gigi with my mom and grandfather, standing by the pool. They're framed and placed side by side on the floor.

Then my gaze turns to Gigi and James Jenkins, who are standing in the middle of the room with their backs to me.

James Jenkins . . . here right now, with Gigi.

James Jenkins.

What in the world is happening?

"And I don't want these portraits," Gigi says to him. "I don't know why you bought them from Candice."

"What do you mean?" James asks, incredulous. "I bought them for you. I thought you'd want them."

"You don't listen! You never do." Gigi shakes her head, furious. "You started this whole mess, and you even pulled Evie Marie into it. Now she's under pressure to present an award to me that I don't even want." Gigi crosses her arms over her chest. She's wearing a loose-fitting cream sundress, her gray curls tied into a low bun at the nape of her neck. She's a petite woman, but right now she stands up tall. "This is your way of trying to make amends, but I wish you would stop. It's been eight years, James—"

"Eight years of you refusing to forgive me," he says fiercely. "I'm sorry for what I did, Peg. I will spend the rest of my life apologizing to you if that's what you want."

Gigi shakes her head again. "If you would let me finish, you'd hear me say that I *have* forgiven you. I shouldn't have reacted so harshly at the FCCs when you were being honored. It was childish, and I've regretted it every day since. What happened between us was unfortunate, but that's just the way of things. I forgive you, and I want to move on."

"I don't." He takes a deep breath and steps forward until there's no space between them. "I've never stopped loving you. Not for one second. If you don't still love me too, I'll leave. But just say the words, Peg. That's all I need to hear."

Gigi stares at him, bringing a hand to her chest, breathing quickly. "Of course I still love you, you fool."

Then James Jenkins takes my grandmother into his arms and kisses her with more passion than I've ever seen in any of their movies, and my mouth falls open in shock. Gigi breaks the kiss and pushes him away, slapping his shoulder.

"I didn't say that you could kiss me!" she hisses. "Really, James. Why do you always have to take things to the next level?"

"Because I love you and you love me," he says simply. "What else matters?"

"Oh my God."

This is said by me. I don't mean to say it, but I cannot believe what I'm seeing right now.

James and Gigi quickly spin around to face me.

"Evie Marie?" Gigi says, eyes wide. "What are you doing here?"

"What am I doing here? What are *you* doing here?" I point at James and shout, "And what is *he* doing here?"

"It's not what it looks like," Gigi says, coming toward me.

"Is this where you've been all week? Hiding here in Brooklyn, waiting for James, of all people?" I ask, backing away. "You disappeared out of nowhere and couldn't call to tell me that you were okay, but somehow you found time to tell him?" To James, I say, "You told me you didn't know where she was. You lied."

He walks toward me too, and I take another step back.

"I didn't lie," he says. "For years Peg has wanted to buy this place and fix it up. I came here on a hunch. I didn't know if I'd actually find her."

"I've been on a wild-goose chase, looking for you every day,

Gigi," I say, feeling stupid. "And you've been here this whole time. You abandoned me when I needed you the most. Just like when you left LA." I only saw what I wanted to see: the possibility that I could find Gigi and bring her back home. That's what wishful thinking will do to you. "You abandoned me just so that you could be with him?"

"That's not what this is, Evie Marie," Gigi says. "It's not what it looks like."

I suddenly don't know if I even want an explanation. My feelings are too big, and this room is too small. I turn around and walk back into the living room, forcing myself to breathe in and out, and Gigi and James quickly follow behind me. Milo is standing in the middle of the living room, and he starts to approach me, but I hold out an arm to keep him at bay.

I can't trust any of these people, and they're closing in on me.

"I didn't come here to be with James," Gigi says. "I came here because the thought of going to the FCC ceremony was too much. For years, I've kept the industry out of my life, and here you were trying to force me back into it. I left so that I could come to my old home, where I feel grounded and calm. Years ago I bought this place because I thought one day I'd move here myself. But once I was here, I realized what I should do is give this place to you."

"What?" I say, shocked. I look around again at the pastel

blue walls, at the portrait leaning against the wall of Gigi and me. Now it all makes sense. "Me?"

"I thought maybe it could be a home to you," she says. "I've been so worried about you, Evie Marie. And for the first time in your life, you wouldn't let me help you. You wouldn't talk to me. You were so caught up in getting approval from everyone, approval that you don't need. I thought maybe if I could offer you a safe space of your own, a place where you could start over and find a sense of peace, then maybe you'd gain some perspective about your career. About your life. You're so *young*, baby girl, and you have so much time on your hands. You don't have to rush into anything. This place is for you, and this way you can be close to me without having to be under the same roof if that's not what you want. I'd planned to tell you everything this morning, but then James came and threw everything off."

Beside her, James mouths, *Sorry*.

I just stare at Gigi, unable to put how I feel into words. But one thought is clear: This is just another empty house. Just like her townhouse in Manhattan this week. Just like my house back in LA. I'd be left alone all over again. For once in my life, I'd like for someone to stick around and show up for me. For someone to *stay*.

"Gigi, I can't tell you how grateful I am that you thought to do this for me," I say. "But the FCC ceremony is starting soon, and we need to be there, both of us together."

She shakes her head, looking at me sadly. "Evie Marie, I don't need this award. That was all James's doing. He persuaded the board to honor me, and it was his idea to have you as the presenter. He's trying to atone for what he's done, but I will tell you the same thing I told him: I don't need to stand up in front of a crowd to know my worth, and neither do you. That's what I want you to understand."

"It's not just about your award." I point at James. "He's remaking *Every Time We Meet* and he offered me the role of Diane. But only if I got the two of you to meet and if you gave your blessing."

Gigi turns to James sharply. "Really, James? In your gallant plan to come here and woo me, when were you going to reveal that you were *blackmailing* my granddaughter?"

"I was getting around to it." He backs away sheepishly. "And I wouldn't necessarily call it blackmailing."

Gigi heaves a sigh, turning to face me again. "Eight years ago, James and I planned to purchase the rights to reproduce *Every Time We Meet*. People were *still* in love with that movie even forty-two years after it had first premiered, and it meant so much to us—a symbol of a love that would always come back to you." She stops and smiles sadly. "Producing the movie was supposed to be something we did together, but James went behind my back and secured the rights on his own. He was going to remake our movie without me." James takes a step forward to hold Gigi's hand, and she tries to wave him off, shooting him a pointed look. "And as I've said, I've already forgiven him for this."

But James manages to capture her waving hand and holds it to his chest. He picks up the story where Gigi left off. "After everything we'd been through, everything *I'd* put us through, I wanted to make my big comeback while standing on my own two feet." He smiles sardonically. "I ended up breaking your grandmother's heart and, therefore, mine as well. When she found out what I'd done, it was the final straw. We had separated privately, well before the FCC ceremony. The board didn't know that, of course, so they asked your grandmother to present my lifetime achievement award."

"I was still so hurt and angry that instead of saying no, I agreed to attend the ceremony," Gigi says. "And I yelled at James on live television. When it was all over, I was so embarrassed by what I'd done that I never wanted to talk about it again. We divorced, and then I moved to New York." She shrugs her elegant shoulders. "That is most likely why he wanted my blessing for the remake, because he didn't ask for it the first time around."

I look back and forth between her and James, my head spinning. "I never would have agreed to play Diane if I knew that backstory."

"I know you wouldn't have, baby," Gigi says softly. "It's a story I should have told you a long time ago."

"Is that the only reason you gave me the role?" I ask,

looking at James. "To make up for what you've done to Gigi?"

"No," he says, frowning. "I meant what I told you yesterday. You're talented. You deserve the role."

I barely absorb his words as I back toward the hallway. I don't know what to believe anymore. What I do know is this: I'm going to the ceremony, and I will make things right for myself with or without Gigi. I don't know what any of this means for my deal with James, but going to the ceremony is my chance to prove to everyone that I'm all right. To erase the terrible impression I left in their minds when that video leaked. Even if I'm never in another movie for the rest of my life.

Milo moves to follow me. I almost forgot he was here. But now I'm reminded of another reason that I have to be hurt. He reaches out to touch my shoulder or maybe give me a hug. I'm not sure—all I know is that I don't want it. I step back to evade him. Gigi catches the motion with a frown.

"I'm sorry, Evie. Don't be upset with him," she says. "I just wanted Milo to look out for you." Her eyes widen when I walk toward the stairs. "Where are you going?"

"I have to get ready for the ceremony." I pause, waiting to see what she'll say, if she'll change her mind.

"If that's what you want to do, I'm not going to stop you," she says. "But you don't need it. All you need is to believe in yourself. You'll realize that the opinions of those people don't matter."

Numbly, I turn around and walk downstairs. I hear the sound of Milo's heavy footsteps following me, but reality doesn't snap into focus again until I'm outside.

I start walking, trying to understand everything that just happened. Then I'm gasping for breath, and I realize that at some point I started running.

"Evie," Milo calls. He runs ahead, coming to a stop in front of me. "Are you okay?"

"No." I stop him before he can say anything else. "Milo, please."

I'm surprised when he steps back and lets me pass him.

Gigi isn't coming to the ceremony. Maybe I should feel some way about this, but I don't. I don't feel anything.

Chapter Twenty-Two

I do feel something as we're on our way to Rockefeller Center for the ceremony. What I feel is panic.

"So let me get this straight," Kerri says, an email draft open on her phone. "You found your grandmother, but she still isn't coming to the ceremony, you're accepting the award on her behalf, and now you're not sure about the remake anymore?"

When I finally returned to the hotel in even worse shape than when I first showed up, Kerri didn't freak out. She sat me down and gave me a few minutes to breathe, and then I went straight to the makeup chair. I'm wearing a black gown that she and I chose before I left LA, designed by Christian Siriano. The bodice is a sleeveless V-cut, and the skirt billows out like a dress made for a princess. I look beautiful and put together, but I feel like an absolute mess.

"That's right," I say, trying to remain as calm as possible. It's not working. I'm sweating in this dress. And I'm wearing a big curly wig so no one will know that I actually cut off all my real hair.

"I'm sending an email to the FCC committee right now to give them a heads-up," Kerri says, moving her thumbs at the speed of light.

My breathing is getting heavier, and I'm starting to feel dizzy.

"Am I having a panic attack?" I say.

Kerri breathes slowly in and out and encourages me to copy her. She puts her hand on my arm. "Evie, look at me. Are you sure you want to do this? I've been behind you every step of the way, not only because it's my job but also because I believe in you, but if this isn't what you want to do, I can reach out to the committee right now and tell them that you can't make it."

I almost take her up on this offer. I'm so tired. I've been running on empty for months. But I've made it this far. What kind of sense would it make to turn back now?

"No, I'm going to do it," I say. "I can do this."

Kerri squeezes my hand, searching my face. "All right."

Originally the plan was for me to walk the red carpet, but I bow out of that. I don't want my picture taken, and I don't want to do any interviews. The FCC committee freaks out when Kerri tells them that Gigi isn't coming. They pull us into a back room and create a game plan for what I'll say when I accept the award for her. Brianne Thompson, the president of the FCC, advises, *Just say something good.* She's tall and white with blunt blond bangs and a very serious demeanor.

Someone gets tasked with writing what I'll read from the teleprompter, and I'm told to make it as personal as possible while reading. It sounds a little ironic, since the words won't be coming from me.

Soon the show begins, and Kerri goes to find my parents, who have just arrived. I promise her that I'll be okay finding my seat, that an FCC employee will be able to help me. She looks apprehensive but leaves, handling one issue at a time as deftly as she can.

With as much nerve as I can muster, I head to the auditorium, passing by all my idols, who are dressed to the nines. No one even notices me or spares much of a second glance, unless they're looking at my gown.

I think about how Milo didn't believe that everyone hated me, how he thought that was a stretch. And I think about the way no one at his party mentioned anything about Paul Christopher. *Has it all been in my head this whole time?*

But then, right as I reach the auditorium doors, I see

him. Paul Christopher. He's with Simone. She's wearing a tight-fitted pantsuit, somehow looking better than the last time I saw her. Of course they're here together. Paul doesn't even look in my direction, but Simone sees me. She freezes, missing a step.

I was trying my best to make it through tonight, but seeing them is what finally breaks me.

A nauseous feeling builds in my gut, and I turn around and rush to the bathroom. Nothing happens when I push through the door and run into a stall. I don't even throw up. But somehow I manage to stay there for the next forty minutes, trying to calm down. The ceremony has started by now. I think about how the camera has probably panned to my and Gigi's empty seats, and I start sweating all over again.

Kerri texts, **Where are you? Is everything okay? They just announced that your grandmother's award is coming up soon. I'm worried. So are your parents.**

I text back, **I'm here. In the bathroom. Everything is under control.**

Do you need me to come and find you?

No, I'm okay.

There's been a steady stream of people coming in and out of the bathroom, but no one has stopped to wonder why a girl in a black ball gown is monopolizing one stall. I wait for the moment that the bathroom clears, and I finally emerge. My cheeks are blotchy, and my eyes are red. I look *terrible*. I can't go on live television like this!

"No, no, no," I mumble, opening my clutch and grabbing my concealer. My stupid, shaky hands drop the bottle, and when I bend down to grab it, all I can do is put my head in my hands and try to breathe.

I stand upright and look at my reflection. I don't recognize myself. Aside from the red cheeks and blotchy makeup, I have a wild look in my eyes, a look of desperation. I've gone to so many lengths to change myself just so that I could be liked. So that everyone would find me worthy of my parents' and grandmother's legacy. That they would find me worthy at all. I've become so obsessed with it I didn't realize what it was doing to me.

I think back to the other night, when Gigi and I argued. She said that my behavior was unlike me, that she didn't understand why I cared so much about what people thought. I told her that she didn't understand where I was coming from; she's always been loved by everyone.

But maybe I don't need everyone to love me. Just the ones who matter. James and Gigi both said that I need to learn my worth. Maybe I should start trying now. By taking off this stupid wig.

I drop it in the sink and look at my matted curls.

Breathe, Evie. Just breathe.

"I thought you might be in here."

I turn and find myself looking at Simone. The second time we've met in a bathroom this week. Seriously, what are the odds?

"You look terrible," she says. "Well, not the dress. The dress is gorgeous. *You* look like you're about to have a nervous breakdown."

Ignoring her, I focus on applying the concealer to the areas underneath my eyes.

"Everyone's looking for you and your grandma, you know," she says, coming to stand behind me. "It's all anyone can talk about." She glances back at the stalls. "Where is she?"

"She's not here." No point in keeping the secret. Everyone will find out soon enough.

Simone's eyes widen, but she doesn't say anything, choosing to watch me silently as I attempt to make my face presentable.

"Here," she says, agitated. She grabs my shoulder and spins me around, taking the concealer from my hands and dotting my face herself. Deftly, she uses her thumb and index finger to smooth the concealer over my skin.

I feel a pang in my stomach, thinking of how we used to do each other's makeup all the time.

"And this hair," she mumbles. She wets her fingers with

faucet water and runs them through my hair, trying to give my curls as much volume as possible.

"Why are you helping me?" I ask.

"I don't know." She frowns. "I feel bad for you." She places my concealer back inside my clutch. "And I guess I feel bad about what I did to you."

I blink. "That is not what I was expecting you to say."

"I wasn't expecting to say it either." She's completely straight-faced.

"You never answered me when I asked why you leaked the video," I say quietly.

She stares at me for a beat, then sighs. "I saw a way for me to get a leg up, and I jumped at the chance. I don't regret what I did, because it worked out for me in the end, but the consequence is that our friendship was ruined. That's just a decision I'll have to live with."

I stare back at her, taking in the open and honest expression on her face. I miss us. But I know we'll never be an *us* again. That doesn't mean that I can't learn to forgive her. Someday.

"I really hope you get everything that you want in life, Simone," I say.

She doesn't respond to this. Instead, she steers me toward the door. "No more hiding in the bathroom. It's time for you to get out there."

We step into the hallway.

"Thanks," I say to her.

She's already walking back to the auditorium, pretending as if she didn't hear me, but I know that she did.

Everyone is frantic backstage. When a woman wearing a headset spots me, relief washes over her. "Evie Jones is here," she says into her headset's microphone. She listens for a moment. "Got that. We're on our way."

Right now, I really wish I were holding Milo's good-luck pick.

"I'm so sorry about showing up late," I say to her, but she's barely listening, ushering me through the chaos backstage. Everyone keeps looking in my direction, and I feel the nausea brewing again. But there's no time to run and hide. We've reached the wings.

"Thank God," another headset-wearing woman says, anxiously standing by the curtain. She clutches a clipboard to her chest. "Ms. Jones, you need to look straight at the teleprompter. Make sure to speak clearly and directly into the microphone. Got it?"

"Got it." I don't got it. I'm terrified.

The auditorium darkens, and a large screen lowers onstage. A slideshow begins to play, featuring pictures of Gigi throughout her career, from when she was only a couple of years older than me to when she stopped acting a few years after my mom was born. The video is accompanied by a narration that lists her accomplishments. And then it ends all too quickly.

"That's your cue." The woman with the clipboard nudges me out of the wings.

The ceremony emcee says in a deep voice, "Please welcome Evie Jones."

The crowd applauds as I walk to the microphone. All I can do is focus on putting one foot in front of the other. I try not to pay attention to how my heart is hammering in my chest. Or the faces of all the people I thought I'd impress tonight, how their eyes widen at the sight of my short hair. The people whose opinions I thought I cared about.

I spot my parents and Kerri in the second row, seated right behind where Gigi and I were supposed to be. My parents smile proudly yet look a little apprehensive. I'm sure Kerri's caught them up on how Gigi won't be here tonight. I wonder just how much she's told them.

The teleprompter clicks on in the distance, and I clear my throat.

I begin, "My grandmother Evelyn Conaway . . ." Then I stop.

Say something good. That's what they told me.

But where do I even start? How am I supposed to praise Gigi when I'm so upset?

And anyway, what does a teleprompter scriptwriter know about my relationship with my grandmother? What do any of these people know? They don't know her life story. That she moved to Los Angeles on faith, with no guarantee that she'd become a star. They don't know that she was intensely private for good reason.

They don't know that she's managed to find a sense of peace, that she refuses to submit herself to her peers for their approval.

I've wanted to be like Gigi my entire life, but I've been approaching it the wrong way. I was so stuck on her success, the ways I measured up to her and the ways that I didn't.

I wanted tonight to work in my favor, to give me the comeback I've so badly wanted. I wanted to prove to the world that I was worth more than being cast aside. But I don't have to be a movie star to know my worth. I don't need to make appearances at fancy award ceremonies or wear wigs or get the perfect role with the perfect director. I spent this week looking for Gigi when she didn't need to be saved or found. I should have been trying to find myself.

I take another deep breath and start again, this time ignoring the teleprompter.

"My grandmother Evelyn Conaway isn't perfect. But she is, and always has been, my favorite person. I learn from her even when I'm not expecting to. She's taught me how to be confident and strong. Through her example, I've learned the importance of self-respect and what it takes to persevere. She's shown me time and again that her love is something I will never be without. I've learned more about her this week than I have in years."

I look at my parents and Kerri when I say, "She isn't here tonight to accept this award."

A collective gasp overtakes the audience, but I continue on. "She doesn't need to be here, and she doesn't need an award to prove that she's worthy. She's always deserved each success that has come her way. And regardless of what I've been through, and regardless of what you all have seen, I don't have to prove anything either. I am proud to accept this award on my grandmother's behalf."

Kerri is the first to clap, *loudly*. She stands, and my parents quickly follow. Kerri gestures to the rest of the audience, and they're slow to join in, but that's okay. I don't care about receiving a standing ovation. I'm accepting the award for Gigi like she asked, and that's all that matters.

A woman walks toward me, holding Gigi's award, but she pauses and glances into the audience. I follow her line of sight and watch as everyone swivels their heads to the back of the auditorium. Suddenly they begin to stand and clap, and I have no idea what's going on until I see Gigi coming down the aisle straight toward the stage, toward me.

She's wearing one of her white suits and pearl necklaces. Her gray curls frame her face.

She climbs the steps confidently, not bothering to focus on the crowd that's giving her a standing ovation. Her eyes are on me.

I stare at her, completely in shock.

"Gigi—" I say, and she wraps me in a tight hug.

"I'm not here for them," she whispers in my ear. "I'm here for you."

The applause surrounding us is deafening as Gigi continues to hold me in her arms.

Then she pulls away and turns to the microphone. "I'd like to thank the Film Critics Circle for this esteemed honor. I'm forever grateful for my late husband, Freddy Stevens, who started me on this journey. And also to James Jenkins, who is more deserving than I give him credit for." She pulls me forward. "And I want to thank my granddaughter for reminding me that we all have to start somewhere."

She loops her arm through mine, and we walk offstage together.

Brianne Thompson rushes toward us. "Oh my goodness, you saved the show. That could have been a complete disaster. Ms. Conaway, thank you so much for being here tonight."

"Of course," Gigi says serenely.

To me, Brianne says, "That was perfect, Evie. Just perfect. Everyone will be talking about this tomorrow."

I look at her and shrug. "You told me to say something good."

"Please let me escort you both to the audience." Brianne smiles at Gigi and says, "You have front-row seats."

Gigi looks at me. "Do you want to stay for the rest of the ceremony?"

"No." I feel like the heaviest weight has been lifted from my shoulders. "I'd really just like to go home."

Gigi smiles in the warm and lovely way that only Evelyn Conaway can. "Let's go, then."

Chapter Twenty-Three

My parents have a ton of questions, but I don't have nearly enough answers.

We're sitting at Gigi's kitchen table. After we left the ceremony, we came back to Gigi's town house, and she cooked dinner. Mark Antony and Cleo keep meowing at her feet. They haven't left her side since she walked through the door. Kerri sits beside me, her phone placed facedown on her lap.

"Why didn't you answer any of my calls this week?" Mom asks Gigi. "Are you feeling any better?"

Gigi glances at me and smoothly says, "Loads better. And something was wrong with the landline, but it's all fixed now."

"What made you change your mind about the ceremony?" Dad asks. "Why weren't you already in your seat?"

Mom follows up with "And, Evie Marie, why weren't you in your seat at all?"

Gigi and I exchange a look. I can either keep them in the

dark about what happened this week, or I can tell the truth. I decide to go with the latter. And when I'm done telling them *everything*, they look so confused.

"Why would you keep this from us?" Dad says, frowning.

"And how could you leave Evie Marie here alone?" Mom asks Gigi.

"Wait," I say, stepping in. "It's not entirely fair for you to point a finger at Gigi when you and Dad have left me alone too. I didn't tell you the truth because, after this summer, I was so tired of being a disappointment. I didn't want to let you down even more or for you to blame me for Gigi having left."

"And that wasn't her fault," Gigi says across the table. "It was my decision alone."

My parents look at each other, then look at me. "I'm sorry we've made you feel as though you're a disappointment," Mom says. "You're *not*."

"We love you, Evie Marie," Dad says. "Whenever you find yourself feeling that we don't have your back one hundred percent, I want you to tell us."

I nod, and the weight that has been sitting on my chest all summer lightens a little. I can't help but think that their work will always come first, but if they're willing to try, I'm willing to believe them. I have to start somewhere. "I love you too."

A silence passes over the table. Gigi is the first to break it.

"Marie, baby, why don't you tell us about Botswana?" she

says. Unable to resist discussing their work, my parents launch into a long discussion about their documentary.

While they're talking, Kerri fidgets in her seat beside me. Now that she doesn't have any emails to send, she doesn't know what to do with her hands.

When Gigi and I said we were going to forgo the remake discussion, Kerri smoothly and quickly had it handled. James wasn't surprised. He said he basically expected as much when Gigi decided to go to the ceremony.

I don't know if I'm going to do the remake anymore. I really need to take a step back and figure out what I want to do for *me*. I don't want to make decisions based on my family's legacy, and I'm done with trying to figure out what will make other people happy. I won't pretend that this doesn't frighten me, just a little. Since I started at McKibben, I always had a plan for what I wanted. I have no idea what my future looks like now.

I told Kerri as much, and she understands, even if it means her life will be a little less busy.

"Thank you," I say now, leaning into her.

She stops fidgeting and smiles at me. "For what?"

"For being great at your job. And for being a good friend."

She squeezes my hand but doesn't reply. This is a lot of affection coming from her.

"I'm going to get changed," I say, excusing myself from the table.

I lift the skirt of my ball gown as I walk upstairs. My French bob wig is the first thing I see when I enter my room. I hold it in my hands as I sit on my bed. This is a great wig, and it served me well. But I don't think I'll wear it again anytime soon. Not unless I need it for Halloween or something.

A knock at my door makes me raise my head.

"Can I come in?" Gigi asks.

I nod and move over to make room for her on my bed. She settles down beside me, light as a feather.

"I'm so sorry, Evie Marie," she says. "For keeping things from you. I thought I was doing what was best. But I should have trusted you to understand where I was coming from. And I know that it's not right for me to disappear whenever I feel stressed. I'm going to work on that, I promise."

I look down at my hands in my lap. "I should be apologizing to you. I was only thinking about myself. I should've listened the first time you said that you didn't want to go to the ceremony."

She softly runs a hand over my head. "I understand why you did what you did. But you should know that none of those people can keep you from reaching your full potential. If you're meant to be the biggest star the world has seen, then that is what the future holds for you, and nobody will be able to change that. Take it from an old lady from Brooklyn who thought she'd spend the rest of her life singing in speakeasies."

"I hope I'll be able to follow your path," I say.

She smiles. "You'll be better than me, surely."

"That's a lot to live up to, but we'll see."

"I meant what I said about moving into my house in Brooklyn," she says. "It's there for you if you want it."

Her offer sounds tempting, and maybe I would have taken her up on it weeks ago. But I don't want to run from my problems either.

"I think I need to go back home to LA," I say. "I haven't really given myself a chance to start over there."

"I understand," she says, nodding. "I'll support your decision either way, and I can rent the brownstone out and get a lot more money in the process."

She winks, and I laugh. Then I remember something. I get up, grab Candice's USB and the two old photos, and hand them to Gigi. "Candice wanted me to give this to you."

She looks at the photos in surprise, then smiles. She inspects the USB, turning it over in her palm. "What's this?"

"It's a USB drive. Your old home videos are saved on it. James is in a lot of them."

"Ah," she says quietly.

Hesitantly, I ask, "Are you going to get back together with James now?"

"No. I'm not concerned about that at the moment. We need to learn how to be friends again first."

"Do you think he'll still move forward with the remake even if I don't want to play Diane anymore?"

"Don't worry about that. He'll get over it, whatever you decide." She puts her arm around me, and I lean into her. "I've forgiven him. It took me years, but I've done it. People are going to hurt us throughout our lives, Evie Marie. We can't control that. But we can control how we respond. We can choose to forgive people. I know you'll be able to forgive the people who've hurt you too."

I pull away and look at her. "Okay, forgiving is one thing, but what about finding a way to trust that person again, or other people in general?" I ask. "How can you trust that James won't lie to you in the future, that he won't break your heart?"

"I don't know," she says honestly. "And I can't say for sure what he'll do. But I believe that he will try his best. Sometimes trusting another person simply starts with believing that they want to do right by you."

I think about Simone and the way she helped with my makeup in my moment of need. I've already decided that I will try my best to forgive her, even if we won't be friends again.

But she isn't the only person I need to consider forgiving.

Kerri knocks on the door, sans her towering high heels, and she looks so much smaller.

"Hey," she says softly, "sorry to interrupt. Evie, Milo is outside, waiting for you. I know he kind of lives here, so I wasn't really sure what to tell him." She glances at Gigi, who then glances at me.

I bite my lip, unsure of what to do.

"Maybe you should just listen to what he has to say," Gigi gently encourages. "He reminds me of your grandfather, and I've always thought that was a good sign."

"He reminds of you him how?" I ask.

"He's patient and doesn't give up too easily." She smiles softly, giving me a long look, waiting for her meaning to sink in.

With my heart in my throat, I stand up. "Okay."

Milo is standing on the front stoop, waiting for me, just like he's done countless times this past week.

"Hey," he says.

"Hey." I close the door behind me.

He takes a step down to give me room. His gaze travels from my head to my toes, and I feel silly for not having changed out of my gown.

"You look nice," he says.

"Thank you."

I lower my eyes and stare down at his Vans. "How did your meeting go with the record company?"

"I missed it," he says.

"What?" My head snaps up. "Why?"

"I went with you to find your grandmother." He says it matter-of-factly, not like he wants me to feel as though I owe him.

My voice is quiet. "Milo, you didn't have to do that."

"It's okay," he says, shrugging. "Helping you was more important. I told Adam I had a family emergency. Apparently he likes us so much he was willing to reschedule."

"That's good," I say, so relieved I descend a stoop stair, moving closer to him.

"I watched the ceremony," he says. "You gave a dope speech. Everyone is talking about it online."

"Are they?" I ask wryly. I still don't think I'll bother to check. At least not for a little while.

He nods. "Yeah, all good things."

"Oh."

We fall quiet again. I can't stand the awkwardness between us.

"I'm sorry, Evie," he says, breaking the silence. "I should have been honest with you from the beginning."

The sincerity in his voice shakes me. I look at him, standing here on Gigi's front stoop, apologizing and putting himself out there for me again.

"I shouldn't have said that you were like Simone," I say. "That's not true."

He's quiet for a moment. Then he asks, "Do you ever think we'll be able to move past this?"

"Um." I hate the way that my voice wobbles. Move past this to what? A future where the two of us are together? I can forgive Milo. I'm strong enough to do that. And I understand why he did what he did; he was being loyal to Gigi. But I'll never be able to forget the way he lied to me so easily. How could we ever have a future if I can't trust him?

Maybe Gigi has found a way to put her trust in James again. But theirs is an epic romance. They're practically soul mates. The thought of comparing Milo and me to them is ridiculous. What we had barely lasted a week, and this is what happened.

"It's okay, Milo. I forgive you," I say, and I find that I truly mean it. "I wish you luck with the band. I really do think you guys will take off."

He frowns, picking up on the finality in my tone.

"I guess we were never meant to be friends, huh?" His voice sounds so sad I can't even take it.

"Thank you for your help," I say, unable to look at him. "Really. Regardless of why you helped me, I liked having you there."

"You're welcome," he says quietly.

"I have to go. We're flying back to LA tomorrow." I turn, but he quickly climbs the steps until he's right in front of me. He reaches out and wraps me tightly in his arms. I breathe deeply, inhaling his cinnamon scent, committing it to memory.

I hold back a sob as I pull away. "Bye, Milo."

His hands gently linger on my waist, then he lets go. "Bye, Evie."

Chapter Twenty-Four

MONDAY, AUGUST 17

Gigi goes with us to the airport on Monday morning. There aren't any paparazzi around, and no one else is trying to take photos of us. I guess we're old news now. I can't say that I'm upset about it.

My parents have decided to stay in LA for the unforeseeable future. They'll edit what they've already filmed for their documentary and head back to Botswana sometime next year. I'm going to stay in LA and try to figure things out. Whatever that means.

Kerri is busy making sure everyone has their boarding passes, working even when she doesn't have to.

"You are quite the worker bee," Gigi says to her.

Kerri freezes. She still has moments when she's completely in awe to be speaking with Evelyn Conaway. "Oh, um. Yes, I guess so."

"That's a good quality," Gigi says. "You remind me of my friend Esther."

At this, Kerri beams. Then she hustles my parents toward security.

It feels weird to leave New York now. I'm still sad over the way things ended with Milo and me. Maybe in the future, he and I will eventually become friends. Maybe we need years between now and then, like Gigi and James Jenkins.

And I don't want to leave Gigi just yet. I barely got to spend any time with her this week. But I have the portrait from my eleventh birthday that she bought from Candice, and I'm taking it back to LA with me. I'll return to see Gigi soon. I promised her this.

"You're always welcome to stay here in the city with me," she says as we hug goodbye. She kisses my forehead. "You'll find your happiness soon, my love. And once you do, watch out, world."

"Thanks, Gigi." I hug her again, tighter this time.

Once we're on the plane and in the air, I look down at New York City, the city where I wasn't necessarily able to start over, but where I learned that starting over is possible.

"A TRIUMPH!"
Helena Carson, *Mahogany* magazine

BENJAMIN STYLES • VERONICA SMITH • EVIE JONES

in the new comedy

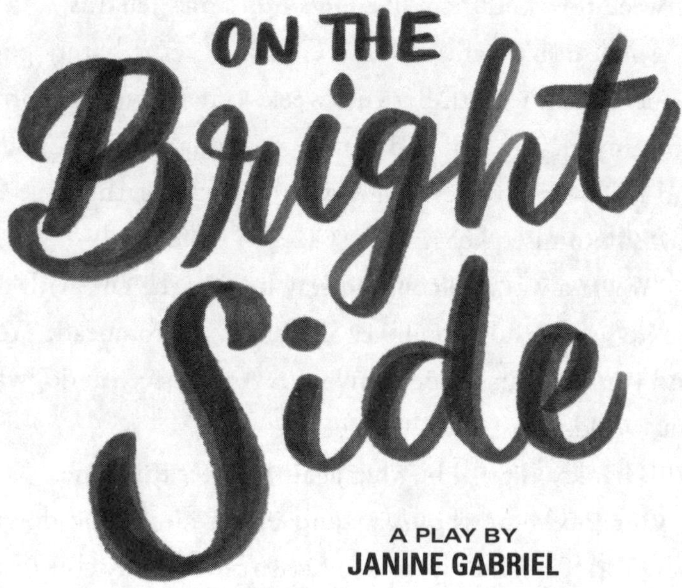

A PLAY BY
JANINE GABRIEL

Opening Night: October 9, 2020, 7:00 P.M.

Kirk Douglas Theatre
9820 West Washington Boulevard
Culver City, CA

Chapter Twenty-Five

FRIDAY, OCTOBER 9

My cast mates and I hold hands and bow onstage. We receive a standing ovation. Not too bad for opening night. Not too bad for my first-ever professional stage performance.

When I first came back to LA, I took a few weeks to figure out what it was that I wanted to do. For a while, I actively didn't think about it. Then Gigi called because Mr. Gabriel wanted to know if I'd ever reached out to his niece. Not wanting to break the promise I'd made him, I called Janine. I didn't think much would come of it, maybe just that I'd make a connection. But it turns out Janine was working on a play that sounded really cool, a love triangle between three college students. I read the script and fell in love with the character of Renee. Something about the way she begins the story so closed off and eventually opens up to love appealed to me. She's not the lead, and she doesn't even get the guy at the end, but that didn't matter. Kerri and I had a meeting with Janine, and then I was cast. According to preview reviews, it seems like people like my performance. But I try not to pay too much attention to what people are writing anymore.

Kerri is waiting backstage with my family. My mom and dad, and Gigi and James, even Mr. Gabriel too.

Gigi is the first to hug me. These past few months have been good to her. She's practically glowing. I still can't believe she's here, that she actually came back to LA after all these years. She and James still aren't together—at least that's what she says. Right now, he splits his time between New York and LA. He takes me out for lunch sometimes when he can fit it into his schedule. He's in the middle of filming the last Aliens Attack Earth movie. He's shelved the idea of an *Every Time We Meet* remake for now. I'm happy he found the time to see my show tonight.

"You did good, kid," he says, giving me a sideways hug. "I bet you'll get a Tony for this."

I give him a look. "Yeah, well, don't go making calls to anyone just yet. I know how you are."

He holds up his hands, laughing. "I won't. I promise."

My mom and dad hug me next, and Mr. Gabriel gives me an enthusiastic pat on the shoulder. "I told you to call my Janine, didn't I?"

I nod, laughing. "Yeah, she's great."

Kerri places a bouquet of roses into my arms.

"Oh my gosh, thank you, Kerri!" I start to wrap my arms around her, then stop, remembering that she prefers not to hug. But to my surprise, she reaches out to hug me instead.

"You're welcome." She smiles and straightens out her blazer when she pulls away. "You deserve them."

Beside me, Gigi gently grabs my hand and places something small in my palm. "I meant to give this to you before your show, but we arrived late." When I unfurl my fingers, I stare down at a small black guitar pick covered in tiny nicks.

I look up at her, speechless. "How . . . how did you get this?"

"Milo gave it to me." She looks at me closely. "He said you'd know what it meant."

"Oh." I fall silent, staring down at the pick again. My family watches me, saying nothing.

Finally, my mom breaks the silence. "Ready to go, baby?"

I look up at their expectant faces. "Um, yeah."

But I don't move. I haven't talked to Milo since that night in August when we said goodbye to each other. I've thought about him, though. I still think about him all the time, actually. I heard that Doves Have Pride ended up getting signed to Vivid Music Group. I even made my own Spotify account so that I could listen to the band's new music. I love what they're doing now, but I can't bring myself to reach out to Milo and say so. There are so many times that I've almost texted him. But I never follow through, because it's been months since we last spoke. I wouldn't even know where to begin.

To Gigi, I say, "When you get back to New York, can you please tell him that I said thank you?"

"Oh, he won't be back in New York for a little while," she says. "The label decided to send the band on a small tour."

She waits for me to let this sink in, then she adds, "He's in LA tonight, actually. It's their first show."

I blink. "Really?"

Beside me, Kerri says, "Seriously, you didn't know? I thought you purposely weren't mentioning it because . . . well, you know."

"I still don't have social media," I say weakly. "Isn't that where most people get their news?"

Putting on her agent hat, Kerri pulls out her phone and shows me a flyer for the band's show. It's at a venue about thirty minutes away, and it started at 8:00 P.M. It's most likely almost over now.

My heart starts beating a little faster. It's telling me something, but I don't know what it's saying. I look at Gigi again, the same face I've turned to time and time again for advice. She meets my gaze and nods.

That's it, just a nod. It could mean anything.

It's up to me to interpret it however I wish.

"Um," I say, "I think I'll go to the show . . . now."

James drives like a bat out of hell, but I don't care. I wish we could fly to the venue in a high-speed spaceship like in his Aliens Attack Earth movies. I just need to get there.

Kerri and I are squished in the back seat with my parents, who are both understandably confused by tonight's recent turn of events.

"Fill me in, please, Evie Marie," Dad is saying. "Who is this Milo person, and why is he so important to you?"

"Um, he's just this boy I know," I answer.

Kerri turns to narrow her eyes at me. "I think that is a severe understatement."

"He's her star-crossed musician boyfriend," James says from the front seat. "Come on, Andrew. Get with the program."

Dad blinks like he didn't know there was a program he should be getting with.

"You have a boyfriend?" Mom says to me. "Is this the boy from the *US Weekly* article? How long have you been dating?"

I shake my head. "James is exaggerating. Milo isn't my boyfriend, and we aren't star-crossed lovers."

"I guess that depends on how you define *star-crossed*," James says.

Kerri huffs. "I'll settle this and look up the definition right now—"

"Everyone, please be quiet!" They all turn to look at me, and I hold a hand over my stomach. "This is already nerve-racking enough."

Gigi twists in the passenger seat and gently pats my knee. "It's all right, my love. It'll be all right."

Her words calm me, but only briefly.

My heart is beating out of control, and the pace doubles when James pulls up to the venue.

I hop out of the car like it's on fire.

"Should we wait for you?" Gigi asks.

"No, no," I call as I run toward the door. "I'll figure out a way home!"

There isn't a line anymore. Two security guards stand outside, smoking cigarettes. When they turn to face me, a bit of the tension in my stomach eases.

"Adrian?" I say, looking at him in surprise. "They brought you all the way from New York?"

"Of course they did," he says. "I'm officially on their security team." His expression softens as he looks at me. "It's good to see you again. Your hair is different."

I run a finger through my curls, which are a bit longer now. "It's growing back."

"I meant you're not wearing a wig."

"Oh yeah. That too." I take a breath. "Look, Adrian, I don't have a ticket, but I really want to see him—"

"Go ahead," he says, interrupting me. "It's packed, but I have a feeling you'll find a way to get to the stage."

"Thank you." I squeeze his hand, trying to show just how grateful I am, and he waves me on.

The venue is at least three times the size of The Goose's Egg, and it's three times as packed as any of their previous shows. And it's dark. The only things I can see are a mob of people and the stage in the distance.

There they are, playing like they've been doing it forever. Raf crooning into the microphone. Ben and Vinny playing the drums and saxophone as if their lives depend on it.

And Milo staring down at his fingers, strumming his guitar. He's biting his lip, in the zone. The sight of him, here in front of me all these months later, makes my heart beat so hard and fast it's a wonder I don't pass out.

"All right, this is the last song of the night," Raf says, smiling widely. They start to play "Leather Pants," and the crowd cheers.

The stage is so far from here. It's insane for me to think I can somehow push my way past all these people so that Milo will see me. What if he doesn't even care anymore and I'm too late? What if I'm not even ready to trust him yet and I'm just being ridiculously impulsive?

But I didn't come all the way here just to chicken out at the door. I made a promise to myself back in New York, and I'll stick to it. No more running.

Well, except for the literal running that I'm doing right now.

As I force my way through the crowd, I feel like Diane in the final scene of *Every Time We Meet*, when she ran through Penn Station for Henry. It looks so fun and romantic in the movie, but in reality, it's nothing short of madness trying to get through all these people.

Raf is on the second verse now. I continue to squeeze my way through and accidentally knock into a boy, causing his drink to splash down the front of his shirt.

"I'm so sorry!" I shout as I keep moving.

"Watch it!" he yells, glaring at me. Then his eyes widen. "Hey, wait, you're Evie Jones!"

That gets others to turn and look. Suddenly, more and more people are noticing me, stepping aside to get a better view. I already see them angling their phones to take my picture. But I don't care where these photos end up. And I don't care what they think about me. I'm not here for them; I'm here for Milo. So I smile at everyone as I keep pushing through, finally reaching the front.

The song begins to wrap up, and I see an opening right in front of Milo. He's looking at Raf as he plays the last few chords. And then his gaze fans out over the crowd. He looks down and sees me.

He blinks, and his eyes widen, not leaving my face. He strums the last chord, and then the song is over. The crowd is shouting all around us. Raf is speaking into the mic, thanking everyone for coming out. But it might as well be silent. I don't hear any of it. There's just Milo and me, in this moment right here.

We stare at each other for what feels like a lifetime. Then he takes a step forward and crouches down. I step forward too, swallowing thickly. My stomach is doing flips like an acrobat.

I open my mouth, but no words come out. What do I want to say? Anything, everything.

I'm sorry for the way I left things. I want to trust you if you'll give me the chance.

I'm afraid to say it. Gone is his friendly and easy smile. He's watching me with an unreadable expression, waiting. I want to turn and run. This is the scariest thing I've ever done. But I have to be brave. *No more running.*

"Milo . . .," I manage to get out. I take a deep breath, searching for the right words. Helplessly, I dig into my pocket and hold up his lucky pick. Like it will speak for me.

He stares at the pick and inches closer. Slowly, his hand closes around mine, pulling the pick from my fingers. The corner of his mouth twitches as his eyes find mine again. Then his easy smile appears on his face. He sighs.

"Well, darling," he says in a slow drawl, "I'm sure glad you showed up."

I laugh, surprised and relieved, and his smile grows even bigger.

He says, "I think, according to the movie, this is the part where we kiss."

I nod, heart completely full. "It is."

I stand up on tiptoe. He leans forward, meeting me halfway. When we kiss, it's better than any scene in any movie. Maybe that's because it's real.

Acknowledgments

I love this story with all of my heart, but writing it was a struggle. They say that's the nature of second books. I'm lucky that I've been surrounded by the best people along the way.

To Mekisha Telfer, my brilliant editor. This book literally would not exist without you.

To my agent, Sara Crowe, the best partner to have in this business and who always has my back.

Thank you to Cassie Gonzales and Avia Perez and Allene Cassagnol. Also, a special shout-out to my publicist, Brittany Pearlman, for partially inspiring Kerri.

To Alison Doherty, my critique partner and friend, for reading every draft and sharing a love of all things romance. To Charlotte Davis and Maya Motayne for the book-two moral support.

To Dana Carey, my work wife, who spent yet another year making me laugh and listening to my tales of woe.

To all of my best friends for inspiring the bond between the members of Doves Have Pride.

To my mom, dad, and brothers, Steven, Matthew, and Mikey. Thank you for your support and love.

To Jason, yes, this time you did inspire Milo. Maybe you should learn to play the guitar?

To Grandma Naomi, the most stylish person I know. Thank you for all the clothes and inherited fashion sense. And to Grandma Peggy, for all of your love, wisdom, and guidance. And thank you for letting me borrow your and grandpa's names for this story.

And to Kitty, my sweet girl, who passed before I could finish writing this book. You are and will always be my favorite.